FROM DIFFERENT WORLDS

She was infinitely aware of the intimacy of the situation. The hay rustled and gave off a sweet aroma with every movement of their bodies. Jason was so handsome, with his obsidian dark eyes and velvety brown hair. He was very different from everything she knew. There was a worldliness about him, an undeniable element of unpredictability.

She needed to keep some degree of sensibility, forcing herself to remember that he had all but shunned her in the past days. She spoke through unexpectedly dry lips. "Why does thee treat me so distantly?" Their mouths were so close that her breath was mingling with his, and she had to try not to think about the fact that she was breathing in air that had been inside him, warmed by his body.

"For your good as well as mine." Was his voice slightly unsteady or was she imagining things?

"I don't understand."

Jason's lips were so close to hers she could feel their warmth. "Right now, neither do I," he whispered, just before he kissed her.

Other *Leisure* books by Catherine Archibald:
HAWK'S LADY

LOVING CHARITY

CATHERINE ARCHIBALD

LEISURE BOOKS   NEW YORK CITY

A LEISURE BOOK®

April 2000

Published by

Dorchester Publishing Co., Inc.
276 Fifth Avenue
New York, NY 10001

ISBN 0-8439-4704-7

The name "Leisure Books" and the stylized "L" with design are trademarks of Dorchester Publishing Co., Inc.

Printed in the United States of America.

To my father, Russell Bennett, who is the first hero in my life and to my mother, Wilda (Jean) Bennett, who taught me it's what's inside that matters.

LOVING CHARITY

Chapter One

Jason took off his hat and banged it against his thigh before stepping through the open kitchen door behind his new employer. He ran his other hand over his dark hair and found it stiff with dirt. The ride from town in Elija Applegate's wagon had been dusty.

From the kitchen, beyond Elija's broad shoulders, came the aroma of cooked beef, boiled potatoes, and yeast, underlain by the clean scent of pine oil. Jason's gaze took in whitewashed walls and a gleaming wood floor. It was as if farm women felt a need to make up for their homes' lack of elegance by polishing everything with elbow grease.

There were several darkly clothed women working at the cast-iron stove and long countertop. From the look of the baking pans covered in snow-white cloths, which rested upon the shelf over the stove, and the mound of dough on the counter, it appeared they were making bread. One of the women was pouring water from a pitcher into a metal basin filled with dishes. As he watched, she took a bar of homemade soap and lathered a scrap of cloth before tackling the stack. The women were so caught up in their tasks that none of them seemed to take any notice of the two men.

Jason was glad for the moment to orient himself somewhat to his new surroundings before meeting them. He told himself that it was the hot August day, which was made even more so by the fire burning in the stove, that made him feel so worn. He was as deter-mined to find Grisak as he had been from the moment of leaving his home in Boston. Since that day he'd fol-lowed each lead along the way, sometimes missing the bastard by mere hours, until a chance meeting with a drunken gambler who claimed he knew the man had brought him here to this small town in Wisconsin. The drunk insisted that Grisak might have family here.

Squaring his shoulders, Jason wiped the sweat from his forehead with his dirty sleeve. If the man had a family here, odds were he'd show up sometime and Jason would be lying in wait for him when he did.

Elija hung his flat-brimmed black hat on one of sev-eral hooks beside the door, then stooped to take off his boots.

Jason hurried to follow the example set by the older man. His gloves caused him to fumble over the laces, but Jason didn't want Applegate to see his bandaged right hand. If Elija thought he wouldn't be able to work, the Quaker just might send his newly hired man packing.

Elija Applegate had insisted that he could use a hand when he'd overheard the man at the livery telling Jason that he didn't need any help at the moment.

Jason had been more than a little relieved after being turned away at several other businesses as well.

He needed this job, wanted to blend into the community so he could learn as much as he could about Grisak, make sure he was the right man, the man who had . . .

Jason's muscles clenched around the hatred in his gut. Determinedly he forced the sensation away. He had to be sure before exacting his revenge. And though everything inside him told him that Grisak was the one, he would not act—not until he was sure. Although he had lost his respect for the law, a profession he had once been proud to practice, he wasn't prepared to kill Grisak until he had some proof. Or, possibly, he thought with a cold smile, even a confession of what he had done to Daphne. That would make the killing easy.

Soon now, soon! Soon he'd have his revenge. He jerked a knot in his bootlace tight, then realized what he had done and began to undo it again.

As Elija set his boots on the braided rag rug directly beneath the hooks beside the door, he called out, "I'm home, daughters."

A flurry of female voices erupted from across the room.

"Papa."

"Welcome home, Papa."

"Are thee hungry, Papa?"

"Would thee like some coffee?"

Glancing up, Jason found himself facing a wall of dark skirts and sturdy black shoes. From the looks of the healthy size of their feet, these girls took directly after their father. His lips twisted without humor. How

11

was it that his mother referred to this particular variety of farm-bred lass? Oh yes, "Milk and Butter Miss." Much as he hated to agree with anything his very superior mother said, Jason thought she might not be so far off the mark with Elija Applegate's offspring.

Laughing, Elija stood, hooking his thumbs in the suspenders that held up his brown homespun pants. "How could I be hungry after eating all the sandwiches thee sent with me? I even had enough to share with my friend here, Jason Wade."

Jason felt the eyes that fixed expectantly on him, looked up, and stared.

All resemblance to the young women's bearded father ended below the ankle. His vision beheld a blur of creamy skin, cornflower-blue eyes, and blond hair that ranged in shade from wheat-gold to moonlight-silver. Not that he could see much hair, only a fringe was allowed to escape the confines of the girls' four neat buns. But it was enough to detect color and the fact that the tresses shone with health and cleanliness.

They made him think of beautiful rain-washed buttercups. The girls' collective gaze remained fixed on Jason, though they withheld the questions that danced on the ends of their tongues.

Elija grinned and hooked his thumbs in his pockets, obviously understanding his daughters were interested in the newcomer. Clearly he meant to tease them just a bit before satisfying their curiosity. "Now, about that coffee? Never can get too much coffee. Don't thee agree, Jason Wade?"

Jason's mouth was as dry as the old tomes he'd once read with such reverence as he studied the law, the profession he'd abandoned to take up this quest for revenge. Realizing he hadn't replied he muttered, "Yes, thank you. I could use some coffee." He then bent to work at his laces again. The compelling warmth that existed between this man and his daughters made him feel awkward. His own heart had long been devoid of such warmth.

An amused female voice interrupted his troubled thoughts. "It might help, if thee took off thy gloves."

Jason kept his head down a moment, forcing himself to concentrate, to behave normally—to keep his dark thoughts from shadowing his thinking.

He looked up into a delicately lovely face framed by a fringe of golden hair. "I'm Charity," she introduced herself without a hint of the self-consciousness he usually associated with young women. And suddenly everything, Elija, the other three daughters, even his painful thoughts, faded into the background.

Instantly he amended his assumption that all resemblance to Elija ended at the ankle. This daughter, at least, had his ready smile and on her it was very becoming, lighting her wide cornflower blue eyes with genuine mirth. That light seemed to come from a place of warmth and vitality inside her.

For an inexplicable moment, Jason found himself responding to her smile, felt his lips curve upward in an expression that had been foreign to him for months. He was lost in those wide eyes; they held an ingenuousness and trust in the future that he had long ago forsaken.

Jason knew a sense of yearning that was dizzying. She was clean through and through, this young Quaker, peaceful as he only wished he could be and he wanted to draw that peace into himself. He closed his eyes,

13

attempting to still the reeling world, and he took a deep breath.

Was he mad? He didn't want peace, only revenge. He didn't even know this woman, or any of them. He was tired, just tired, nothing more than that. He opened his eyes and ran a deliberately assessing gaze over Charity Applegate, wanting to see her as the simple farm girl she was and nothing more.

She wore a high-necked dress made of faded dark gray homespun. The garment was simple, long-sleeved, and without any particular style, but it gave a tantalizing hint of full breasts. Clearly realizing the path of his gaze, she blushed and wiped what appeared to be unsteady hands on the white cotton apron that was tied around her narrow waist with a wide bow.

To Jason's surprise, his thorough assessment had not eased his interest and her restless reaction only further fascinated him. He watched as she raised long slender fingers to smoothe a strand of hair that had escaped her bun to lay along the white curve of her neck. He found himself wondering if the flesh along her delicate nape was as velvety as it looked.

Jason swallowed, hard, looking back into her face and the flush deepened along her high creamy-skinned cheekbones. Her tongue flicked out across her lovely wild raspberry mouth.

His body tightened, heated, responding to that unconscious seductive gesture with alacrity.

In instantaneous horror he checked himself, turning away. Daphne was dead, never to see or taste or feel anything again. Jason had no right to the smallest of pleasures, especially that of enjoying the sight of a pretty young woman. He was here for one reason and one reason only, to find out if Wayne Grisak had murdered her—and if he had, to kill him.

"My girl's right, thee are only tangling things. Take off thy gloves, boy," Elija chided.

Slowly, Jason drew off his left glove, then his right.

There was a deep penetrating silence at the sight of the grubby cloth wound around his right palm.

Elija reached out, taking Jason's left hand, and pulled him to his feet. The older man's beard effectively covered his expression, but his voice was gruff as he bent to get a better look at Jason's bandaged right hand. "Why didn't thee say thee were hurt, Jason Wade?"

Squarely, Jason faced the bigger man, drawing the injured palm back. "Don't misunderstand, Mr. Applegate. I can work. My injury won't interfere with my performance in any way."

"Now, there'll be no Mr. Applegating around here, Jason Wade. Quakers don't hold with Mistering. I'm Elija to both God and man."

"Elija . . ."

But the big man wasn't listening. He turned to his daughters. "Prudence, where's Mother?"

An odd shadow seemed to pass over the girls' faces. The one with wheat-colored hair stepped forward. "Levi came right after you left. He had to take a *delivery* north to Springfield." As she sniffed, raising her brows and giving her father a meaningful look, Jason saw that her nose was slightly narrower than her sisters'. "He had to. He had visitors this morning. From down south. They were looking for *escaped slaves.*"

Suddenly a silence as dense as stone settled in the room, as all eyes went to Jason. He felt their anxiety as to what he might make of this information, which sep-

15

arated him from them as surely as a barricade. He frowned.

The golden-haired beauty no longer wore her father's smile. Charity glared at her sister as she cast a meaningful glance toward Jason. "Why don't thee just come out and say where mother's gone? Thee are that good at keeping a secret, Prue."

Prudence flushed, though she made no reply. Reaching into her pocket, she drew out a pair of wire-rimmed spectacles, which she placed on her nose. Her next comment was directed toward her father. "Mother decided to go with Levi. She left me in charge until thee returned. I'm trying to finish the baking."

Their father's face gave away much less, but Jason could see traces of concern in his slightly pursed mouth.

For a moment, Jason allowed himself to wonder at the danger of the game these Quakers might be playing. No matter that slavery was deplorable, helping escaped slaves was a crime.

Jason checked his thoughts. Politics was his father the judge's area of interest. He was plagued by his own demons.

He faced them squarely. "What you do is your own concern. Anything I learn about your private lives will go no further."

Elija continued to study the younger man for a long moment, his brow furrowed. Then, as if the honesty he saw in Jason's face were enough to appease him, he turned to his daughter. "That's fine then, Prudence. Thee must go on with what thee were doing. We will trust in the Lord to look after Mother."

Elija looked toward his other daughters, his gaze

taking in the two who were obviously the youngest and, if Jason didn't miss his guess, twins. "Constance, Purity, help thy sister finish the baking."

They nodded, smoothing back silver-blond hair in unison. "Yes, Papa." They scrambled to obey him.

Elija turned to his remaining daughter. "The coffee can wait until that hand is taken care of. Charity, fetch Mother's ointment and some cloths. Look after the lad's injury." He turned and Jason saw that he again wore a faint frown. "I'll put thy horse in the barn with my Daniel."

Jason took a step toward him, his chin set firm with determination. "Let me do that, Mr. . . . Elija. I intend to earn my way."

For a moment, Elija stared at Jason, an odd speculative look in his eyes. Suddenly, he grinned as if having measured Jason and found him worthy. "There'll be time enough for that, young man." Then he was gone.

Jason stood there like a hitching post as they all moved to their appointed tasks. His eyes lingered on one slim back as its owner opened a door leading into the other part of the house, then disappeared.

Charity hurried to her parents' room to get the things she would need. She was aware of her father's concern for her mother. Their work on the underground railroad was difficult for all of them at times, knowing as they did just what danger they faced from those who made it their business to recapture escaped slaves.

Yet she could not help thinking about the stranger as she stood in the familiarity of her parents' room, which was sparsely furnished with a wood-frame bed, a chest, and a wardrobe. The hardwood floor shone from a recent polishing, the patchwork quilt lay smooth upon the bed, and the starched white curtain fluttered in the breeze from the open window.

Charity closed the door and leaned back against it, her heart racing, her thoughts centering on the man in the kitchen. They'd hired men before, but never anyone even remotely as fascinating as this Jason Wade. When he'd looked at her, she hadn't been able to quell the flutter of nervous excitement in her belly, no matter that she'd told herself she was being as silly as Martha Wyeth, who flirted with all the young men after Sunday Meeting.

Jason Wade didn't look like the usual drifters who came through the farming community looking for work. He was dirty all right, covered in a thick layer of grime and sweat. But his speech was refined, like that preacher who had come from back East. There was a quiet reserve to his manner. And his hands. Those weren't the hands of a farm laborer. They were rough all right. But rough from accumulated blisters and cuts, not from years of hard work.

Even his clothes were different. It was true he was wearing a simple shirt and dungarees. But they had not come from any dry goods store. Those denim pants were cut to hug every line of his long legs and narrow hips. The shirt was of a quality rarely seen around Helmsville. And he was so lean and spare, as if his muscle and bone had hardened into rock from constant use. Charity had also been surprised to see that he was as tall as Papa, who was like a large, warmhearted bear.

For a moment, when she had smiled at him, she had felt that he was responding openly to her amused comment about his gloves. Then, without warning, his expression had changed, his gaze focusing inward, the burning fire of what she could only describe as despair coming into his eyes. Somehow she knew there was a hurt in him so deep and strong that it had scarred his soul.

Surprisingly, the intensity of emotion had made his eyes all the more compelling. They were a startling gray, almost black, like an arrowhead Papa had once found in the fields.

As the clatter of someone dropping a pan below intruded upon her thoughts, Charity realized she had lingered here too long. She gathered everything she needed and hurried down the stairs. It was not her place to be worrying over the stranger. Whatever his secrets, they were between the Lord and himself.

Jason Wade was still standing by the kitchen door where she had left him. She set the ointments and clean cloths on the oft-scrubbed rectangular pine table.

It was obvious to Charity that her three sisters were attempting not to stare as they went about their work. For some reason, Charity did not care for the notion that her siblings were reacting to the stranger as strongly as she was.

Charity was careful not to look at the man directly. "Would thee come over to the table?" But she was infinitely aware of him, and the very maleness of his presence, just inside the kitchen door.

The sound of his soft footfalls told her he had finished removing his boots while she was upstairs. Careful to keep her eyes on the top button of his dirty cotton shirt as he approached, Charity pulled out a simple, but well-made bow-backed pine chair. "Would thee like to sit?"

"Thank you," he answered with what sounded like a hint of amusement in his voice.

She lifted her gaze to his face, saw a glint of sardonic humor in the depths of his dark eyes as he answered by raising his hands. "I had meant to be of some use to your father, not to take advantage of his charity."

Charity heard Pru gasp aloud and her own eyes widened at the implication of his words. Even as she realized that she was reacting far too strongly, Charity spoke somewhat sharply, "Are thee poking fun at me?"

For a moment there was a devilish gleam in Jason's dark eyes and she felt an unexpected answering warmth inside herself. Then too quickly he sobered, bowing toward Charity, and his gaze slid away from hers. "I'm very sorry. There was no pun intended."

She realized that she had best get control of herself and without delay. There was simply no explanation for the way she was reacting to this stranger. "Thy apology is accepted, though not necessary if no insult was meant." Charity had been one to speak her mind even in early childhood and had long since become accustomed to making apologies for being too frank. "It is I who should beg thy pardon for taking offense."

Jason Wade must surely think her childish. The heroines in the books she borrowed from the library spoke with poise and intelligence. If only she could do the same. With what she hoped was self-possession, Charity indicated the chair she held. "Please sit down and I will tend thy wound."

Jason took the offered seat and placed his bandaged hand, palm up, on the table. His dark gaze met hers, and for a long moment Charity could not look away. She felt an odd tightening in her chest. Then, even as she watched, his expression grew questioning. Immediately she focused her embarrassed gaze on the tabletop.

Hoping he would not notice the rise of color in her cheeks, Charity quickly took the chair next to him. Reluctantly reaching out for Jason's large hand, she reminded herself that she was just treating his wound, nothing more. But it didn't seem to calm her agitation, as Jason's warm rough fingers settled on hers. The hairs raised along the back of her arm all the way to her neck, and Charity had to make a conscious effort not to let go. She'd never touched a man this intimately—oh, her father and other relatives of course, but not anyone like Jason Wade. No one who made her feel as though it was hard to breathe just by looking at her.

Inhaling slowly, keeping her eyes downcast, Charity unwound the handkerchief, which was grubby with dried blood, dirt, and sweat. Concentrating on the man's injury did much to calm her agitation. It was a shallow, clean slice, such as a sharp instrument might make.

As if in answer to her unspoken question, he muttered, "Scythe. I thought the blade was the handle."

"Oh." It was the only reply Charity could make. No experienced farmworker would mistake the blade of a scythe for the handle. The more she knew of Jason Wade, the more of an enigma he became.

With an act of sheer will, Charity set her thoughts to the matter at hand. "I will try to be as gentle as possible."

It was a long moment before Jason could reply. "I'm sure you will." He wanted to stop looking at her, but he couldn't seem to manage. In spite of the fact that he didn't want to admit it, he couldn't deny that there was just something about this young woman that drew him.

Desperately he studied her, trying to understand what was wrong with him. Her lashes were surprisingly dark against the curve of her cheek as she examined the injury. There was something very appealing about her forthright manner, and her fingers felt cool and capable as they moved against his own. It had been some time since he'd been touched by a woman. Obviously too long, if the tightness in his lower belly was any indication. He tried to distract himself from such thoughts by allowing his gaze to move over the heavy coil of golden strands at the base of her neck. Jason had a sudden impulse to pull the pins from her hair so he could watch the heavy mass tumble down to frame her face.

He shifted in his seat, feeling perspiration bead on his upper lip. He swiped at it with his free hand, telling himself it was just too damned hot in here.

Charity glanced up from her ministrations. "I am sorry if I hurt thee."

His reply was low and rough. "You didn't hurt me."

It had been months since he had even thought of a woman in this way. Months since Daphne had been attacked. All through the ineffectual investigation by the authorities in Boston, and then during his own, he had thought of nothing beyond finding her attacker.

Now, here, hundreds of miles from his home, he had met a woman who made him think of something, if only briefly, besides his rage and obsession for vengeance. But Jason did not want this.

Revenge was his god. It had sustained him in his efforts to find Grisak, and he couldn't forget that now, even for a moment.

He glanced around the kitchen to where the other

three sisters were baking bread. They were doing their best to keep from watching what was happening at the table. And failing miserably. The one they called Prudence opened the heavy oven door and nearly lost her glasses as she turned to look at Jason at the same time.

He had to fight to keep back a smile. On this ground, at least, his thoughts were safe. Prudence was pretty enough, but she had a hint of distance and superciliousness in her manner. The traits reminded him of his mother and though he loved her he was not blind to the truth of her nature.

Though the twin girls promised to be exceedingly lovely women, they could not be over thirteen. One of the two took that moment to peek in his direction.

Without thinking, Jason smiled at her.

She blushed deep rose to her hairline and ducked her head, paying undue care to the pan she was greasing. As if sharing her sister's discomfiture, the other twin glanced from Jason to her embarrassed sibling with a blush of her own.

Jason looked away. He had not meant to disturb the child. It seemed that he had best keep his attention to inanimate objects. Jason ran his free hand, the one that was not held by Charity Applegate, over the smooth surface of the table. It was simple carpentry, nothing to rival the workmanship of the furnishings in his mother's Boston mansion. But the large table, chairs, counter, and cupboards had been fashioned by a careful and patient hand. It was the work of a man who loved his woman.

As if responding to Jason's thought of him, Elija took that moment to reenter the kitchen. He still had a slightly preoccupied air, but he smiled in greeting. He crossed to the table in long strides, taking the seat across from Jason and his daughter. "How bad?"

Charity moved her hands aside so her father could see the injury. "The cut is inflamed, but hasn't festered."

Elija reached to hold Jason's hand still while he took a closer look, then turned his warm grin on him. His huge callused hand was, surprisingly enough, as gentle as his daughter's. "Hear that, young fella? Thee'll be right as rain in no time."

Jason looked from daughter to father, feeling warmed by their care. As a boy he had been tended by nannies and servants, all paid to look after the only child and heir of the Trentons of Boston. His mother insisted that it was the proper way to rear children and she must do everything the proper way. She did these things in the hope that she would eventually convince her husband's family that she was no longer the daughter of the late Patrick O'Bannion, who was rumored to have made his fortune in questionable trade in the far east. She was now Frances Trent, who had married her fortune into one of the oldest and most respected families in Boston. Jason's father, Robert, who was the youngest son, had inherited little from his father. But he did love the law. Trenton & Trenton had been founded by his father, and had demanded the full attention of both Jason and his father, who had never made secret his desire for Jason to join his practice.

Yet making contrasts was useless, especially because Jason had had no complaint with his life until Daphne's death. Only when he'd seen the cost of his selfish existence had he questioned it.

Grimly, he realized he could not allow himself to be drawn too close to these people. Even if he did feel he had a right to the friendship they seemed to offer, he knew that if they found out why he was here they would no longer feel the same about him. Quakers did not believe in violence of any kind, killing was surely the worst kind of violence—even when done in the name of justice.

Jason drew himself up. "Mr. . . . Elija. I'm here to work. I have no intention of lazing around for days. As I said earlier, I'll earn my keep."

"The work will wait for thee. Have no fear." Elija chuckled softly, hooking his thumbs through his suspenders. "But not until thy hand is healed."

Charity spoke in a tone that was filled with affection and respect for her father. "Thee had best resign thyself. Papa will not let thee win."

Looking up, Jason saw she was smiling at him again. It was smile sweeter than mulled wine on a frigid December day. That expression reached inside him to where his heart was hard and cold and warmed him. He looked from her to her father, for a moment overcome by the feelings of acceptance.

From across the room, the other three joined in, as they added their own warnings regarding their father's stubbornness.

Never in his twenty-eight years had he felt such love and joy in any people he had known. It wasn't just that they were Quakers. He had met others of their faith. None had the inner light that lived in this family.

There was a peace in them that came from someplace he had never been and was not likely to go.

And rightly so, he reminded himself. The destruction of another human being had become his reason for existing.

* * *

The sun was low over the barn before Charity heard Levi's wagon rattle into the drive.

Running to the door, Charity felt her shoulders sag with relief. Her sisters' faces mirrored the same emotion as they joined her.

The wagon moved past the barn and corral to halt a few feet from the kitchen door.

Papa ran from the barn, where he had been showing Jason the layout, and where he was to sleep. His joy at seeing Mother was clearly written in his eyes. Assisting escaped slaves get to Canada was not without hazards.

When their elder sister Hope's husband, Levi, had ridden over to say that bounty hunters were in the vicinity, they'd all known the hiding place beneath the barn would no longer be safe for Lizzy, the woman they had secreted there most recently.

There had been many temporary residents in that hiding place since her father had come back from a special Meeting some two years ago. He'd explained the dangers of being caught to all of them, but the family had agreed that they must not stand by and allow their fellow men to be held in bondage. They also knew that they were only one step along the way. No slave was safe until they had crossed over the border into Canada, and Lizzy was no exception, though she had stayed longer than anyone before her.

Papa reached up and swung Mother's slim form from the wagon, planting a sound kiss on her lips. "Thank the Lord thee are safe." The late evening sun cast a golden glow on her pretty features and Charity knew a renewed sense of peace as she moved close. Her mother was the real core of strength that held their family together.

Mary Applegate patted her husband's hairy cheek. As usual, she had a religious quotation to fit the situation. " 'The path of the just is as the shining light.' " She swung around to face her daughters, who clustered around them. "We had no problems. Lizzy is safe."

It was then that Mother's cornflower eyes came to rest on Jason, where he stood in the open doorway of the barn. Charity had tried her best not to think of him since he'd left the house with Papa for a tour of the farm, though in all honesty she had not quite succeeded.

He approached the little group slowly.

Like the others, Charity turned to watch him. She felt her heart thud in her chest at what she saw.

Obviously, Jason had taken the time to wash up. His hair was not as dark as she had at first thought. In the last dying rays of the sun, she could see red and gold tints that glowed vibrantly. His skin, she felt certain, was tanned by the sun rather than naturally dark, but it still served to enhance the angular lines of his face. Supple lips softened the hard visage with a devastating effect on Charity's senses. Jason Wade was definitely more attractive than any man had a right to be.

With a concerted effort, Charity focused her attention on her mother as Mary spoke to her husband. "And who is this, Elija?"

Elija waved Jason forward. "Mary, Levi, meet our new hired man, Jason Wade."

Charity could see wariness in her mother's eyes, but Mary nodded. "Jason Wade."

Levi nodded with equal stiffness.

Jason's reply was carefully polite. "How do you do?"

Mother watched him for a moment, then turned to

Papa with raised brows as she sighed. "We will discuss the day's events more privately later." She looked up at Levi, who was still on the wagon seat. "Will thee come in for a bite of supper, son?"

Levi shook his blond head and looked west across Elija's fields, where they butted up against his own. The home he shared with Hope wasn't visible from here, but Charity knew he was seeing it nonetheless. "No, I think Hope will be wondering if everything is all right. I'd best get back."

With a long look at Jason Wade, he waved stiffly and headed the team toward his neighboring farm.

Elija gave his wife another hug, then rubbed his belly. "Suddenly I'm hungry as a polecat at midnight."

Mary's startled gaze took in her four daughters. "Did thee not prepare the meal?"

Her husband hurried to put her concern to rest. "They cooked, but none of us was of a mind to eat." He looked into his wife's eyes with love. "We were worried."

Mary gazed up at him for a long moment, then patted his arm. "Put thy trust in the Lord," she said, but Charity could tell her mother was pleased by her husband's concern.

"Now," Mother told them all brusquely. "Let us eat."

Charity's eyes focused on the stranger again as he took a step backward toward the open door of the barn. "Thee, too, Jason Wade."

He halted abruptly, appearing uncomfortable with her invitation. "There isn't any need for that bother, Mrs. Applegate. I can eat in the barn."

"Thee may call me Mary, and it will be no bother. Join us." Her tone, though quiet, was also adamant.

Jason Wade nodded, though the frown did not leave

his handsome brow. Charity wondered at his reluctance. Yet when his troubled gaze met hers, all
thoughts of why he did not wish to eat with them were
lost in her own unprecedented reaction to his dark,
strangely hypnotic eyes. In that instant Jason's gaze
softened for one brief moment and Charity's heart
turned over in her breast. The sensation was so intense
and so uninvited that it brought her abruptly to a realization of how inappropriate it was.

Immediately she turned away, telling herself she
must get control of her racing pulse, her unexpectedly
trembling knees. Yet as they went forward she
remained fully conscious of the man as he followed
slowly behind them.

The kitchen was still overwarm from baking bread,
and the back door stood open to admit any hint of
breeze. Unfortunately there was none. The air
seemed unusually still, as if nature knew that something was about to happen and was waiting with
baited breath. Even the crickets seemed to sense it;
they croaked in an off-beat chorus that made her feel
oddly restless.

Papa had lit a lamp and set it on the table because it
was growing dark. The soft light caught in the red and
gold highlights of Jason's hair where he sat across
from Charity at the end of the table closest to her
father. While Elija talked to him about the work on the
farm, she found herself watching the newly hired man.

He seemed genuinely interested in what Elija had to
say, though he added little to the conversation himself.

Quietly polite to the other members of her family,
he spoke not at all to Charity—a fact which made her
feel worse than it should have.

Unfortunately, though, Jason seemed to take little notice of her. Charity sighed, looking up to see her mother watching her with considerable interest.

At that moment Elija, noticing that the plate of buns was empty, asked for more. Grateful for the opportunity to escape her mother's scrutiny, Charity leapt to her feet.

After lingering at the counter for as long as she reasonably could, Charity brought the plate of fresh buns to the table. She held out the platter for her father.

He took one, then bit into the soft bread with relish. "Jason, have another."

Charity turned to the young man, politely holding out the plate. But when Jason reached for a bun, they inadvertently touched. It was just the merest grazing of his hand against her forearm, but the contact caused both of them to start.

The plate fell from her hands to crash against the floor, shattering into many pieces.

Her face flushing scarlet, Charity dropped to her knees. Hurriedly, she began to pick up the scattered shards of crockery.

Then Jason was beside her, reaching to take the broken pieces. "Let me help."

Charity was completely and absolutely mortified. What an impression she was making! "No," she whispered. "I . . . I can manage."

"I insist." Why oh why didn't he just go away and leave her in peace?

She refused to look at him, knowing those eyes would be dark with concern. His hand closed around her wrist as she reached for a particularly jagged piece of glass and involuntarily she jerked, as a tingling sensation raced up her arm and into her chest. The glass sliced into her finger, which started to bleed.

She could feel his warm breath on her cheek as he leaned forward to look at the cut. "Here . . . let me . . ."

"That will not be necessary, Jason Wade."

Charity looked up to see her mother standing over them, her hands on her hips. There was a smile on her lips, but her tone brooked no argument. "Charity, go and tend to thy finger. Jason Wade, thee must be tired. Why not go on out to the barn now? The girls and I can clear this up in no time."

Neither Charity nor Jason said a word as they did what they had been told.

It was much later that night when Charity crept down the steps to use the privy. Carefully she avoided the creaky third step in the dark, then made her way past the seven samplers she and her sisters had made after they'd first learned the alphabet.

Prudence, who shared a room with her, was long asleep. Unfortunately, Charity had not managed to join her in slumber. Even in her short-sleeved cotton nightdress, she was too hot and restless, her thoughts filled with visions of a lean, tanned jaw, supple lips, and mysterious dark eyes that held secrets she could only wonder about.

Coming to the bottom of the stairs, she noticed the square of light that slipped from the closed sitting room door. Frowning, she crept forward in the narrow hallway. It was then that Charity heard her parents' voices coming from inside the parlor. Her concern

2222222222

over what would keep them up so late overrode her embarrassment over the way her mother had spoken, not only to herself, but also to Jason, as if they were small children. That her mother might have taken note of her reaction to the hired man, Charity would not allow herself to even contemplate.

As she raised her hand to knock, she heard her mother's voice saying Jason's name, and she realized her parents were in fact discussing the new hand. Taking a deep breath, Charity hesitated. Never before had she deliberately eavesdropped, but this subject was one which was nearly driving her to distraction.

And not her alone. Prudence, who was happily engaged to Albert Whitehead, had talked of little besides Jason after coming up to their room. Her speculations included comments on how uncharacteristically clumsy it was of Charity to have dropped a plate and made herself look ridiculous.

Now, standing right outside the parlor door, there was no way she could force herself to turn away. Though she knew she'd feel penitent later, Charity listened with bated breath.

Mother said, "We don't know that young man. It may be dangerous for us to have him here. He must know what we were doing today."

Elija's answer was earnest. "Thee are right on that count. It wouldn't have been hard for him to guess. I don't know why, Mary, but I believe the boy won't tell anyone. It isn't just that he said as much, I just feel it here . . . in my heart."

Mary sighed, obviously weakening. "But why bring him here, Elija? Thee were putting Lizzy and all of us in danger."

"He was just wandering around Helmsville, going from business to business looking for a job. I don't know why, but something about this boy tugged at me. I just closed my eyes and waited for His light. It came to me then, Mary, that I had to help him. I knew that the Lord wouldn't think kindly of me if I let that young man go in want when we have so much."

Charity knew Papa had said the one thing that Mother couldn't argue with. Mother would never interfere with the Lord's work. Quakers trusted in divine guidance as an active force in their daily lives. It was the cornerstone of their beliefs.

"If thee are bent on having this man here—" Mother let out one of her long-suffering sighs. "—just remember that one does not set a fox to watch a henhouse."

Her father coughed. "Just what does thee mean by that?"

Charity felt herself blush to the roots of her hair as she took three steps backward and came up against the opposite wall. She raised her hands to cover her quivering stomach, understanding perfectly what her mother was saying.

"Thee has very comely daughters, Elija Applegate, as thee well know."

"And why should I not?" There was a pause, and Charity felt sure her parents had kissed. "I have a very comely wife."

Mother giggled like a girl. "Just mind what I say."

Her father's voice turned serious. "Does thee need to be told, woman, that my girls are more precious to me than jewels? I trust Jason Wade, though I cannot say why. He wouldn't try to force himself on any of them. I know it."

"It's not the forcing I'm worried about," Mother interjected.

Elija answered gently. "I've a feeling Jason Wade will not be staying long. That boy is searching for peace, and he doesn't know that it's only to be found inside himself."

"I would be less than honest if I were to say that I am sorry," her mother interjected. "Though there is one of our daughters in particular who might be far less pleased to hear you say that."

A deep flush heated Charity's cheeks and she put her hands up to cool them as she turned and fled back up the stairs, completely forgetting her errand. She didn't know what disturbed her more, the supposed danger to herself, or her father's certainty that Jason would soon be moving on.

Chapter Two

Over the next days, Jason did his very best to stay away from Charity Applegate. He would not risk a repeat of what had gone on that first day.

He was here for one reason and one reason only. He would find and kill the man who had raped and murdered Daphne. It was all he could do when he knew that he was to blame for her death. Even though theirs had been an arranged marriage, Jason should have made more of an effort to fit her into his life.

If he'd spent more time with her she wouldn't have ever gone to work in her brother Michael's clinic. A girl like Daphne couldn't just sit and wait day after day for a husband who was more intimate with his work than his own wife. Why, he'd never even taken her on a honeymoon, promising that it would take place as soon as he found the time to leave the firm for a few weeks. By the end of a year there had still been no date on which she might plan. Daphne, who'd seemed unhappy and listless from the day of the wedding had only shown her first hint of happiness when Jason had agreed to her going to help in Michael's clinic in one of the poorest sections of the city.

His lips twisted in self-derision. She'd wanted to give something. And if it couldn't be to Jason, it would be to the poor Irish immigrants who Michael had decided to spend his life helping. If it weren't for Jason's neglect, she would not have been there to volunteer to take that poor unfortunate girl home after her miscarriage.

The sick girl, Angie Monahan, had been the last person to see Daphne alive. She'd been found the next morning in an alley, raped and murdered. The authorities had wanted to question Angie's lover. It was he who had beaten Angie so severely that she lost her child. He had not been seen since the night Daphne was killed. But even after months of searching the authorities had not been able to find him for questioning. The man, Wayne Grisak, was a bit of a drifter. Angie had insisted that she never knew when she would see him next.

Frustrated with the police's inability to find answers, Jason had known he must act. Posing as an officer, Jason had questioned Angie. She had been unwilling to tell him anything new, but the fear in her eyes when speaking of her lover had left Jason with a cold certainty that she was hiding something. He'd told the police but the authorities had refused to act on his suspicions, even with the force of the name Trenton behind him. They had said they lacked the manpower to search the entire United States to find the drifter for questioning. He had known then it was up to him to follow his lead. Fate's way of telling him that he personally had to avenge Daphne's death. He could atone—at least partially—for not caring enough while his wife still lived.

Jason had no intention of letting himself forget, even for a moment, exactly why he was staying at the Applegate farm.

He bided his time, waiting for a chance to go into town and see what he could find out about the man he sought. He worked in the barns, doing everything Elija would allow until his wife, who had taken over the tending of Jason's hand, said he was healed.

He was just hanging the bucket he'd used to water the cows on its customary hook, when he heard a wagon rattling to a halt on the east side of the barn. Elija entered a moment later, calling out a greeting to Jason as he came inside, his booted feet clomping a steady rhythm on the wooden floor as he made his way down the aisle between the rows of stalls. A cow, kept in because of the birth of her calf the previous day, bawled out a hello, and Elija paused to give her a quick pat. Jason smiled slightly, appreciating this interaction between man and animal, watching as Elija then moved to the ladder and climbed to the loft above.

Hearing a loud grating noise above him, Jason realized that Elija was opening the loft door.

Without waiting for an invitation, Jason followed him up the ladder to the upper floor. The morning sunlight poured in through the open loft doors, warming the golden hay and its sweet rich scent. Pitchfork in hand, the Quaker was shoveling hay into the wagon below. Grabbing the other pitchfork, which hung on the wall, Jason pitched in alongside him.

Jason was growing tired of doing only light duties. His hand was much better and he was prepared to do his share. He already felt as if he were accepting the Applegates' hospitality under false pretenses. Jason was sure Elija's attitude toward him would change if he knew why the stranger he had befriended had come to Helmsville.

But Jason couldn't let that bother him, no matter how much he had grown to like and respect his employer.

If this lead on Grisak turned out to be rootless, Jason would simply begin again—no matter how long it took, or how far he had to go.

Suddenly Jason became aware that Elija had stopped. The Quaker had pushed his black hat back on his head to watch him. "What are thee doing, young fella?"

Jason returned the farmer's gaze. He squared his shoulders with determination. "I won't do the easy work anymore: weeding the garden, feeding the cows, carrying water, brushing down the horses. My hand has healed very well over the past few days. Last night when she dressed it, Mrs. . . . Mary said the wound's almost healed. If you don't believe me, you can go ask her."

Elija's answer was stern as he took his handkerchief out of his back pocket and wiped the sweat from his forehead. "I do not doubt thee, Jason Wade. I just don't want thee to overdo thyself. What use will thee be to me if thee don't heal properly?"

Jason smiled, knowing the gruff words were only a cover for the older man's concern. He had learned quite a lot about the Applegates since arriving on their farm.

The family's prayers before meals were sincere. And sometimes Jason would come upon one of the

Applegates and find them sitting silently, their eyes closed, a look of utter peace on their face.

Just yesterday he had intruded on Elija where he sat on a stump in the field behind the barn, his face turned toward the warmth of the sun. Jason tried to back away quietly, but Elija heard him, and opened his eyes with a smile of welcome.

The older man had shown no embarrassment, he'd simply told Jason that it always did a man good to give a moment to the Lord.

Though he did not understand their ways, Jason was coming to respect them. The Applegates' kindness to him left him in no doubt as to Elija's true feelings when the older man asked what use Jason would be to him if he didn't heal. The Quakers' generosity only increased his guilt for being at the farm under false pretenses.

To cover his self-derision, Jason answered matter-of-factly. "Have no fear of that. I'll be fine."

Elija gave the hired man another long, measuring look, but his only acknowledgment was a nod of assent.

When the wagon was loaded, Jason followed Elija outside and climbed into the driver's seat. The horses stood quietly swatting flies with their tails while he loosened the reins. "Where is the load going?"

"To the livery in Helmsville." Elija scowled with worry. "How is thy hand after filling the wagon? Will thee be able to unload?"

Jason nodded. "Fine. I'm sure there is someone at the stable who helps with the unloading."

"Yes, Henry Tucker." Elija took off his hat and wiped his brow with that big white handkerchief. "But he's none too eager to work, and has to be prodded at times."

"Don't worry. I can prod with the best of them. My

assistants . . ." Jason stopped, realizing he was saying more than he'd intended.

It was apparent from the farmer's thoughtful expression that Elija had caught the slip, but he didn't comment. Going around the wagon, Elija pulled himself up into the seat. "Drive around to the house. Mary asked me to stop by before I went into town."

Jason headed the team around to the west side of the barn, then across the yard to the side of the neat, two-story house. He was careful to skirt the ends of the rows of vegetables that grew behind the structure. He was very familiar with both those plants and the flower garden that flourished in the front yard. Though his work there had been light, Mary Applegate was exacting in her standards.

As they halted, the kitchen door opened and Charity emerged. She was dressed for traveling, wearing a plain gray bonnet with her dark high-buttoned dress, and she was carrying a pocketbook over her wrist.

The young woman was obviously surprised to find Jason at the reins of the wagon. She looked up at him, the dark bonnet framing her sweetly curved cheeks, her wide eyes rivaling the summer sky for intensity of blue, and winning. Jason felt a strange tugging sensation in his chest. Abruptly he turned away, not wanting to see the fresh sweetness of her, not wanting to feel—anything.

Yet his gaze quickly found her again. Even as he watched, she flushed and bit her lip, then looked down at the toes of her black boots. As her father jumped down, Charity glanced up at him, her expression questioning.

"Does thy mother need some supplies from town?"

Elija asked his daughter, clearly not noticing the exchange between her and Jason.

"Yes, she thought I could go along with thee . . . Papa." Her gaze was doubtful as she looked from her father to Jason.

Elija frowned for a moment as his eyes met those of his hired hand. Jason knew what was on the other man's mind. Could he be trusted with Charity? For a moment the uncertainty in the other's gaze prickled, but he pushed it aside, knowing that Elija simply wished his daughter safe. And Jason couldn't deny to himself that he did find Charity more than passingly attractive.

Yet he was not the kind of man who forced himself on any woman, no matter how appealing. And he'd known the pain caused by those men that did. He faced the older man directly, unwaveringly, and the farmer seemed to come to a decision. "Thee can ride with Jason. He's taking the hay to the livery stable."

She frowned, and Jason could tell Charity wasn't pleased at the thought of going with him. He felt an unexpected sense of disappointment and quickly dismissed it. With Charity along it would be more difficult to make inquiries about Grisak. He didn't want to have to explain himself to her. He also realized that he would not be able to purchase a gun as he had intended to do when he reached Helmsville. He knew in the same instant that he would wait for that, wait until he had actually found Grisak. He did not wish to further betray the Applegates by bringing a weapon back to their farm. It should not prove difficult to obtain a gun when the time came. He had more than sufficient funds in his saddlebags and could wire for more from his accounts in Boston if need be.

The money, a change of clothes and a few toiletries were all he carried with him. He had left possessions and his care for them behind him in Boston with his respect for the law. He required nothing but his anger now.

With that thought in mind he watched Elija help his daughter into the wagon. Elija then came around to Jason's side and spoke softly so that only Jason could hear. "Look after her." There was a gentle hint of warning in his blue eyes. Apparently, Jason had not been completely successful at hiding his attraction to Charity.

Jason nodded, his expression direct in spite of his irritation with himself. "I will, Elija." He meant it. No attraction, however powerful, would sway him from his true purpose, which was finding Grisak. Once he had settled that score, Jason would be going back to his old life. His father, who had been shocked at his decision to abandon his life and his principles to go after the man who had killed his wife, still counted on him to return.

It was a life that was far removed from the Applegates' farm in Wisconsin and a beautiful young Quaker girl with eyes the color of the sky.

As the wagon rattled down the road Charity set her mind to ignoring Jason Wade, just as he had ignored her over the past days.

Since the moment she had realized Jason would be driving the wagon into town, her thoughts had been chaotic. Her own reactions to the strangely compelling way he had of looking at her sometimes made her feel . . . well, she wasn't quite sure. She only knew that she had never experienced anything like it.

Charity couldn't help wondering what her mother would say when she found out Papa had sent her off alone with him. Though Mother had never even questioned her riding along with their previous hired man, Jake, her opinion of hired men seemed to have changed.

Admittedly Jake had been missed since he'd gone to live with his married daughter in Nebraska. Yet he'd offered nothing that could make a young girl's heartbeat quicken.

Jason was another matter entirely. Acutely aware of the man beside her, she risked a quick peek out of the corner of her eye. The breeze ruffled his dark hair and the sun gilded its red and gold highlights, making her wish she could touch it. But he sat straight and stiff beside her, his hands white-knuckled on the reins, making it clear he would not accept such a familiarity, even if the idea was proper. Which it was not!

Yet, Charity could not stop her wayward thoughts or the surreptitious glances. Her yearning eyes saw that Jason was neither old, nor unattractive. After eating her mother's excellent cooking, there was now even a bit of flesh on his bones. And if she had to say so herself, he had filled out very nicely. His cheeks were not quite so hollow, his shoulders wide and sturdy. Those dark denim pants of his were clean, and hugged distractingly the muscular lengths of his legs.

To top all that, he was intelligent, hardworking, and had an easy manner when dealing with others. That is, with everyone except Charity. With her, he was reserved and distant.

Even Prudence liked him. And goodness knows, Prue didn't often approve of men like him—drifters with no roots or ties.

Just yesterday, Charity had seen them coming

43

across the yard together. He'd had Prue laughing and blushing like a schoolgirl. And her promised to Albert Whitehead. Jealousy as frustrating as a tangled embroidery thread had made her hurry away before they'd seen her in return. She didn't want to feel that way, but Charity just couldn't seem to help herself as far as this man was concerned.

Clearly oblivious to her, he drove on. His lean jaw was set in a firm line, and he looked neither right nor left as he urged the horses down the road. She sighed. This could turn out to be a very long ride indeed.

Determinedly, Charity turned her thoughts away from Jason.

It was a perfect day in early August, and the sun was hot on the back of her head. The sky above the trees was a rich azure, and she knew she should enjoy this outing, for it was a busy time of year and such an opportunity wouldn't come again soon. She breathed deeply of the heady scent of the wildflowers that lined the road.

Summer was always welcome after the cold Wisconsin winter, and Charity obeyed the impulse to remove her bonnet. What had felt hot through the dark cloth now became a warm caress, and she sighed with pleasure, leaning back.

From where it nestled close to the well-used wagon trail, the forest appeared cool and deep. It smelled of rich moss, dry oak and sharp pine. At fairly regular intervals, these patches of wood gave way to ripe golden fields that rippled in the gentle breeze. Butterflies fluttered their delicate wings among wildflowers that were beginning to bloom in a riot of pinks, blues, purples, golds and reds along the road. There was even an occasional glimpse of a farmhouse and once the sound of children's laughter rising sweetly in the distance.

The horses moved along at a steady pace over the smooth track and the wagon rocked only slightly in a soothing rhythm. Charity found it harder and harder to remain aloof as the beauty of their surroundings engulfed her, spoke to her senses and heart of the Lord's great abundance. Surely she could spend the next few hours with Jason without making a fool of herself, treat him as any other man. She refused to acknowledge the twinge of uncertainty in her belly as she turned with deliberate casualness and said, "Isn't this the most beautiful day thee have ever seen?"

Jason had been concentrating on not letting his arm come into contact with the warmth of her side, and it took him a moment to hear the question. He glanced her way and gave a start of surprise. Obviously Charity was not nearly as tense at this forced contact as he. She was leaning back against the wagon seat, her eyes closed, a gentle smile curving her mouth. Unconsciously, Jason's eyes lingered on those lips, his tongue coming out to wet his own, which were suddenly dry. Charity had taken off that horrible bonnet and the gentle breeze teased the fringe of gold hair that had escaped her bun, and a strand fell forward to caress her sun-warmed cheek.

He felt again that increasingly familiar tightness in his chest. His lips thinned in derision.

But then she opened those blue eyes and looked at him, her expression completely ingenuous, and Jason was ashamed. That one look at her open face made him realize he could not continue to be so withdrawn.

It wasn't Charity's fault he was attracted to her and

hating himself for feeling anything when Daphne could not. It was his own responsibility to control himself.

Jason took a deep breath of the sweet summer air and felt it seep into his being, relaxing him and filling him with a small portion of her pleasure in the day. "I'm not sure I could be that definitive, but it is certainly a beautiful day."

Charity grinned, seeming pleased at his words. "I love summer. It's my favorite time of year. Everything is so bright and good. In summer almost anything is possible."

Jason couldn't remember how long it had been since he'd seen so much enthusiasm and faith in the world around him.

Looking at Charity beside him, so young and warm and innocent, Jason couldn't keep from answering her smile with one of his own. "You could be right. I find myself almost believing anything *is* possible at this time of year."

"Hope's youngest, Jacob, was born last August."

Her smile widened, her eyes fairly glowing with approval and another emotion he didn't want to name. His heart thumping, Jason felt himself dangerously close to the edge of a precipice that he could not cross. Desperately he searched for something to take his mind off of those lovely blue eyes, his own wildly racing pulse. "Hope is the sister who is married to Levi?" he asked, trying to think of something, anything to distract himself from the beauty of her eyes.

"Yes, and Hope is the oldest. She lives just up the road from us. They have three children, two boys and a girl." Charity made no move to lean away from him as the swaying of the wagon repeatedly brought her slender shoulder into contact with his. Every time they touched, he caught the scent of her sun-warmed hair and his pulse responded with a double beat.

He knew he should move away. But there was no place to go on the narrow bench. He took a deep breath. "I take it there are no sons, as I've never heard your parents mention anything but female names."

Charity went on thankfully oblivious to his torment. "There are seven of us." She counted on her fingers as she said the names. "Hope, Felicity, Patience, Prudence, myself, Constance and Purity. Constance is the older of the twins."

Jason tried to relax as she chatted on, telling himself this attraction was nothing he couldn't control. He urged her to go on, "Hope, Felicity, and Patience are married?"

She looked down at her hands. "Yes, Patience lives with her husband, William, a few miles south of Helmsville. William works his father's farm. Someday it will pass on to him. We haven't seen much of them lately. Patience is expecting her second and doesn't travel well."

"And Felicity," he prodded, although he could not help noticing that with her hands pressed together like that her the fabric of her dress tightened distractingly over the swell of her bosom. Even when he deliberately turned away, he still could just see out of the corner of his eyes—if he looked.

At that very moment, Charity paused, glancing at him, then away. He felt himself flush at the inappropriateness of his thoughts. Though he told himself she couldn't possible read those thoughts, her hands moved to twine around the string of her purse. Finally she answered. "Yes, Felicity is married, too."

* * *

Charity heard the breathlessness in her own voice and knew that she was doing a poor job of thinking of anything besides the heady male scent of Jason Wade, the strange look in his eyes that made her belly tighten. He was so close and so very masculine in a way that made her more aware of her own femininity than she had ever been before. She looked down at her own hands. They seemed so small and fragile in comparison to his, which were strong and capable on the reins.

Desperately she scanned the forest beside the road as she tried to breathe more evenly—to concentrate on something besides the way she was feeling. She found no answer to her agitation in the lush vegetation, nor in the occasional patch of light where the sun pierced the canopy in splashes of dappled brightness. Then out of the corner of her eyes she caught a flash of scarlet in the woods to her left. Without thinking she cried out, "Please, stop."

She leapt to the ground before the wheels had stopped turning. A few feet into the forest she stopped and knelt on the ground, which was soft with a padding of moss, leaves, and small plants.

Charity turned with a brilliant smile as he came up beside her, indicating the deep red wild poppy she'd cupped her hand around. "Isn't it beautiful?" she asked, knowing she was overreacting and that it was due to Jason's nearness, not to finding the poppy.

His answer came slowly as he ran a hand through his hair, his gaze raking her with an expression she could not name. But that expression brought a flush of heat to her cheeks and an intensification of the fullness in her lower belly. His voice was low as he said, "Well, yes. But you startled me out of three years' growth. Please don't do that again."

Looking up the long length of him beside her, Charity suddenly found herself laughing aloud, emboldened by his nearness, and by some inner sprite that seemed to have been awakened by the strange light in his eyes. "Thee don't seem to have lost any inches from where I am."

His brows rose and he rested his hands on his lean hips, as his lips twisting mockingly. "Infant, hasn't anyone ever told you not to talk back to your elders?"

That inner sprite only seemed to be taking more control of her mind and senses as she found her gaze travelling up the length of that long, lean form. "Thee don't seem so very old to me, Jason Wade."

Jason's lids became hooded and he swallowed—hard. His voice was even deeper when he spoke, "Watch yourself little one. I don't think you know quite what you're about. After all, I'm only human."

Charity flushed as the meaning of his words washed over her. Her gaze dropped to the ground even as a strange sense of power swept through her. Jason might not be as indifferent to her as he had seemed in the last few days.

She looked up at him, her gaze searching, yearning.

He took a sharp breath, stepping backward. "We'd best be going. I don't want your parents to worry."

"Why should they worry?" Charity shrugged, giving him a look from under her long lashes. "Aren't thee trustworthy?"

Jason gave her a long searching glance, started to say something, then obviously thought better of it. His voice was now tight, controlled. "Let's just go."

She felt a stinging sense of disappointment that could not be explained, turning to dig into the soft dirt with her fingers as she fought the sensation. "I am sorry to inconvenience thee, but I have to bring the poppy." He continued to stand there as she pulled up the flower, earth and all, then stood with it cradled in her palm. Though she tried for matter-of-factness, her voice betrayed an excess of emotion as she said, "May I use thy handkerchief? I want to take it for Mother's garden. Thee don't see very many of them wild and red is my favorite color."

Reaching into his pocket, Jason produced a clean kerchief. Charity felt his gaze on her as she wrapped it around the roots and earth but didn't look at him. His slightly teasing voice startled her. "Is that a proper favorite color for a pious Quaker girl?"

It wasn't his question that surprised her, but the teasing tone after his abrupt coolness. The somber grays, browns, and blues of her wardrobe certainly didn't reflect this love of bright color. Still stinging from his rudeness she shot back a retort. "God made the flowers the way He wished them to be. Humans are not born in such finery."

Jason know he deserved derision. He had reacted very badly to her innocent efforts at flirting because they had effected him far more than they should. Because of this he found himself answering her softly. "I don't think the Lord would hold it against a pretty girl for wanting to wear the colors she liked. I'm sure you'd look lovely in red." Her blush deepened until he wasn't sure she was right about the Lord not seeing fit to grace humans with bright color.

God, but she was beautiful, and shy, and sensuous—and far too compelling.

Wordlessly and without knowing why he did so, he reached out to her. When she placed her hand in his, he raised her slowly, to her feet. Charity's skin was cool in his and he couldn't help feeling the way her fingers trembled. Jason looked down at that slender hand, long-fingered and sensitive, yet strong. It was the hand of a woman who could be many things to a man, friend, partner, lover. His throat went dry and he fought an overpowering urge to press his lips to the pale skin of her palm.

As if sensing his thoughts, her eyes locked with his for an infinite moment. Her breathing became shallow.

Time seemed to stretch and Jason suddenly knew that more than anything he wanted to kiss her. He knew that she, without being aware of it, wanted it too. He was also very conscious of the fact that if he did kiss her he would make her think . . . well . . . things he didn't want her to think.

Again Jason brought himself back from the precipice, breaking the intimate silence, though it cost him no little effort. "We'd better get that hay delivered for your father."

Charity blinked, then swung around and hurried toward the wagon. He was not sorry that she climbed onto the seat without waiting for his help.

Jason followed the road straight into Helmsville. Having been there once, he could do that much on his own. And he was glad that he didn't have to ask Charity for directions. Too much had been said already. He kept his attention on where he was going. Yet when they passed the train station on the outskirts of town, he was forced to ask for assistance.

A noticeably subdued Charity directed Jason to the livery stable, which was a large red structure right at the east end of Main Street. Jason could only guess that her feelings matched his own. Glancing over at her impassive profile, he told himself he had no right to miss her former warmth. Yet he did.

The barn was located at the back, and Jason went around to where they would unload.

Charity still didn't look at Jason as he helped her from the wagon. "I'll just go along to the dry goods store," she said.

Jason's hand tightened on hers and a deep line of worry appeared beside his mouth. "Alone?"

Surprise at his vehemence widened her blue eyes. "Why, yes," she answered. "There's nothing to be concerned about. No one will bother me. I've lived here all my life."

Jason's lips tightened. Daphne had died because she was too trusting. "That's no reason for you to be careless." She started to speak, but he hushed her by saying, "And don't tell me the Lord will look after you. He sometimes has his eyes shut."

Sorrow filled Charity's gaze as she looked up at him. Her gentle voice made his chest tighten. "Thee shouldn't speak so, Jason Wade. I don't know what happened to hurt thee so, but thee mustn't let it get the best of thee. Troubles come to every life. Thee must learn to go on from whatever has happened."

He heard the gruffness in his own voice as he replied and knew that he was more moved by her concern than he would ever have expected. "You don't know what you're talking about. Some things are impossible to forget."

To his utter and overwhelming amazement she reached up and put her hand to his cheek. "Nothing is worth letting it eat thee alive."

As in the forest, when he'd held her hand, her fingers were cool against his flesh. He felt his heart thudding against his ribs and a pulling in his lower stomach. Jason could hardly breath past his own sudden and inescapable longing. The desire to give in to her sympathy, her goodness, was strong. Instinctively, he turned his lips to her soft palm.

With a startled gasp, she drew her hand away, holding her tingling palm against her bosom.

Jason swallowed hard, silently cursing himself. Why had he forgotten himself enough to kiss her that way? She was an innocent, without the means to understand what was happening between them. And Jason was not free to teach her. He was bound to his hate and need for revenge. He laughed at his own foolishness, a dry chuckle without any mirth. "Just be careful that you don't get burned, little one. I'm on fire with hate, and you're coming too close. I've got enough hate in me to destroy you."

Silently she watched him for a long moment, her gaze confused and decidedly thoughtful. Then, to his surprise and grudging admiration, Charity raised her chin and said, "Thee can't destroy me with thy hate, Jason Wade. Love sustains me, the love of the Lord and the people I care about. Love is stronger and will always win out over hate."

Before he could say another word she turned and stalked away from him, her straight back and gently curved hips distracting him far more than he would have wished.

Only after the wagon had been unloaded, the hard work unfortunately doing little to ease his frustration over what had just occurred, did Jason stop to talk with the livery hand who'd offered very little assistance. Henry Tucker was a wiry little man, whose obvious laziness might be explained by the scent of rye whiskey on his breath.

As soon as he was finished, Jason moved to where the bleary eyed Tucker stood holding up a post. He kept his tone deliberately even. "You lived around here long?"

Henry Tucker rubbed a grubby finger along the side of his nose. "All my life."

"Then you know most of the people who live around Helmsville?"

He shrugged. "I'd say I do. Though most of those I'd call friend, I know from Francine's Place. Best Saloon in town and if you've a mind, the girls are willing to go upstairs for a dollar. Clean, too, you don't have to worry about catching nothin'. Not like at Joy's Palace. No tellin' what you might get over there." He scratched at his groin gingerly.

Jason wondered if the man had first hand knowledge of what might be contracted at Joy's Palace. He didn't ask. Jason concentrated on saying what he wanted to say without revealing too much. If Grisak was around Helmsville, Jason didn't want him to hear that someone was asking about him. He'd taken great pains to keep his presence and inquiries discreet along the way.

Yet what could he do but ask? "You know of a fellow by the name of Grisak?"

Henry Tucker's watery eyes widened. "Do I know? Why he's my own dead Liza's boy." He nattered on, unknowing of the jolt of shock that rolled through Jason's body. "The boy never took to me much. She had him when she come. And when she died . . . well I ain't seen much of Wayne since then."

With deliberate and profound care, Jason slowed his breath, forced himself to think clearly. "Do you know if he's around town?"

Tucker drew a tin of tobacco out of his pocket and offered it to him.

Jason shook his head, trying not to let his impatience show. "No, thank you."

"Suit yourself," Tucker put a generous pinch between his gum and lip, then returned the tin to his pocket.

"Nope I ain't seen him fer some time. He a friend a yourn?" He looked at Jason with new interest.

Jason shook his head. Not even for such a worthy purpose could he claim such an evil beast as his friend. "No, not really. I just ran into someone who told me to look him up and have a drink when they heard I was coming this way."

The older man nodded, casting a surreptitious glance about, then taking a flask out of the inside pocket of his tattered jacket. "Yer welcome to have a swallow with me."

Jason took the flask and feigned taking a drink. He didn't want to seem to be anything other than what he pretended to be, a careless drifter. No threat.

Tucker reached for the flask and took several long gulps before sticking it back into his pocket. "Yep, less'n you mean to stay awhile, you ain't likely to see him. I hear tell he does a bit of travelin' in the south, if you know what I mean?"

"What do you mean?" Jason asked though he did in fact have suspicion.

"He ain't above trottin' escaped property back south on his trips to make extra money."

Jason wasn't surprised to hear such things about Grisak. "I see," he kept his tone carefully neutral.

The other man nodded. "So, are ya stayin' long?"

Jason shrugged. "That depends on how long long is."

Tucker seemed to take this noncommital answer well for he offered, "Hear tell he's got a wife and kids someplace out along Silver Creek."

A wife. His lips thinned. The scum had beaten his woman in Boston so badly she'd lost their baby, but Jason shouldn't be surprised at anything a man like that would do. The scales of judgment tipped a little further. Jason was more and more sure he had the right man. He straightened. "Well, I'd better be going. I have to get Miss Applegate home. Do you mind if I leave the wagon here while I find out what has to be picked up and where?"

"No, no, go ahead. This here is a livery stable anyhow." Tucker gave a crusty chuckle. "Won't even charge you no rent."

"Thank you," Jason answered, impatient to be off now that he had learned all he could. If Grisak wasn't in the area, the decision had to be made whether to stay or move on.

"Don't blame you for wanting to get off after that Applegate girl. Ever one of them girls is as purty as an unopened bottle of rye." The way he smacked his lips thirstily made it apparent that his words were high praise indeed.

Jason didn't reply, though he felt unaccountably offended by the comment. He told himself that what the old codger thought was of no consequence to him. He had overcome the madness that made him react so strongly to Charity.

As he stepped onto the boardwalk an empty wagon rattled by, throwing a cloud of dust over him as Jason's booted footsteps echoed hollowly along the boardwalk. Belatedly, he noticed that he was dirty and covered in straw. Self-consciously, he dusted himself off as he stopped outside a building with a sign that read WILBURT'S DRY GOODS.

He went inside, only to be told by the mustached young clerk that Charity Applegate had left some time ago. Jason might be wise to try Hilda's Emporium, which was just down the main street and across the road.

Jason continued on his way, encountering more people now that he was in the busier part of the town. Well-dressed ladies strolled by on the arms of tidy gentlemen. Occasionally Jason noted someone dressed in the more somber manner of the Quakers. He passed a druggist's and a milliner's on the right-hand side of the street, and a doctor's office, the sheriff's, and Western Union on his left. Helmsville was quite the little metropolis.

Directly across the street from Lola's Parisian Fashions he found Hilda's Emporium.

Like all shops of its type, Hilda's was crowded with stock from floor to ceiling. Shoulder-high rows of shelves held cloth, shoes, sewing notions, pots and pans, and gardening tools, not to mention a myriad of other articles.

A rather robust blond woman stood at the front counter. She came toward Jason with an appreciative smile in her deep-set eyes. When she spoke, it was with an unmistakable German accent. "Ach, can I help you?"

"I'm looking for Charity Applegate," Jason said, remembering not to address the Quaker girl by any title.

The woman's disappointment was obvious. "Ja, she is at the back." She waved a dramatic arm covered in lilac muslin. "But if you should need anything else?" Her dark-lashed eyes held an open invitation. There was a certain earthy charm in her looks and manner.

Jason simply nodded. The last thing he needed was trouble of that kind. The woman probably had a large German husband who would be happy to pummel any man who so much as glanced at the lovely Hilda.

Talking a few steps toward the back of the store, Jason stopped dead in his tracks as he noticed the lady standing behind one of the shelves. She stood before a mirror, tying on the wide ribbon of her ivory silk bonnet adorned with fully bloomed pale pink roses, which had also been fashioned from silk. She tilted her elegant head as she smiled at her reflection in the mirror and he saw her delicate profile more fully.

He gasped. This elegant lady in the decidedly beautiful but worldly bonnet was none other than Charity Applegate.

Charity swung around to face him, her hand coming up to cover her pink lips as her eyes widened in shock and horror. Hurriedly she nearly tore the bonnet from her head and placed it on the counter. She stood, clutching her handbag with both hands as he moved toward her. "Jason Wade, I did not expect thee so soon."

"Really?" he could not resist teasing her as he indicted the hastily discarded bonnet. "It's lovely."

She frowned. "I . . . is it?" She hurried past him. "We must go."

Jason drew himself up short. Then slowly he followed, his gaze trained on her rigid back as they left the store. He would remember that teasing was not allowed, nor was recalling how beautiful she'd looked in that bonnet.

Chapter Three

Charity gave a groan of frustration when she scraped her knuckles on the lamp shade. She knew it was her own fault for not paying attention to what she was doing, but that man was nigh on to driving her crazy.

The day they had gone to Helmsville, Charity had managed to make a fool of herself, flirting with him in the woods and allowing him to kiss her hand in the stable. The very memory made her shiver. Heaven knew why he had done that, other than the possibility that she had unknowingly invited him to by touching him.

Whatever had possessed her to do such a thing—even out of sympathy, which was surely why she had done it? And then to be caught trying on that ridiculous bonnet! It did not help to know that she had been thinking of Jason when she had done so, wondering if he would find her beautiful in it, if he would no longer call her an infant.

His reaction of amusement had not reassured her. Her cheeks heated more with each mortifying memory. Her self-possession had only disintegrated further with each moment that Jason had ignored her on the long, long ride home.

She had even tried to convince herself that he was silent because the rumbling of the wagon beneath them made conversation difficult. For the ride home was just a bit rougher than the one to town, due to the fact that the flour, sugar, coffee and other supplies Charity had purchased in Helmsville were not nearly as heavy as the hay.

Yet her explanation did not ring true. There was a stiffness in the set of his shoulders that gave away a certain tension. She told herself it didn't matter what he thought about anything, including her. She didn't want to talk to Jason, anyway.

In spite of this resolution, she was not pleased by the fact that he had continued treating her as if she were invisible over the last few days. She dropped her cloth to the floor, nursing her injured knuckles even as she acknowledged that the hurt could not match the one inside her. For as Jason remained open and friendly with her sisters, she found it impossible not to wish. . . .

Charity sighed, glancing up, and realized that she had allowed her thoughts to slip too far down an unwanted path. She had allowed them to make her forget where she was, and with whom.

Across the sitting room, her mother was making

short work of dusting the bookshelves. She swung around to frown at her daughter. "What ails thee, Charity Applegate? Thee seems to be having trouble accomplishing the simplest tasks. 'Good for the body is the work of the body,' " She said, quoting Thoreau.

Charity blushed, not looking at her mother. "I scraped myself. I guess I was . . . thinking."

Mary Applegate dropped her duster and went to the parlor curtains, opening them with a jerk. " 'Whenever God gives us a cross to bear, it is true that he will also give us strength.' We will pray that all will be well with Lizzy." Until a slave reached Canada there was always danger of recapture.

Obviously, Mother thought she was worrying about Lizzy. Charity opened her mouth to confess that her thoughts had not been so selfless, then she shut it again.

There was no way Charity could tell her mother she was mooning over the hired man. "Yes, Mother, we will pray," she agreed, although the words burned in her throat, feeling like a lie.

Her mother was the strength of the family, and they all knew it, even Father, who was twice her size. Mother's absolute faith in God and His wisdom had always kept them all stable. Never had Charity kept anything from her.

When the older woman spoke again, she was once more in command of her emotions. "Thee finish up the parlor now, Charity. I'm going to see how the others are coming in the bedrooms."

As Charity watched her mother bustle out, she realized how much she had changed of late.

Before, Charity had been fairly happy with her life

as it was, chores, prayers, time spent with the family. Oh, she daydreamed of some of the faraway places she'd read about, but her life seemed, if not completely fulfilling, then content at least. Real fulfillment would come when she married and had children—children who would be raised in the true light of the Faith.

Since the day Jason walked into their kitchen, that had all changed. He was her first thought when she woke, her last before she fell into restless sleep. All day she wondered where he was, what he was doing—thinking.

And when he was nearby, it was even worse. Everything about him fascinated her. Charity would find herself staring at his mouth as he talked, his long fingers as he reached for his hat, his slate-dark eyes as he looked at her. He made her feel alive and aware as she'd never felt in her life. It was as if she'd been winter-dormant, and Jason was a warm rush of spring air sent to awaken her.

He barely seemed to notice that she existed. She told herself she was glad, at least he didn't know how foolish she was being. But her self-assurances did not quite ring true.

Charity sighed and looked at the cloth in her hand. The dusting. Determined not to think about Jason Wade anymore, and almost succeeding, Charity finished her cleaning.

The next few days continued on much the same path. Charity did her best to concentrate on what she was supposed to be doing, but it grew more difficult rather than easier.

Every time she heard Jason's voice, or saw him

smile at one of her sisters, she felt her insides go tight, as if they were being squeezed with fencing wire.

The hayloft was a special place, one of the few spots on the farm where Charity could go and be alone. One hot afternoon, book in hand, she climbed the ladder in the barn and made herself a nest of hay near the edge of the sloping roof. But not even here was she to find any peace. She found herself studying the motes of dust sparkling in the light that filtered through the cracks around the doors, and it reminded her of the way sunlight shone on Jason's hair.

She dropped her book on the hay beside her, realizing it was hopeless. Charity had read the diary of George Fox before. Quite a lot of the work, like much of the literature of the Quaker faith, was written in the form of essays. These writings, which were on finding and listening to the voice of the Lord that is inside each of us, usually gave her a sense of solace. But today she couldn't concentrate.

Her thoughts wouldn't leave her alone.

Just that morning, before he'd come in to breakfast, Jason had been washing at the pump. Charity had watched him from the kitchen window as he hung his shirt on the pump handle and splashed water onto his face and bare torso. The morning sunlight turned his wet, well-muscled chest a warm gold, and her gaze had lingered unashamedly over every supple curve. She'd watched one glistening droplet as it slipped down his body to disappear in the dark hair below his navel, and she'd grown unaccountably warm.

Just as Jason was reaching for his shirt, Purity and Constance had come along, together as always, each carrying a basket of eggs.

Jason had greeted them with a cheery smile as he buttoned his shirt, and they'd stopped to talk. Something, some teasing remark he made, had caused Purity to laugh, and she'd reached into the bucket beneath the spout and flicked cold water onto him.

Without hesitation, Jason had returned fire, then chased the girls around the yard. Neither Purity nor Constance had tried very hard to get away.

The game had ended when Elija had come from the barn and good-naturedly ordered them all in to the morning meal. Then, over breakfast, Charity listened while Jason had asked a not-so-innocent question about whether or not Albert Whitehead had managed to win Prudence's affection.

Prudence's cheeks had grown rosy as ripe apples, and she'd looked at the floor. Everyone knew the young woman had taken a walk with her fiancé last evening. Jason must have inadvertently come upon them together. From Prue's demeanor, they must have been doing more than making wedding plans.

But no one minded. Mother and Papa had just laughed. Albert was a welcome addition to the family, and just the pragmatic, steady kind of man Prue wanted.

In comparison to all this teasing and familiarity, for Charity, Jason had managed nothing better than a tight "Good morning" and a "Please pass the biscuits"? Yet she'd pushed her loneliness aside, knowing it was best to ignore it.

As if these events weren't enough to make her feel left out, later in the morning Hope had driven over in her buggy. Usually Patience would have come with her, but she was experiencing a great deal of motion sickness with this pregnancy.

Hope was a tall slim woman, like her mother and sisters. She had a sweet, settled air about her that Charity envied, and she was a strict but loving mother to her three children.

The visit had begun well enough; Charity had been enjoying herself, chatting as they baked apple pies together. But when the talk had turned to marriage and childbearing, she had been asked, along with the twins, to take herself off. Before today she hadn't greatly minded leaving them to talk of such things, which were not yet her concern, but now she found herself yearning to be included, to be thought of as a woman.

Charity turned her face to the sweet-smelling hay with a sigh of frustration. What secrets did these women share, these who had experienced the mysteries of a man's love?

As though her thoughts had conjured up the sound, she became aware of a masculine voice singing "Rock of Ages," and the clump of boots coming across the floor below. Her lips turned upward as Jason stopped beneath the loft. There was the unmistakable sound of hay being raked in the stall below her as he continued singing. His rendition of the hymn was low and slightly off-key, yet strangely endearing.

She wondered why he would have left the field so early. For a few short moments, Charity was inordinately pleased to just sit and listen to him. Then she began to feel a trifle guilty. There was something unseemly about lying above him without him knowing she was there.

She was just sitting up so that she could go down the

ladder and make her presence known, when she heard another voice. This one she knew very well.

Purity. And something about the breathless quality of her tone made Charity's brow crease in a disapproving frown.

"Good afternoon, Jason." The voice was simpering, and Charity could just imagine the way her sister was standing, close by the handsome hired man.

"Good afternoon . . . Purity."

Charity was surprised. Most people couldn't tell the twins apart, especially when they weren't together. Charity had known which sister was speaking by the slightly higher tone of her voice. By the way, where was Constance? The twins were always together.

"I saw thee and Papa come in from the field."

Charity frowned. And what had that got to do with her sister following him into the barn?

"One of the reaper blades broke," Jason answered easily. "Your father had to go into Helmsville to the blacksmith."

"Thee didn't go with him?"

Charity's eyes rolled heavenward. Clearly, Purity was desperate to make conversation.

"No, I thought I'd stay here and do some mucking out in the barn. So, if you don't mind . . ." Then there was only the sound of Jason's exertions for a few moments.

"Thee are very strong." Was Charity mistaken, or was Purity's voice just a little too breathless?

"Why, thank you. I haven't been doing this kind of work for long. I'm afraid it takes some getting used to."

"Oh—" Purity obviously took what Jason said as an

opening for questions about his past. "—what did thee do before?"

Charity leaned forward, very interested in the answer to that question herself.

Jason gave an uncomfortable laugh. "I . . . it doesn't matter. Nothing you'd be interested in."

"Oh, but I would be interested," Purity told him.

Charity could hear the openly flirtatious quality in her younger sister's voice. She wanted to shake her. Jason was well over twenty-five. Besides, fourteen was too young for Purity to be acting this way with any man, no matter his age. What was her sister thinking of? But there was nothing Charity could do at the moment. It was too late to let them know she was there. She could never explain why she had remained hidden for so long.

There was a short, perfect silence, then she heard Jason speak, his tone puzzled. "Purity?"

It was too much for Charity. She just had to see what was going on down there. Rolling over onto her belly, she crawled over to the edge of the hayloft and hung her head over. From there the warm scent of cow dung and soiled hay stung her nostrils, but she didn't allow that to deter her.

To her utter disappointment, all she could see were Jason's brown boots and Purity's black ones, facing each other in the aisle between the stalls. They were very close together. Jason's rake leaned against one of the posts that held up the wooden floor of the loft.

Losing all thought for her safety, she leaned even farther over the edge. Bits of hay moved with her, to fall to the lower floor, and she held her breath, hoping she wouldn't be noticed. When the blades settled onto the pile below without incident, she allowed herself to breathe again.

Straining for all she was worth, Charity could just make out their bodies to the waist. Purity was standing in front of Jason, her arms around his narrow hips.

Purity whispered, "Jason, I think I love thee."

Charity lips tightened with shock and horror. Desperately, she shifted once more, crawling out until she was hanging out of the loft from the ribs up. Her balance was precarious, and she was barely hanging on with both hands, but she just had to see.

Her efforts were rewarded.

Charity's heart thudded with shock when she saw Jason's hands clasping Purity's shoulders.

Purity stood on tiptoe, leaning forward, obviously meaning to kiss him, just as he drew back. It was then that Charity realized Jason was holding her younger sister away from him.

The thought must have occurred to Purity at the same moment, because she stiffened. Her expression became that of a hurt puppy. "Jason?"

Jason's voice was kind. "Purity, honey, you don't love me. You don't even know me."

"Oh, but I do. I thought thee loved me too."

"Listen, little one." He wiped a tear from the corner of her eye. "Don't cry. I'm not worth one of your tears."

"Thee are. Thee are wonderful and kind and funny."

His jaw tightened and a muscle worked in his cheek. "No, I'm not. I'm hard, and cruel, and so miserable you'd hate me if you only knew."

Even as Charity heard her sister reply, "Then let me help thee," she wondered what could have made him describe himself so harshly.

And even as she watched, he ran a gentle hand over Purity's cheek, belying his own words without being aware of it. Charity felt an unexpected pang in her chest as he went on. "Don't ever take on a man for that reason. Wait a few years and find someone who's worthy of all that devotion you have inside you. Someone good and honest, like yourself."

"Thee just say that because thee think I'm a little girl." She pouted up at him, her blue eyes full of a feminine guile Charity hadn't even known she possessed.

Jason smiled, making Charity's own heart thump in reaction. "No, I don't. I just know that I'm not the right man for you. I also know the right one will come along soon enough. Don't rush. Take time to get the very best. You deserve it."

Unbelievably, Purity seemed mollified by what he said. She even looked flattered. And, if Charity wasn't mistaken, her sister was just the tiniest bit hopeful as she said, "Maybe thee'll wait for me." Charity couldn't help wondering for one brief second how she would feel if Jason were to look at her that way. Why, just the thought was enough to make her cheeks get warm.

Mesmerized she saw Jason reach out and tucked a strand of silver-blond hair behind the girl's delicate ear. "Purity, by the time you get around to really wanting a man, you won't even remember this. I'll be far too old."

Purity giggled at the thought, her gaze running over his darkly handsome face in obvious disbelief. "Don't be too sure," she murmured, sounding far older than her years.

Jason laughed, and gently pushed her away from him. "Now, go on and let me finish my work."

Backing away from him, Purity stopped and said, "Thee won't tell Papa?"

Deliberately, Jason's expression grew blank. "Tell him what?"

Purity smiled brilliantly and scampered away like the child she was. Jason moved to stand directly under Charity's perch, staring after her sister, a fond smile on his lips. With the twin gone, Charity now felt a dawning realization of just what a precarious position she was in.

Looking down at the top of Jason's head, Charity began to rue the curiosity that had gotten her there. Her arms were beginning to ache so badly they were shaking. She couldn't hold on much longer, but neither could she move for fear of drawing his attention.

Why didn't he go back to work?

But Jason didn't move. He just stood there with that ridiculous grin on his face.

Charity's whole body was trembling now. She knew she could delay no longer. Desperately, she shifted, tried to ease herself backward, and realized her arms had gone to sleep. They felt no more useful than leaden sticks. To make matters worse, a shower of hay accompanied the slight movement.

Jason looked at the falling hay as if puzzled. "What the . . ." Then he raised his head and stared, his startled gaze wide, directly into Charity's frantic eyes.

Too late for stealth.

A sob of frustration passed her lips as she tried to push herself farther from the edge. But it was no use. Her arms cramped and tingled painfully. Helplessly she teetered.

Charity's gaze never left Jason's face as she pitched

forward into his reaching arms. The impact of his body forced the air from her lungs. In a tangle of limbs, they fell backward into the hay.

From her prone position atop him, Charity took a gasping breath. For a long moment she could think of nothing else besides feeding her starved lungs. The sound of Jason doing the same was clearly audible with her ear pressed against his solid breast.

Slowly, she became aware of where she was. Jason, firm and warm beneath her, made her aware of her own body: her breasts pressed against him, her hips on his. . . . A strange tension tightened her chest and she knew a different sort of breathlessness. Coloring, she placed her hands on his chest, raising herself to look down at him. A flush of utter embarrassment washed through her, along with another even more troubling sensation of . . . Charity didn't know, only that it seemed to come directly from this contact with Jason's hard form.

Jason seemed totally oblivious to her discomfort. The whites of his eyes showed all around the irises, as if he could not fully accept the fact that she had just fallen atop him. His expression would have made her laugh had the situation been any less distressing.

Even as she watched, his gaze darkened in a way that only added to the tightness inside her.

Sucking in a breath, she rolled off of him to lie at his side in the hay, her head on his sinewy arm.

Taking another deeper breath, Jason ran a hand over his face.

"I am sorry," Charity sputtered, putting her hand over her mouth. "I did not mean to . . ."

Her gaze went to the edge of the loft above them.

The eight feet looked much farther from here. He must think her completely senseless.

Jason quirked one dark brow as he shifted on the hay-strewn wood floor beside her. "You were listening to Purity and me."

Her cheeks flushed even more hotly as an explanation tumbled from her lips. "I didn't mean to. I was reading. And then thee came, and I was just listening to thy song . . ."

As Jason's expression changed from one of surprise to another that she could not even begin to read, she blanched, realizing that she was admitting to eavesdropping not only upon him and her sister, but to Jason alone. What he would think of that she did not even wish to contemplate.

"But why were you leaning over the edge like that, peeking at us if you hoped that no one would discover your presence? You could have just waited in perfect comfort and safety with your book."

Charity knew the only way she could even partially redeem herself was to tell the truth. She took a deep breath, her eyes focused on the clean line of his jaw. "I thought I heard the sound of . . . kissing, and I just had to see what was happening. I know it was wrong . . . but at the time I didn't think."

Jason threw back his head and laughed, the sound deep and rich so close beside her, and her nape prickled pleasantly. "I can't blame you for human curiosity. I would have been more than tempted to find out what was going on myself."

Charity felt something warm moving inside her at his nearness and the understanding words as she looked up into his dark eyes. *Jason.* She couldn't even remember what she had been like before he arrived. He now seemed to be the source of all her thoughts, and certainly these strange overwhelming feelings she didn't understand.

As their gazes held, a lock of golden brown hair fell across his forehead, and she wondered what it would be like to touch it. Then all thoughts stopped as Jason's eyes roved slowly over her upturned face and he murmured, "Do you know how beautiful you are?"

Her heart leapt. "Thee think I'm beautiful?"

Jason rolled toward her, his face mere inches from hers, and he reached up to graze her cheek with one gentle finger. "How could anyone not?"

To Charity's chagrin, her voice was as breathless as Purity's had been earlier. "I thought thee didn't like me."

His smile was self-mocking. "Not liking you has not been the problem." He leaned closer to her. "The facts are quite to the contrary."

She was infinitely aware of the intimacy of the situation. The hay rustled and gave off a sweet aroma with every movement of their bodies. Jason was so handsome, with his obsidian dark eyes and velvety brown hair. He was very different from everything she knew. There was a worldliness about him, and an undeniable element of unpredictability.

She needed to keep some degree of sensibility, forcing herself to remember that he had all but shunned her in the past days. She spoke through unexpectedly dry lips. "Why does thee treat me so distantly then?" Their mouths were so close her breath was mingling with his, and she had to try not to think about the fact that she was breathing in air that had been inside him, warmed by his body.

"For your good as well as mine." Was his voice slightly unsteady, or was she imagining it?

"I don't understand."

Jason's lips were so close to hers she could feel their warmth. "Right now, neither do I," he whispered, just before he kissed her.

For a moment his firm smooth lips felt foreign, then suddenly it was as if that very foreignness became right. It was almost as if they had always been meant to touch in this intimate way.

Charity's mouth softened against his, and Jason gave a deep-throated groan of encouragement. Slightly emboldened, yet tentatively, Charity moved her lips as Jason was doing. In response he put his arms around her, drawing her close to the hard, lean planes of his body.

It was then that she felt something spark, as if someone had lit a candle between the two of them. The heat of it flowed from her lips downward to settle like liquid fire in the pit of her belly. She became aware of her breasts, pressed against the hardness of his chest. They felt swollen and achy, and she found herself wishing he would reach up and touch them.

She squirmed, instinctively trying to get closer to him, the source of her pleasure. He shifted above her and her legs parted slightly, putting his thigh into more direct contact with her body. Despite the fact that they were separated by the layers of her dress and petticoat, Charity arched, feeling the liquid warmth move lower, to settle between her legs. She moaned against his lips, unable to contain her pleasure.

Nothing in her life had prepared her for the passion of her response, and she was totally helpless to hide it.

His mouth left hers to trail gentle kisses across her cheeks and forehead. "Charity, sweet Charity."

She pressed her lips against his throat, feeling the pulse beating there with a sense of wonder. "I didn't know it would be like this to kiss a man."

His arms tightened around her. If only he had met Charity sooner, before he'd married Daphne and made a mess of their lives. If only he could have felt this awareness when he'd looked at his wife, held her in his arms. But he hadn't and now Daphne was gone. When he spoke, Jason's tone was hollow with loneliness and guilt. "I can't do this. It is wrong."

Startled and confused by his sudden withdrawal, Charity lifted her gaze to his face. What was he saying? Why was it wrong? Was he worried about Mother and Papa? They would come around. When her parents saw how much he meant to her, they would allow Jason to court her. For surely that was what he meant to do if he wanted to do these things with her, had admitted that he *liked* her.

She put a shaking finger up to his lips. "Thee should not talk like that. What I feel is not wrong."

Jason took her hand and drew it down from his mouth, his eyes as bleak as a prairie in winter. He sat up slowly, drawing her with him. "Maybe not for you then, but for me."

She was beginning to know some panic now. "Why are thee saying this? Are thee promised to another?" Her eyes widened. "Married?"

"No, Charity, no." He put his hand to her cheek. "There is no one else, but that doesn't mean I'm free."

Shaking her head in confusion, Charity said, "I don't understand."

"Then let me try to explain." He took a deep breath to allow himself time to think. "A few months ago, my life was ordered and, other than my love for and great satisfaction in my work, dispassionate. I'm ashamed to say I preferred it that way. She . . . As I said, I had my work and I really didn't have time for much of anything else."

His jaw grew tight and hard. "Then something happened, something that has changed everything I ever believed about myself and the thing I had been reared to believe in most. I had been so wrapped up in myself and my own needs that I failed to protect and care for someone who needed me. And now she is dead."

"How did she die?"

When he turned to her his eyes had narrowed with hatred, and she shivered even though she knew his rage was not directed at her. "Suffice it to say that she deserved far better than the end she met." He drew himself up. "The circumstances of her death have left me with a debt to pay. I can find no rest, no peace, no comfort until that debt is settled."

Though she felt frustrated by this cryptic reply, she knew he would say no more. She also felt a sense of envy for this dead woman, even though she knew it was wrong. "Did thee love her very much?"

His tone was heavy with self-hatred. "I should have been a better man." He thumped his fist against his chest. "I have no right to just forget her, get on with my life as if I've done nothing wrong, as if she didn't exist."

No right to make love to a pretty girl on a pile of hay, even if that girl did make him aware of the fact that he was a man for the first time in months.

Charity felt a wealth of emotion rise up inside her: sympathy, regret, sadness, shame. Charity backed slowly away from him in the hay. "Then thee were only trifling with me."

A look of pure regret passed over his handsome face. He raised up beside Charity and looked down at her. "No, Charity, I . . ." But even as hope rose up inside her he dashed it by turning away. "I'm sorry."

Springing away from him, she stood, her hands going to her hips. There was nothing Charity could do besides speak from the honesty of her heart. "And thee think that because thee choose to punish thyself, that thee will not even speak of that, I am to go on as if nothing has happened? Thee have only turned to me in thy pain; I have made a fool of myself by thinking it was more."

He reached toward her, saying, "Don't think that of yourself. You were simply caught unaware."

But she avoided the contact. "Keep thy sympathy to thyself. I do not require thy pity, nor thy efforts to make me feel better about my own foolish actions, Jason Wade. I am a big girl and you need not concern thyself that I will expect anything of you. I . . . thee need not feel that I will try to make myself believe that thee forced anything upon me. To my detriment, I wanted what happened to happen."

With that said, she turned and stalked away.

Yet even as she strode away, Charity felt a wave of self-directed horror wash through her. Whatever had made her speak that way? Was she mad?

She had admitted far too much with those words. Dear heaven, she had admitted that she had wanted him to kiss her. Well, she raised her head high, she could only hope that he was equally as clear on the fact that it would not be occurring again.

In spite of the aching tug of regret that tightened her chest, she was determined that she would never again give Jason cause to think he had been anything to her but a brief foolish attraction.

For that was all he had been.

Chapter Four

At the evening meal, Jason tried repeatedly to meet Charity's gaze.

She wouldn't look at him, not after what had happened in the barn, the things they had done, the things she had said. Still, unaccountably, she was annoyed when he stopped trying to get her attention and sat back in tight-lipped silence.

At first no one seemed to notice his withdrawal.

Her family was busy talking to Papa about his trip into town. He had only returned from Helmsville just before the meal began.

Her father finished the news by telling them that the mower had been repaired and was ready for work. He focused on his hired man with a crooked smile. "What say we start at the eastern edge of the barley field in the morning?"

There was no reply. Charity watched as Jason simply continued to push the thick slices of ham, boiled potatoes, fresh greens, and biscuits around his plate.

Papa raised his shaggy brows and peered around the table. His gaze came to rest on Charity's plate, which was also full, then moved to her face.

Charity blushed and looked away.

"Jason?" Elija repeated calmly, but in a slightly louder voice.

Jason looked up at the older man, his eyes slow to focus. "Yes?"

"I said we could start at the eastern edge of the field in the morning."

The hired man's neck colored. He glanced at Charity, then away. "Has the mower been repaired?"

Constance laughed. "Papa already told us it was, Jason. Thee were right here. Whatever are thee thinking of?"

Jason gave a tense laugh. "I suppose I'm a little more tired than usual tonight."

"Perhaps thee should turn in early," Mother said firmly, but not unkindly.

Jason glanced up at her and away. "I'll do that, ma'am."

Mother didn't say anything else, but Charity could feel her perceptive gaze on her.

Charity felt her throat burn as she fought back tears. Despite her attempts to hide her attraction to Jason, it was apparent that both her parents had noticed. This only made her shame over the way she had behaved in the barn even worse. What would mother and father say if they knew? Her stomach churned and she thought she might became ill. Charity whispered, "I don't feel very well, either."

"Maybe thee should lie down," her father answered gently.

Charity cast him a grateful glance. "Thank thee, Papa." Without looking at anyone else, she rose and went up to the room she shared with Prudence.

Throwing herself on the bed, Charity let the tears fall. She cried until no more would come, and she was physically as well as emotionally exhausted.

Rolling over onto her back, Charity was grateful for the faint hint of breeze that stirred the lawn curtains and soothed her heated cheeks. Her gaze traced the veinlike crack above the dresser in the whitewashed wall. Over the dresser hung a sampler she had made when she was seven. She thought of the cedar chest at the end of the bed, her hope chest. Inside were the linens and household items she had collected for the home she would have someday.

But she found no comfort in these familiar things. A restlessness had grown in her, a feeling that left her with a certainty that nothing would ever be the way she had imagined.

Jason had changed things. Changed her.

Never could Charity remember feeling so distant from her parents or sisters—her life. The peace had been shattered like broken crockery. By a man who didn't even want her. Well, not in the way that a man should want a woman. He was lonely and grieving for the woman he had lost, vulnerable to any kindness, nothing more.

Yet even as she told herself this, Charity found herself recalling the way he had treated Purity when she tried to kiss him. He had been very gentle and kind in his rebuff, but it had been a rebuff nonetheless.

Why would Jason turn her away if he only wanted . . . ? She shook her head in confusion. It made no sense.

Charity wasn't very experienced. In fact, she had no experience with men, but surely to a man who was simply desperate for comfort, any woman would do.

And the way he had kissed her. He had made her feel so . . .

In utter frustration, she punched her pillow. Men shouldn't just go around kissing young women when they didn't really have any feelings for them.

And that left her to ask herself a question. Whatever was wrong with her, responding to Jason the way she had? She would never behave so badly again, not that there would ever be a chance. She was grateful for that fact, as it had been wrong for her to react so openly to Jason's kisses.

Deep within herself Charity could not help wondering why nothing else had ever felt so right.

The next day, Jason only saw Charity at meal times. She managed to be just as coolly polite with him as he had been with her.

It should have made him glad, for he had nothing to say that could make her feel better. It was best for her if she did resent him, if she did feel that he had responded to her because of his grief.

Surprisingly, he was anything but glad. In some deep part of himself, Jason wished that he could tell Charity that, real and painful as his grief might be, it had not made him kiss her. He had done so because he could not stop himself. The both simple and complicated truth was that he was attracted to her, and had reacted to her with an intensity that he had not experienced before.

He told himself that it was because Charity was different from anyone he had ever known. She had responded to him so openly, so quickly, with no holding back. Her passion had moved him and left him shaken, especially in the face of her inexperience. Jason was both amazed and humbled, knowing that he was unworthy of her eager and innocent passion even if he had been inclined to return it.

Jason had not seen or experienced that kind of open sharing between a man and a woman. His own marriage had been characterized by the same civil politeness his parents had always shown each other, in and outside of the bedroom. Daphne's attitude toward lovemaking had been shy and forbearing, not encouraging him to display any true passion.

Instinctively, Jason knew things would have been different had Charity been his wife. But he couldn't allow himself to even think about it. There was nothing for him down that path. He would not give up his quest for vengeance for any reason, even if it were possible for him to contemplate life with a simple Quaker girl—which it was not. His life was in Boston. His father, with whom he had once shared a love of the law, and his mother, whom he also loved, despite her need to do what was socially correct, counted on him. He would not fail them as he had Daphne.

Nor could he forget his duty to her. He had to find his wife's killer. No matter the cost.

Thus Jason suppressed the urge to speak to Charity, telling himself that it was all for the best, especially as he had not failed to note the steady way her mother and father had begun to regard him whenever he was around her. Hoping to put their unspoken concern to rest, he immersed himself in the physical labor of the farm, which was seemingly unending, until he could get a moment to follow the lead that Henry Tucker had given him.

Under Elija's knowledgeable tutelage, he was beginning to attain a certain level of skill at the work. The more he knew about farming, the more he realized it would take years of training to really call himself a farmer. Yet he found the hard physical work fulfilling in a way he had not experienced before, not even when working on a challenging legal case. There was a real knack in knowing when each stage of the harvesting must be done. Still, he was able to assist with the tasks assigned to him without embarrassing himself.

If Elija thought it odd that a man would hire on for such work with so little idea of how to do it, he didn't comment. The farmer's kindness only made Jason all the more determined to get on with what he had come to do, then go, and leave the farm and Charity in peace.

On the afternoon of the second day after he had kissed Charity in the barn, he asked Elija if he could have a few hours off to go fishing. Jason didn't want to tell the other man his real purpose in going to Silver Creek, where Henry Tucker had said Grisak's family might be living.

Elija agreed without any hesitation.

After saddling his gray gelding, Jason left the farm. He had found out from Elija that Silver Creek was the very watercourse that he had crossed a few miles this side of Helmsville.

* * *

Charity looked down at the almost full bucket of raspberries with a sigh. Soon she'd have enough to go home and make jam.

It was such a relief being out in the woods by herself. She didn't have to be on constant guard against letting anyone see how miserable and distracted she was. She didn't have to worry about running into Jason—though Charity couldn't decide if that was a blessing or a torment.

Intruding on the stillness of the afternoon, she heard the sound of a horse snorting. Startled, she looked toward the road, which was some fifty feet away, through the trees.

It was *him*, on his horse. She'd heard Papa come in as she was leaving with her bucket to pick berries. He'd informed mother that Jason would be going fishing this afternoon. Charity had told herself that she was glad. As long as he was working around the farm, she risked running across him.

In spite of her happiness at the thought of not seeing him, the sight of him, tall, lean, and handsome in the saddle, made her heartbeat quicken. Angry with herself, she was careful to stay hidden behind a tree until he had gone on without noticing her.

Yet even as he passed out of her sight, she cocked her head, frowning, as something, some inconsistency prodded at her. Papa had said Jason was going fishing.

He didn't have a pole.

Why would Jason go fishing without a pole?

Without giving herself time to think, Charity went to where her own mount, old Dan, was tied to a tree. After hooking the handle of the bucket around the saddle horn, she pulled herself up onto his back. She gave him a gentle nudge and headed out.

There was no sign of Jason when she reached the road. She urged her horse to a trot and hoped she'd see him before he saw her.

It was then that her conscience began to war with her actions. It was no business of hers where the man was going or what he was doing. She should just turn around and go home, but she couldn't. For some reason Jason and what he did *were* important to her.

It was a couple of miles before Charity finally spotted him up ahead of her on the road. Her heart was pounding with fear that he might see her, and something else she could only call anticipation, a thrill of adventure. Surely there was no harm in this. Jason Wade would never even know she had been there. She simply could not resist the temptation to find out what he was up to.

Another undeniable thrill of anticipation washed over her. Even a week ago she would never have imagined that she could be following such an interesting man to some unknown destination, let alone that he would have kissed her—held her close to the hardness of his masculine body. In spite of the fact that there was no future for them, there was no denying that she had experienced more excitement since Jason had come along than in her whole life. Perhaps it was this that so fascinated her, not Jason himself.

With bated breath, Charity followed, suddenly realizing that he would see her if he glanced around. Quickly she turned off the road and entered the edge of the trees, staying back until he turned south onto the narrower road that ran along beside Silver Creek. As old Dan plodded over the uneven ground, Charity grimaced. *Road* was too generous a term for the narrow rutted track.

Whatever could Jason want way back there?

No one even lived along the route—that is no one except for Louisa Grisak.

What would Jason want with Louisa Grisak?

Charity really didn't know much about Louisa, except that she had several children and her husband was rarely home. It was rumored that she had come from someplace down south—a slave state. It was also rumored that Wayne Grisak was a bounty hunter who took escaped slaves back to their owners. That in itself was enough to tell Charity she didn't wish to know the man better.

Mother sometimes took outgrown clothes to the children, as she did for other poor families in the vicinity, but Charity had never met Louisa.

It was surprisingly easy for Charity to follow Jason until he turned into the yard of a small plank shack. Keeping Dan just out of sight in the trees, she watched as Jason rode up to the sadly neglected dwelling.

Several grubby children were playing a halfhearted game of tag in the yard. None of them could have been older than six. They stopped, forming an untidy group and staring at the mounted man with open curiosity.

Jason bent forward in the saddle, resting his crossed hands on the saddle horn. His smile was easy as he spoke to them. "Your folks around?"

A little girl of about seven stepped from around the end of the dwelling. Her hair was pulled back from her thin face in a straggly braid, and she wasn't much cleaner than the smaller children. Self-consciously, she wiped her wet hands on the skirt of her overlarge dress. "Can I help you mister?"

Jason's tone was polite but it also bore an underlying gentleness that moved Charity. "Are your parents at home?"

The little girl cast a worried glance toward the door of the cabin. "Ma's inside. She's feelin' kind of poorly today." She straightened her small shoulder. "I'm doin' the wash, so if you don't need somethin', Ye'd best be moving along."

There was a strange dignity to the little urchin that tugged at Charity's heart.

Charity couldn't see Jason's expression, as he had turned his back to her, but the timbre of his voice remained uncommonly soft. "Might I get a glass of water?"

"That I can give you, mister. It'll even be cold." The child stepped up on the crate that served as a stoop, and went inside.

Jason tied the reins to the saddle horn, then swung to the ground and followed her in.

Minutes passed, and the children—Charity had counted four when they were standing still—began to chase each other around the dusty yard again. It was a hot, still, August afternoon. Except for the shouts of the youngsters, and the fly that buzzed around Charity's head, there wasn't a sound.

She shifted restlessly in the saddle. What could be taking so long? Looking toward the open door of the cabin, she made a decision.

What could Jason do to her?

Defiantly, she prodded her horse forward. The children stopped playing to stare at Charity in her

Quaker gray dress and sturdy boots, but they didn't speak.

Charity climbed to the ground and tied her horse to the scruffy bush growing in the yard. Setting her chin at a stubborn angle, she stepped up onto the crate and went inside the cabin.

At first it was too dim for her to see, after the brightness outside, but then her vision adjusted and she found herself staring across the sparsely furnished room into Jason's furious gaze. Taking a deep breath for courage, Charity smiled with forced cheer. "What a surprise meeting thee here, Jason Wade."

He raised skeptical brows, but said only, "Yes, I'm sure."

Relief washed through her. It seemed he was not going to argue with her here. Quickly, she took more careful note of her surroundings. The cabin was very small, and furnished with a stove, a rickety table with two rough benches, and a bed. A pile of straw ticks was piled against one wall. Charity assumed they were for the children.

Jason was standing beside the bed, the little girl who'd been doing the washing at his side. The child was holding a battered tin cup.

"Since you just *happened along*," he told Charity, grimacing ruefully when she blushed, "you might as well make yourself useful."

"What do thee need?" Charity crossed the room in two strides. Looking down, she saw that the bed was occupied, though the slight figure barely made a wrinkle in the worn patchwork quilt.

"This lady is very ill." Jason leaned forward and put

his arm beneath the occupant's shoulders. When he raised her up, Charity could see that it was indeed a woman, though she was little bigger than the child. Her cheeks were hollow and the circles around her eyes were so dark they could have been painted on.

Taking the cup, Charity saw that it contained cool water. She lifted it to the woman's mouth as Jason held her.

When she had drunk a little, Charity drew the cup away and Jason let the woman settle back on the bed. "Water is good to help clean the poisons from the body," Charity told the sick woman. "But when did thee last eat? Thee needs to gain some strength. A good hearty beef broth would be just the thing."

The woman made an attempt to answer, but all that emerged from her throat was a raspy cough. She closed her eyes, obviously too weak to try again.

The child answered for her. "We don't have no beef, ma'am. There ain't even hardly any beans left in the sack, and the flour barrel's almost empty."

Charity wanted to cry out loud at the thought of this woman and her children going hungry, but she knew it wouldn't help. "What is thy name, child?"

She simply stared at Charity for a moment, her eyes uncertain. Then softly she whispered, "Sarah."

"Now, Sarah." Charity smoothed the fine hair back from her brow. "How long has thy mother been ill?"

"Ever since the baby come a few days ago." Sarah pointed toward a box in the corner.

Jason met Charity's eyes, his expression registering the complete shock she felt. Clearly, he hadn't known about the baby.

Charity and Jason moved forward as if led by the same rope.

Kneeling down beside the box, Charity reached in and took out what appeared to be nothing more than a bundle of rags. Quickly, but carefully, she unwrapped the bundle to find a bone-thin baby boy. His skin was the color of bleached ashes, and he hung limp like a broken flower stem in her hands. For a terrifying moment, Charity thought he was dead, but she touched her ear to his tiny chest and felt the tenuous beating of his heart.

Jason watched her with wary eyes. "Is he . . . ?"

Charity replied with forced calm. "No, but he will be soon if he doesn't have some nourishment." It was her guess that the sick woman had no milk. Which wasn't all that surprising if she'd had no food.

Using a stained but dry rag from the box, Charity changed the infant, then rewrapped him. Expertly she cradled him in the crook of her arm. "When did thy mother last feed the baby?" she asked Sarah, who was watching the proceedings with concern.

"Just this mornin'. But Jacob don't seem much interested in feedin'. He fussed about eatin' right from the start." She shrugged her narrow shoulders. "Now he don't make no noise."

Jason ran his hand through his hair. "We've got to do something."

"There isn't anything here to cook. The place is filthy. And I don't know how much help I could be for either of them," Charity answered honestly. "I haven't had much practice at nursing sick people."

Sarah drew herself up straight and wiped a hand across her damp eyes. "I done my best."

Going to her, Jason put a hand around her shoulders.

"Of course you did. No one could have asked for more from you."

Charity watched as Sarah leaned in to him for comfort. She couldn't help noticing that even at a time like this, he had a way with females. She also was unable to deny the effect his gentleness and warmth had upon her own peace of mind.

Jason went on, thankfully oblivious to her wayward thoughts. "Can I take you to Henry Tucker, or is there some way to contact your father?"

She looked slightly surprised at his question, as was Charity, but she made no comment on it as Sarah said, "Grandpa don't have nothin' to do with us. Pa's been gone since way before the baby come. He don't never stay long when he does come around."

Charity's curiosity as to Jason's knowledge of this family was forgotten as she heard this last statement with a sense of revulsion and incredible sorrow. What kind of father could he be for his child to talk this way?

Obviously, he was the kind of man who took slaves back to a cruel master where they would be beaten—or worse.

When she looked at Jason, his expression clearly showed his abhorrence, and a fearsome rage that almost frightened Charity. He visibly worked to hold it in check, and she was grateful for the child's sake.

She and Jason had to act with calm—and soon, if Charity didn't miss her guess—or these children would be orphans.

Suddenly, she knew what had to be done.

"Sarah," Charity said, rising with the baby. "Does thee have a horse, a wagon, anything?"

"We got a dog cart. It's hid out in the woods so nobody can steal it. But we can't use it unless Pa's home, cause we got no horse."

Charity turned to Jason. "We're taking them all home with us. We can pull the cart with Dan if thy horse won't harness up. I'll get Louisa and Jacob ready to go."

Jason nodded sharply. "Come on Sarah, show me where the cart is. There's no time to waste."

Charity realized that they were a ragtag-looking little troupe as they rode into the Applegate farmyard two hours later. The sun was just going down, flicking through the tops of the trees like orange flame and adding to the drama of the scene.

Mother and Father came running from the house, closely followed by the twins and Prudence.

From where she was seated atop old Dan, Charity looked down at her mother beseechingly. "Louisa is very sick. They hadn't enough food. She and the baby are both very weak. The children are hungry and worried. I brought them all home to be looked after. I didn't know what else to do."

With obvious pride and approval Mother smiled up at her. "Thee did just the right thing."

Warmed by the words, Charity watched as her mother hurried to the cart and looked inside, assessing the gravity of the situation at a glance. Immediately she took charge. "Constance, turn down the bed in your room. Prudence, fetch that chicken stock from the cellar and warm it up. Charity, you bring the baby in and feed him some warmed cow's milk, but only a little, mind you, or he won't hold it down. Jason and

Elija, carry Louisa upstairs. Purity, you can make the children some sandwiches from the cheese in the larder.

Everyone scrambled to do as they were told.

Charity took the baby to the kitchen. The little boy had to have some nourishment and soon, but she would be careful to give him only a little, as her mother had said. Taking a tall, small-mouthed bottle from the pantry, Charity warmed some milk mixed with water. Jacob's belly would be squeamish from being empty for so long. She poured the diluted milk into the bottle and tied a piece of clean cloth over the top.

They had once fed a calf this way when its mother rejected it. She hoped the same method would save little Jacob's life.

Not once during the process of preparing the milk did the baby make a sound. She hoped it was not too late for him.

Cautiously, she gave the odd-looking bottle to the infant. He had to be coaxed into drinking even a little, but seemed to fall into a more restful sleep after taking some. Only then did Charity begin to take some note of what was going on around her.

Aided by Sarah, who insisted on helping, Purity had managed to make food for the other children. They were all seated at the table with clean faces, wolfing down sandwiches and gulping tall glasses of milk.

As Constance came into the kitchen, Charity said "Please warm some water and bring it to my room." She meant to give the poor little mite in her arms a warm bath, and there would be less chance of a draft in her room.

When Constance nodded, Charity went into the hall

and found Jason coming down the stairs. He slowed when he saw her, coming to a stop on the bottom step directly in front of her. Charity felt a jolt of awareness at his nearness, realizing that it had only been the trying circumstances of the last few hours that had kept it at bay.

Jason reached out to touch the baby's tiny cheek with a gentle finger. "How is he?"

Charity looked down into the pale face with pity, trying not to think of how very close Jason was, of how her heart thudded in her chest. "He took a little milk. We'll just have to see how it settles in his stomach. It's been empty so long."

Clearly he sensed that something was wrong, for she could hear the concern in his voice as he said, "Are you all right, Charity? Your mother sent me down to see if you needed anything."

Carefully, Charity avoided meeting his gaze. She couldn't, not now, when she was feeling so vulnerable because of her worry for this family, because of her own reactions to Jason's nearness, his concern. She spoke without emotion, trying not to give away her own scattered feelings. "There is a crib out in the shed. I'd appreciate it if thee'd bring it up to my room. Prue and I are next to Constance and Purity. Mother put Louisa in their room."

For a long time he just stood there, and she felt him willing her to face him. She did not, and finally he turned to hurry out.

With a sigh, Charity took the baby upstairs. She had to keep her mind on the matter at hand. What Jason thought was of no concern to her. He had his own life to live and was obviously determined to keep it to him-

self. How Louisa Grisak and her family might fit in to
the story he had told her of his wife's death was not
apparent. Yet surely it must, for he'd made it clear that
it was all he cared about. Somehow Jason had known
of Louisa, had gone to the shack for some reason of his
own. But truth to tell, she had too much on her plate to
worry over it at the moment.

There was always a spare supply of changing cloths
and gowns in the linen closet at the top of the stairs,
since her sisters' children visited often. Charity gathered what she needed and went to her room.

Constance met her there with the hot water, and
poured it into the basin on the dresser, leaving again
as her mother called for her. Gently, Charity bathed
the infant and wrapped him in the clean cloths and a
tiny gown that still managed to dwarf his small body.
He was so still and quiet through it all, she was
unnerved.

"Oh God," she offered up a whispered prayer as she
looked down at him lying on her bed. "Please see Thy
way to saving this little child. He has not even known
Thy wondrous bounty."

From the doorway, Jason heard her words, saw the
anxiety on her face. He murmured a soft affirmation,
"Amen."

Charity swung around to face him, her sudden
frown making him recall all too clearly how cool she
had been on the stairs. There had seemed to be a truce
of sorts between them as they had cared for Louisa and
her children. Clearly it was over.

He held the wicker crib in front of him, telling himself it was for the best. Surely if she was not speaking

to him more than she absolutely must, she would not question his interest in the Grisaks.

She definitely would not look at him the way she had just before he'd kissed her in the barn.

Yet in some part of him, he knew that he wished she would do so. Her opinion of him did matter. The more he knew of her the more he felt drawn to the gentle but strong Quaker woman. The way she had responded to the need of Louisa and her children had moved him more than he would ever have thought possible.

At the same time, he knew that she would be repulsed by his reason for going out there. His actions had been based on his own interests. Charity and her family had acted from true kindness and a desire to help.

As if to drive the point home, the boisterous sound of the children, now fed and feeling better, climbed the stairs behind him. In contrast, the baby gave a pitiful mewl where he lay snuggled against the sweet swell of Charity's bosom. Without thinking, Jason shut the door to blunt the noise, even as he dragged his gaze away from that sight. All he wanted now was to finish the task she had set him. He indicated the crib. "Where would you like this?"

"Here beside the bed," Charity said politely enough, though he saw her glance skitter to the closed door and away.

He brought the crib closer and placed it where she'd indicated, beside the bed. "I only wanted to deaden the racket."

Charity would not meet his eyes. "Of course." She carefully laid the babe upon her mattress, then turned to spread fresh bedding in the crib. It was no time at all before she reached down to pick up the baby, and as she did so he felt the weight of her thoughtful gaze upon him.

Jason did not allow himself to look away, in spite of the fact that he knew it was dangerous.

So occupied was he with that thought that her question startled him. "What were you doing there?"

Chagrined, he answered in kind. "Me? Why were *you* there?"

She held the baby between them like a shield. "I followed thee."

He gave a wry chuckle in spite of his discomfiture. She was disconcertingly direct, as ever. "That much I'm aware of. I want to know why."

"Papa said thee were going fishing, but I knew thee weren't." She shrugged, giving a half smile. "Thee didn't have a pole."

Under any other circumstances Jason might have laughed. It seemed he hadn't been very clever, but he hadn't thought anyone would be checking on him. He'd remember not to underestimate this woman again.

"Jason," she asked again as if she couldn't stop herself. "Why did thee go there?"

He stared down at her with consternation.

"Well?" she prodded.

Looking into her determined eyes, Jason suddenly realized he couldn't lie. He was certain that somehow she would know it. But neither could he tell the truth. "I'm not going to tell you. I know you don't like it, but I have good reason for wanting to keep you out of this. Suffice it to say that you don't want to get close to this situation, or me. Beyond that, you must listen when I tell you that Grisak is a very dangerous man."

Her eyes narrowed. "But . . ."

"Please, Charity, just accept what I say for your own good." Even though he knew it wouldn't do any good, he felt compelled to try. "Promise me you won't try to follow me again. And that you won't tell your parents anything."

"I . . . can't," she answered, defiant. "I don't even know what I'd be promising to keep secret."

He'd thought as much. "Then at least say you won't tell your parents I wasn't fishing."

"How can I?" She glanced toward the closed door and back at him. "They're going to ask me how I came to be with thee at Louisa's."

"Leave that up to me." Jason breathed a silent sigh of relief. "I'll tell your father it was my fault. That I got lost and I met you in the woods and you offered to show me the way to the creek."

Her brow wrinkled with regret as she bit her lower lip. "I haven't ever lied to them."

"I told you, I'll take care of the explanations. I'm sorry, but it's the only way. I didn't ask you to follow me, and secrecy is my best hope of succeeding."

"Succeeding at what?"

He frowned. "That is something I won't talk about." He knew he could not face the horror in her face if she was to learn that his sole purpose had become the murder of another man.

Charity was clearly unhappy with the cryptic reply, but her gaze went to the infant's tiny face, where he lay against her bosom. "Then keep what thy will to thyself, Jason Wade. Thee owe me nothing. I know that I had no right to follow thee, but I'm not sorry I did, no matter that thee refuse to tell me what is going on. In a way it's almost as if we had to go there. I hate to think of what would have happened if we hadn't come along. Sarah was doing her best, but it wouldn't have been enough."

He tried to ignore the guilt he felt at being so secretive with her when a crazed part of him wanted to tell her everything. He wanted to take comfort in her sweetness, her passion.

Attempting to distract himself from these wild thoughts, Jason touched the baby's miniature face with the tip of his finger, as he had downstairs. But this time was different. He was very aware of the fact that they were in Charity's bedroom with the door closed, that his knuckles had brushed the fabric covering her breasts.

He saw her face flush even as his own blood heated. But he said nothing about it as Charity abruptly turned and laid the baby in the cradle.

Knowing he must not dwell on the feelings the inadvertent touch had raised, Jason looked down at the baby, doing his best to concentrate. "He'll be all right. They all will. You Applegates will see to it."

Feeling Charity's confused gaze upon him, he turned back to her, his eyes earnestly on hers. Almost against his will, he found himself saying, "I've never known anyone like you and your family. These people are virtual strangers to you and still you took them in. Not just with money or words, but with your home and your warmth. Just as you took me in. That's one of the reasons that I just can't let you become involved in what is going on in my life. It's all too sordid and ugly."

She merely watched him for a long moment, her expression full of hurt and confusion. He returned her gaze, wishing with everything inside him that it could be different. The knowledge that it could not be brought an aching sadness to his breast.

As this feeling washed over him, her expression changed. Her eyes grew round and soft, and God, he couldn't help but see that they were full of yearning.

That yearning called out to the hollow place within himself. Without knowing that he was going to do so, Jason leaned close to her and cupped her chin in his hand, his thumb caressing her soft cheek.

Charity's breath caught, and her tongue flicked out to wet her lips.

It was too much for Jason. For days he had been able to think of little besides the memory of her slim body next to his—her mouth. Even while he worked, the scent of hay as the mower cut it caused his body to tighten with remembrance.

He bent forward to put his mouth to hers.

Charity sighed against his lips, reaching up to put her arms around his neck. The strain of the last few hours, and the shadow of loneliness in his eyes, left her open to him.

She slanted her head, allowing him full access to her lips, moaning with the joy and sweetness of the sensations racing through her body.

Her upraised arms left the slim curves of her waist and hips exposed to Jason's questing hands. He didn't deny himself, running his fingers sensuously over her, encouraged by the way she pressed herself more fully to him. His fingertips searched for and found the rounded undercurve of her breast. He moved his open hand to cup the gently rounded flesh, felt the nipple harden against his palm.

Charity gave an involuntary gasp of pleasure and Jason wrapped both arms around her waist to lift her up against the shockingly hard and straining need of him.

Her arms tightened around his neck, and he felt an overwhelming sense of gratification and pleasure, as he had the first time he kissed her. She wanted him—wanted him as he wanted her.

The sudden sound of loud voices in the hall just outside her door startled him to alertness. He dragged his mouth from hers, taking deep ragged breaths as he fought to regain control. With a great act of will, he set Charity on her feet. Then gently, but insistently, he moved away from her. She looked up at him, clearly bewildered at his sudden withdrawal. Putting a hand on her elbow, Jason steadied her until he saw her confusion clear.

He shook his head with shame. "I'm sorry, Charity. I don't know what came over me. I just don't seem to have as much sense as I used to. This won't happen again. You have my word."

He swung hurriedly away and left the room, shutting the door with a dull finality, like the closing of a book.

Chapter Five

Three evenings later, Jason told Elija he was going in to Helmsville for a few hours. Jason had a hard time meeting his employer's gaze as he did so. He still felt uncomfortable with how difficult it had been to lie to Elija about how he and Charity had come to be at Grisak's shack that day. Elija had simply nodded and commented on how the Lord worked His miracles.

Elija's trusting ways only made Jason feel more tainted by his own inner conflicts, more determined to do what he had come here to do and go.

He would not allow himself to forget the fact that not only was he at the farm under false pretenses, but he couldn't seem to keep his hands and mouth off of Elija's daughter. For that was exactly how he felt. In spite of his resolve to forget what had happened between them, he knew that if he were alone with Charity again the outcome would very likely be the same.

The fact that Charity had responded to him with such enthusiasm did not aid his cause. It only made him think of her, her soft lips, her sweetly rounded breasts . . .

Jason groaned, feeling the now familiar ache of longing in his body. God help him, he knew he had to stop this.

He felt like he was existing somewhere between heaven and hell. On the one end were Charity and pleasure and, this was even harder to admit, the peace he would find in her, the sweet release of losing himself in her body. But taking her would be wrong, for Charity was not the kind of woman who could give herself to a man lightly. Jason would not allow himself to use her and walk away, no matter how badly he desired her.

And he could not offer her anything else, had he even wished to, for on the other end was his own need to catch and punish the man who had killed Daphne, the man his instincts told him was Wayne Grisak. For that was growing more and more obvious. Wayne Grisak was indeed capable of the kind of cruelty that had resulted in Daphne's death.

If he had murdered Daphne, Jason would never rest until he saw the man dead at his feet.

Jason was too different from the people who had made a miracle for the Grisak family. And a miracle it had turned out to be for Louisa and her children. She had gotten much stronger, even in this short time, as had little Jacob. Mary clucked and fussed over them as if they were her own chicks.

Having Louisa and her family at the farm made more work for everyone. The twins now looked after the children. So that left their chores to be done. Even though Charity and Prudence did little outside work, there was extra to be done there as well. Weeding the garden—a task the women seemed to enjoy—had been completely turned over to himself and Elija.

Yet he had heard not one complaint from any of them.

They went on, unconcerned with the fact that they might have put themselves in jeopardy by helping Grisak's wife. Jason even considered, for an instant, that he could help by warning them against the man's violent nature, even if doing so might reveal his knowledge of him. But he knew the effort would be wasted. Neither Elija nor his family would behave any differently.

It was up to Jason to stay a step ahead of Grisak. He had to find out where he was if he could, and go after him, and leave the Applegates in peace. He ignored the tug of sadness in his chest, pressing his horse to a faster pace.

Arriving on the outskirts of town just as the sun was going down, he cast a long shadow in the sparsely populated streets, surprised to find himself there so quickly. Jason realized he hadn't really attended to where he was going since leaving the farm. Luckily the horse, obviously having more sense, had followed the road.

The few men on horseback or on foot seemed to be headed in one general direction and, acting on a hunch, Jason followed. Tucker had mentioned a particular saloon, and Jason would not be shocked to learn that these solitary men were headed there at this time of evening.

The tinny sound of music played on a cheap piano was his reward as he moved into what was obviously a seedier portion of the little town. Where else would lonely men go on a Saturday night?

Remembering Tucker's warning, Jason passed by an establishment bearing a sign that read JOY'S PALACE without stopping. If he hoped to run into Tucker, to see if he could discover even one more clue as to Grisak's whereabouts, he was far more likely to find him at Francine's Place.

The saloon didn't look any different from the other on the outside. Nor did Francine's seem any more elegant on the inside. Jason would just have to take Tucker's word that it was the more reputable establishment, thanking his fortune that he wasn't going to the other.

The bar was the focal point of the place. Its oaken grandeur was reflected by a full-length mirror which hung on the wall behind it. A full-size nude painting hung majestically along the opposite wall. The subject was a little plump for Jason's taste, but she had a come-hither smile and no obvious inhibition.

Most of the clientele looked to be farmers—their homey dress and lack of weapons gave them away.

Two scantily clad females moved through the throng with professional aplomb, plying drink and whatever else they might. Jason had been in more places like this than he could count, in his pursuit of Grisak. He'd begun in the seediest parts of Boston, asking about the man, following one lead after another to large towns and small, for Grisak was not a man who stayed in any one place for long. It had been in a saloon much like Francine's that he'd first heard of Helmsville, Wisconsin, and a possible family connection there. Even to those who claimed to know him, the man seemed to give away little of his personal life, though he was well remembered by those who had met him for his cruel ways and dislike of staying in one place more than a few days.

Always Jason had been one step behind him. Only when he'd learned that Helmsville might indeed be the man's true home had Jason known his best chance was to come here and hope that Grisak showed up. Time didn't matter. Nothing besides learning the truth had mattered to him.

But now, with Charity Applegate . . . He wasn't sure of anything anymore.

Deliberately Jason drew himself up straight and moved to an open stool by the bar. He would find Grisak.

The bartender, a beefy man with a half-clean rag slung over his shoulder, asked, "What'll it be?"

"Whiskey," Jason replied absently, as his gaze scanned the bar for Tucker. When he failed to see the wiry man amongst the clientele, he went on as casually as he could. "Have you seen Henry Tucker tonight?"

The bartender didn't look at Jason as he poured alcohol into a shot glass. "He a friend of yours?"

"You might say that." Jason took a drink. "I'm kind of new in town. I met Henry over at the livery and he asked me to look him up if I was ever at Francine's. Told me it was the finest establishment in town."

"Did he now?" The bartender tried not to let his pleasure show, but he had definitely loosened up as he cast Jason a halfway civil grimace that must pass for a smile. He leaned over the bar and whispered conspiratorially, "Francine up and left me a year ago, but I ain't about to change the name. That's her picture up there." He pointed to the nude with a tear in the corner of his eye. "Draws in a lot of customers."

"I can see why it would," Jason answered with forced interest. He regretted opening this conversation, now that it looked as if it could turn into a maudlin speech about the lost Francine.

"Well, if this don't beat all," a voice called out from behind him, even as a hearty hand descended upon his shoulder.

Jason spun around to face Tucker with more warmth than he might otherwise have felt. "Henry Tucker," Jason said as he shook the proffered hand eagerly.

The bartender, beaming at seeing Jason united with his friend, moved off.

"I see you met Frank." Tucker stared after the big man. "Hasn't got over losin' Francine." His gaze lingered over the woman in the portrait with nostalgia. "Can't say's I blame him. She was quite a woman."

"Lovely." Jason nodded with determined agreement.

"How you been?" Tucker elbowed him in the ribs. "Those Applegate girls treatin' you right?"

Jason felt a surprising tug of resentment at this innuendo. "The Applegates have brought their girls up strictly, Henry. Nothing like you're suggesting goes on out there at the farm."

He had to push away a sudden and vivid vision of Charity warm and pliant in his arms.

Tucker's reply brought his thoughts back to reality. "I'm sure they are, young fella. Them Quakers is fine upstanding people, even if they are a bit straitlaced." This thought seemed to remind Tucker of his reason for being in the saloon in the first place. He signaled to

Frank, who brought him a double shot of whiskey on the spot. It was obviously a standing order. "No harm intended," he crooned as he took a noisy gulp. "Just funnin' ya. One of the girls here would be glad to take care of a good-looking fella like you."

"Not tonight." Jason smiled politely.

As he signaled Frank a second time, Tucker peered closely at Jason with watery eyes. "You ain't sweet on one of them Quaker girls, are ya? Not that they ain't a pretty bunch, but I hear tell they don't hold much with marryin' outside the faith, so to speak."

For a moment, Jason's chest contracted, aching as if an elephant were sitting on it. But he forced himself to breathe deeply, telling himself that this reaction was nothing short of insanity. What was it to him if Quaker's didn't marry outside their faith? Slowly the pain went away enough for him to speak. "Don't worry about me. I'll be moving on before too long, and I wasn't thinking of taking any of them with me."

"Good thinkin', boy," Tucker approved as he started on his second drink. His rheumy gaze drifted over the room as the liquor started to kick in. "Best not to get mixed up with women. They is always causin' problems." He motioned for another drink as his eyes settled on Jason. "Funny thing happened last night, 'specially funny after you wuz askin' about my boy, Wayne."

Jason felt the hairs along his nape prickle, but he tried to keep his voice even as he said, "Really? And what would that be?"

"Why he was here, in Francine's, right mad, and drunk as all get out."

110

Jason felt the blood begin to pound in his head. "Grisak was here?"

Tucker's drink arrived and he downed the double whiskey as quickly as the first two before answering. "Aye, he was, and like I told you, mad as all get out. He had done been out to his place at Silver Creek and—lo and behold—his wife and them kids was gone." His bleary gaze met Jason's and Jason was suddenly very glad Tucker was already feeling his alcohol. Otherwise, he was sure the older man would see the eagerness in his eyes.

Jason raised his hand and signaled to the bartender for two more drinks. It took every ounce of his will to wait until the drinks had arrived before speaking.

"Is he still around?" Jason asked as Henry nodded his thanks and tipped up his glass. He knew he sounded too eager, but he couldn't quite control himself. His blood was pounding so hard he was near dizzy with anticipation.

He'd waited so very long.

Tucker wiped his mouth with the back of his hand before answering. "He left here drunk, and madder'n I ever seen him before. He was spoutin' some kind of nonsense about some trouble in Boston and how he weren't gonna take any stuff from no woman. He said he was gonna find Louisa and show her, just like he done showed somebody else who tried to do him dirt."

Shock drove a heavy fist into Jason's belly, followed by a rage so intense that he could hardly breathe. Forcing himself to inhale slowly, to remember that he had to try to find out where Grisak was, he asked again,

"Where is . . . Wayne?" Jason heard the unmistakable fury in his own voice as he realized that Grisak had revealed enough to condemn himself. The man's death warrant was sealed.

Distantly he watched as Tucker grabbed up a fresh drink that Jason hadn't even seen him order.

"Gone, gone south with a slave he's a-totin' back to its master. Said he caught her just afore she got to the border of Canada. He just stopped by for a little bit of comfort on his way." He tried to focus on Jason, but failed miserably as he went on. "But he'll be back to find that woman, and God help anybody what helped her run off. Wayne don't forgive nothin' fer nobody."

Jason could take no more. He stood without another word and stalked from the saloon. He made no effort to reply as Tucker called out to him. His rage was so great that he feared he might do bodily harm to the man who could so nearly admiringly talk of Grisak's penchant for violence.

It was a sure bet that he had never experienced the depth of hate and rage that roiled inside Jason at this very moment. Jason did not think he would be admiring if he had.

Jason retrieved his horse and headed toward the Applegate farm at a gallop. As the cool wind began to clear his pounding head, he realized one more indisputable fact. He could not wait until Grisak returned to Helmsville, not when he'd all but proclaimed his guilt in the rape and murder of Daphne. He had to go after him, and as soon as possible—before his trail got cold. Surely it would not be so difficult to follow the trail of the man, especially if he was accompanied by a slave.

He was shocked at how much his next thought hurt,

especially in the face of his all-consuming fury. He had to leave the farm. He would never see Charity Applegate again.

Even if he had wanted to return, they would not want him after he had hunted down a man for the sole purpose of killing him—even if that man had murdered his wife. Not that he wanted to come back. Once Grisak was dead, he had to go home to his family and his practice. The thought did not bring him the degree of pleasure he would have expected. Still, he'd finally be free from the guilt that had driven him for months.

What he felt for Charity was nothing but a physical reaction to an admittedly lovely and fascinating young woman. He had simply been too long without softness or comfort. He had not known how fiercely compelling they could be.

For that reason he would never forget Charity Applegate, the strange mixture of passion and innocence that had made him feel again, even though he hadn't wanted to. If only there was some way that he could say . . .

Suddenly he stopped the horse and swung back toward town. There was something he had to do before he could leave.

At the back of the Applegate farm, on a little knoll down by the stream, there was a quiet place where Charity loved to go. It was a place where she felt close to God and His creations, a place of peace. It was the place where Charity had always hoped she might someday, when she fell in love and married, build her home.

A sugar maple grew close to the water there and the

ground beneath was covered in a deep cushion of moss. Fiddlehead ferns, Indian paintbrush, goldenrod, and wood violets swayed gracefully amongst the carpet of greenery.

The morning had been a busy one, but now both Louisa and the babe had fallen asleep. The twins had taken the other children picking wild berries. Feeling that she would not be needed for at least a short time, Charity had come here. She stood at the top of the knoll and took a deep breath of the still summer air, but for the first time, the beauty and solitude of the spot failed to soothe her.

And she knew why, though she did not want to.

Last night, Jason hadn't come home until very late. Charity knew, because she had watched for him from her upstairs window for hours, wondering hopelessly if he was gone for good. The way he had been acting since that day in her room, so restless, his eyes dark with that inner torment that she had recognized the first day he came to the farm, she had somehow known that he was thinking of moving on. When Papa had informed them at supper that Jason would not be joining them, as he had gone into town, she'd felt her heart sink. It had been all she could do to eat even a portion of the food on her plate, and she could not afterward recall what it had been.

As soon as she could, Charity had escaped from the watchful gaze of her mother, seeking sanctuary in her room, pretending to be asleep when Prudence came to bed.

Yet while Prue had slept obliviously in their bed, Charity had sat at the window, unable to sleep or think of anything but the intimate moments she had spent with Jason, the way he had touched her, kissed her, and made her feel like a woman. Her eyes had grown dry and hot with the tears she would not shed, no matter how much she hurt.

Why should she keep crying over him, a drifter, who would come into their lives, then leave without even saying goodbye? He was a man who could kiss her as if he were drowning and she a lifeline one moment, then calmly tell her he couldn't have anything to do with her the next.

Yet when she had finally seen his shadowy figure approaching, relief had nearly undone her, rising up in wave after cleansing wave. Even as she felt it, Charity knew that it was nothing short of insanity to allow herself such feelings.

By his own admission Jason was not the staying kind.

She simply had to make herself remember that. How had she allowed herself to become so dependent upon Jason, for her happiness, her very breath?

She didn't know how or when it had happened, only that it had. Nothing else seemed to matter as much as it once had, her family, her way of life, all faded into the background when she thought of never seeing Jason again.

The very idea of never experiencing the way he made her feel was unbearable.

She moved into the shade of the trees beside the creek and sank to the moss, turning her cheek to the rough wood of the tree at her back. She felt its cooling coarseness against her hot cheek.

"Charity."

She wasn't surprised at her mind's conjuration of the sound of his voice. Even when Jason wasn't with her, he was more real, more tangible than anything else.

"Charity." Her name came again and she realized that it was indeed from outside herself. Unable to collect herself so very quickly, she swung to face him, knowing her eyes were dark with longing and pain.

Jason hesitated as he looked into her face. His gaze searched hers, but he gave nothing away as he took a deep breath before approaching slowly, his hat in his hands. "I saw you heading this way and followed you. It's a beautiful spot."

She nodded, awkwardly. "Yes, I have always hoped that someday when I married we would build a house here."

He spoke softly. "I hope it's everything you want it to be and more."

His tone was distant, his expression unreadable; he was evidently quite unaware of how empty the future now seemed to her. "Why did thee follow me?" she asked, quirking a brow with dry irony, suddenly angry with him for being so cool and with herself for caring. "Wasn't it thee who said we had to keep apart?"

Jason had the grace to flush, then his jaw tightened with determination. "That isn't why I'm here."

She raised her chin. "Then why are thee here?"

He looked down at his hat. "I . . . wanted to tell you something, but I am asking you to keep it to yourself."

"Yes?" She held her breath.

He looked up at her again. "I'm leaving tonight after everyone goes to sleep."

Charity felt the words slam into her. Desperately she fought for control. Hadn't she known this was coming?

She found her voice, shocked when it gave no evidence of the crushing weight of her sadness. "Why are you telling me this?"

He frowned. "I don't know. I just felt that after the way I had . . . after what we had . . ." He shrugged. "I just wanted you to know, to say goodbye." He stopped and looked up at the sky. "In spite of how it may seem, I didn't mean to use or abuse you, Charity. That was never my intention. I just couldn't seem to stop myself." He drew himself up. "Well, I just wanted to say I'm sorry things couldn't have been different."

She took a deep breath and stared down at her own hands, shocked and still uncertain of why he was telling her this. When she looked up, he was gone.

She put her head on her knee, expecting the tears to flow. But they did not. Her eyes remained hot and dry and aching. It seemed she was just too empty for tears.

As the hours passed, Charity began to feel differently about what had happened in her meadow. Jason was leaving, yes, as she had known he would, but he had said goodbye to her.

Why would he bother if he did not care about her at all? He had also told her that he'd not meant to use her, that he was sorry things couldn't have been different. Why would he do that unless it was true? And if it was true, wasn't it an indication that he felt something?

What his feelings might be, she didn't know. She was under no illusions that he loved her. He would not leave her if he did. Yet if what he did feel was even half as powerful as the force of yearning that drew her to him, it was not something easily ignored or discarded.

Restlessly she paced the confines of her room, the

hours since she had spoken with him in the meadow a blur of confusion and longing. He'd not come in to supper, and Elija had told them that he'd said he wanted to turn in early after a late night the previous evening. Her father did not seem to question his excuse, but Charity knew he was only getting ready to leave.

Charity told herself she was glad that Prue had gone to spend the night with Levi and Hope. She was far too distraught to hide her agitation tonight, knowing as she did that Jason would be gone in the morning.

But in another part of herself Charity was not sure that she should be alone just now. Something was stirring inside her, something primitive and raw that could not be ignored.

She wanted Jason—feared she wanted him as a woman wants a man, though she wasn't quite sure what that meant in its entirety. Oh, she knew the basic facts of nature; she couldn't live on a farm and not see. But how could the emotions become so powerful that one actually . . . ?

A deep flush stained her cheeks and throat.

What she was distractingly certain of was that Jason would know. The darkness of his eyes, the sureness of his lips on hers, told her as much. Though she knew she would never actually discover if her belief was true, she could not deny what she wished. . . . The very thought brought a thumping of her heart and a tightness to her chest that left her yearning to experience the passion of his kisses again.

Suddenly she had to see Jason, perhaps for the last time, to be with him even if they couldn't be together as she desired. Jason's very nearness would comfort her. Somehow she knew that he was no more asleep than she, that he too would be beset by restlessness.

Didn't the fact that he had told her he was going, that he wished things had been different, mean that he too would be upset at the loss of whatever lay between them? Before she could consider the wisdom of her actions, Charity left her room and hurried from the house, her passage cloaked in silence and darkness.

She found Jason in the barn with his horse, murmuring as he stroked and groomed it.

As if sensing her presence, he swung around, his expression glad for one brief instant before he masked it. He squared his shoulders. "What are you doing here? Is something wrong up at the house?"

She did not care for the coolness in his dark eyes, but she hurried to reassure him. "No, everything is fine. They are all asleep."

His expression seemed to grow even more remote. "Then why are you here?"

She felt uncomfortable beneath that cool gaze, but could not lie. "I just wanted to see thee one more time before you left."

Jason's lips twisted in a wry grimace. "I don't think that would be a good idea. It's all been said."

Without stopping to consider, Charity moved to stand within inches of him. "But I need to see thee one more time. . . . I . . ." She could not finish, for there was too much inside her.

Jason watched her for a long moment, and as she held his gaze, not even trying to hide her sadness, his dark eyes grew unexpectedly and achingly tender. Her breath caught as he reached out to run his finger over her cheek, making her flesh tingle with awareness all the way down her spine. "I'm sorry, Charity. I forgot how very innocent and straightforward you are."

She felt herself flush again, but this time it was not from discomfort or embarrassment. She shivered. "I'm not so very innocent."

"Oh, but I think you are." Jason watched as her pink lips formed a pout, feeling a tug inside himself even as he realized anew how much passion burned inside her, and how strongly it called to him. He sighed, unable to resist the temptation to move his finger to her mouth. Almost from a distance he was aware of himself running his finger slowly over the top lip, then the bottom. His breath quickened as her lips parted.

His name escaped her lips on a sigh. She swayed, and her breasts brushed against the front of his shirt.

With a groan of need, Jason wrapped his arms around her and drew her close to the warmth of his body. And as he did so, Charity knew that she had only been fooling herself when she imagined that it would be enough to simply be near him. This was what she had longed for, hoped for in the secret recesses of her mind.

"Oh, Charity," he whispered against her forehead. "What am I going to do with you?"

Charity raised her face to gaze up at him, her eyes dark azure and damp with yearning. "Kiss me, Jason, like you did before."

And he did.

This time, Charity was ready for the touch of his mouth against hers, and she responded immediately, putting her arms around his neck to pull him even closer. Her lips softened under his and she returned the pressure, drawing on his sensuality to feed her own.

Jason's arms tightened around the small of her back, and she fitted herself perfectly to the curve of his hard body.

With gentle insistence, his tongue came out to prod her lips, encouraging them to open. Unwilling to deny Jason anything, Charity welcomed the sweet invasion. His tongue moved over hers in an erotic dance, and she raised up on tiptoe, desiring nothing more than to be close to him, to enjoy the languid heaviness in her limbs.

Jason moved his hand up her side, and she felt the heat of his fingers despite the heavy fabric of her dark dress. Slowly he explored the curves beneath until he came to the swell of her breast, and paused to rest his thumb under its gentle weight.

Charity held her breath, all her consciousness centered on that spot where his thumb rested against her. That sure, warm touch only made her want . . . oh, she did not know what.

Then his hand closed over the aching fullness, the nipple hard against his palm, and she knew that this was what she had wanted. Charity gasped aloud as a shaft of the purest sunlight shot down her body to spread in radiating waves from her stomach. A liquid warmth trickled down to pool in the most secret of places at the joining of her thighs.

Jason dragged his mouth from hers, his breathing harsh and ragged. His lips were moist on her temple. "Charity, oh Charity. I want you so much. I've never felt this way about any woman."

Charity heard these words with a rush of elation. Shaking with the tumultuousness of her emotions, she buried her face in the strong curve of his neck, her voice trembling as she admitted, "I . . . I want thee too."

Hearing these words made Jason's heart contract, his body pulse with longing.

His arms tightened in a grip that was almost painful, but she gloried in the feeling as his lips found hers once more. Her heart sang as she returned his kiss measure for measure.

He broke the contact of their mouths, holding her head against his shoulder. He knew that he had to stop this, that it couldn't go on. But he couldn't seem to slow his breathing, let alone take his arms from around her body, which was so warm and yielding against him.

Suddenly, over the hoarseness of their breathing, came the loud rattling of a wagon outside.

Charity gave a start, and felt Jason go rigid as he lifted his head from hers. Her voice was raspy with shock and desire. "What is going on?"

Jason's voice was strained as well as he replied, "I don't know, but they can't find us here like this."

Both hurt and anxious at his words, Charity whispered bitterly, "No, we would not want anyone to know we have been together." Turning her back, she moved toward the door.

She felt Jason follow, but could not bring herself to look at him when he spoke her name, even as she heard the sound of voices coming from the direction of the house.

There was nothing to say. His attitude should not have come as a shock. Had she had time to think, she would have known that a few kisses would not actually change anything.

She nodded, too numbed by disillusionment and shame to feel any more pain at the moment. Although in some deep part of herself, she knew the pain would come again. And that it would come with a crushing and terrible force.

Not now, please not now, she told herself. Not when she must still make her trembling legs take her out to see what was going on, out to face her family. Without another word, that was exactly what she did.

Chapter Six

In the light of the lantern that her father held in his hand, Charity saw that her ears had not fooled her. The sounds had definitely been that of a wagon, driven by Levi.

Keeping in mind the fact that Jason did not wish anyone to know that they had been together in the barn, she moved around the circle of light until she could come up behind her father. Her anger toward Jason was so great that it took a moment for her to fully take in the horrified expression on Levi's face as he looked down at her father, who was clad in his nightshirt.

Her father was not so slow. He spoke with concern. "What is it, son? Patience? The babe?"

Quickly he shook his head. "No, Elija. It's Lizzy. I've just had word that she was taken by a slave hunter."

"A slave hunter?" Mother put her hands up to cover her mouth. "Dear God preserve the poor girl."

Levi nodded, his face grim. "Yes, and it's even worse. It was Wayne Grisak. He passed through Helmsville with her."

"Wayne Grisak!" Papa said, glancing toward the house where Louisa and the recovering baby lay.

Levi nodded again. "They say he was drunk and going on about how he was going to come back and make anyone who had helped his wife to leave him pay."

Mother took a deep breath, raising her chin. "Well, we'll not let that worry us. Those who trust in the Lord have nothing to fear."

Yet even as her mother was speaking, Charity's gaze went to Jason where he stood at the door of the barn. The rage on his face was more than apparent, narrowing his eyes, which were frigid with hatred. Charity shivered. She suddenly felt as if that fury separated her from him in a way that his leaving never could.

Hurriedly she told herself that this made no sense. Jason was Jason. His anger did not deter her, for beneath it was the kind and loving heart that had been so apparent the day they'd brought Louisa and the children here. Yet Jason's expression told her that Wayne Grisak was indeed the connection between himself and Louisa. It was very likely what had brought him to Helmsville in the first place.

She suddenly realized that it was because of Wayne Grisak that he was leaving her. The fact that he was ready to disregard everything and everyone in his quest to find the man, told her that it had something to do with his woman's death. And that man had taken Lizzy. Dear heaven, poor Lizzy, whom Charity had come to love in their time together. Not only was she in that man's clutches, she was on her way back to her cruel master in the south. Though she had the feeling that Lizzy had actually revealed very little of the true misery of her life as a slave, she had talked enough to make Charity's heart bleed with sadness for her. The name of the place she had escaped, Ivy Plantation, offered no clue as to the horrors of life there.

Charity was aware of a sense of desolation and hopelessness. She could do nothing for either Lizzy or Jason.

Sadly, Charity shook her head, her gaze on Jason's now hanging head. With a sigh she glanced away from him and toward her mother, realizing that she must gain control of herself.

She did not want to answer queries concerning her behavior. Jason had asked her to keep what little she knew of his secret, and the only hope she had of doing that was to avoid being questioned. She could not lie to her mother.

She told herself that she didn't want anyone to know that she had gone to him in the barn this very night, yearning for . . . Heaven help her, she had to get such thoughts out of her mind.

Jason was leaving, and she must become accustomed to the idea.

She forced herself to attend to the conversation. Levi was frowning down at her father. "I should have known thee would not heed my warnings, but I had to come and tell thee in the event that the madman had somehow learned that thee had Louisa and the children here. He could come at any time. I know that violence is wrong, Elija, but thee must find a way to avoid this man."

Her father nodded his head, his gaze earnest. "And I

thank thee, son, for thy loving act in warning us. But thee know that we can do nothing different from what we do. As my Mary says—" He put his arm around his wife's shoulders and pulled her close. "—we will put our faith in the Lord."

Levi sighed. "So be it."

Mother smiled up at Levi. "You'd best be getting home to Patience now, son. Tell her not to worry."

Levi sighed again. "Goodnight." With that, he swung the wagon around and drove toward home.

All the while, Charity was completely conscious of Jason, lingering in the background, his expression dark with torment and rage. As her family went on to discuss the matter of Lizzy and her desperate condition, she knew she should be thinking of the recaptured woman, but she could not.

Almost against her will, she found herself turning to Jason. She was shocked to find his strangely and unbelievably sad gaze upon her own face. Her eyes found his dark ones and she knew that her answering pain must be apparent. Yet she could not summon the self-control to disguise it. She could only stare, her heart aching with such longing and anguish that she was no longer capable of even trying to hide it.

For a long moment their eyes held, Jason's dark with what she, even with her lack of experience, could see was need. It was recognizable for the feelings of desire it drew from deep within her. She felt her mouth soften, saw the way his gaze went to it.

Then suddenly Jason swung around and disappeared into the darkness, leaving not even a shadow to ease her longing. Charity put her hand over her aching heart.

Feeling her mother's gaze upon her, she swung around and saw the pitying expression on her face. Putting her hands over her face, Charity ran into the kitchen and through the house to her room.

There she threw herself upon the bed and cried, giving in to the tears that had burned in her for days. She was so overwhelmed by her feelings of loss and hopelessness that she could not seem to prevent herself.

After a time she heard someone open the door behind her, but she feigned sleep, keeping her face turned to the pillow until they had gone. But she could not stop the tears flowing even then. They continued on for so long that her eyes grew heavy, her chest aching from the sobs. . . .

Starting awake, she realized that she had cried herself to sleep. She felt no better for the short and fitful rest. A world without Jason was not one she cared to face.

Rolling over onto her back, Charity wiped her hair back from her damp brow. The room felt closed-in, stuffy. With a sigh, she got up and went to the window to let in the cool night breeze.

As on many other nights, Charity could hear the rustling of the leaves in the trees. Suddenly the sound was the loneliest thing she could imagine.

Charity choked back a sob, unwilling to offer any more tears.

Life on the farm would go on. She would listen to the breeze stirring the leaves outside her window. She'd sit at the same table, do the same chores, sleep in the same bed, but she would never be the same again.

Jason wouldn't be there. She wouldn't hear the sound

of his voice as he talked with Papa over breakfast, wouldn't smell the fresh clean scent of him after he'd bathed in the stream. Never again would she feel the passion he'd awakened in her with his lips and hands.

Nothing would be right without him.

In spite of her resolve, hot tears prickled her eyes.

Then out of the corner of her eye, she saw movement out in the yard. Her eyes rounded as she looked closer.

Her breath caught, for it was a man on a horse. Her heart told her that it was Jason and he was riding away from the farm—away from her, as he had said he must.

The house had grown quiet again, yet Charity was careful to go silently as she hurried down the stairs, then let herself out the back door. As she ran across the yard to the barn, she could think of nothing save the need to see if it had really been him, if he was really gone.

The stall where Jason kept his horse was empty, and yet some senseless, miserable, desperate part of her hoped. Charity moved to the back of the barn, where the room for the hired hand was. There was no sound from inside, nothing.

Knowing that she was only torturing herself by searching for him, Charity turned the knob. The door swung inward. The room was empty.

Her heart heavy, she went into the room, turning about in hopeless loss. She put her hands to her face and sank down on the bed, unable to stand on her suddenly trembling legs. As she did so, she brushed up against something.

Reaching out to push the object aside, Charity realized that it was an oddly shaped box, something like a hatbox in fact. Though she tried to make out exactly what it was—a hatbox made no sense whatsoever—she could not fathom what else it might be.

She was suddenly very determined to examine its contents.

Charity realized that she would have to take it back to the house and her room to really get a good look at whatever it might contain. She also felt a sense of guilt at doing this; it might yield some personal items that Jason had inadvertently forgotten and would wish to keep private.

She quickly dismissed her scruples. Jason had left it and she didn't care what he or anyone else might think of her or her actions. She was going to have a good look inside. There might even be some clue as to who he was or where he had come from.

Did she not deserve to know something of the man who had come to change her so irrevocably? Without another moment of hesitation, she grabbed up the box and raced back across the yard, into the house and up the stairs to her room, where she had left the lantern burning.

Now that she looked at it in the light, Charity saw that she indeed held a hatbox before her. Frowning with curiosity, she took it to the bed and laid it on the coverlet. Sitting down next to it, she took a deep breath, again dispelling a sense of guilt. With a nod that felt like self-encouragement, she reached out and lifted off the lid.

Inside, nestled in creamy tissue paper, was a hat. And it was one that she immediately recognized. It was the same one that she had tried on the day Jason had taken her into Helmsville. The one in which she had wondered very foolishly if he would find her attractive. Puzzled at this strange occurrence she lifted it out of the box, and as she did so a piece of paper fluttered to her lap. Setting the hat aside, she picked it up and read:

Charity:
I'll picture you in it wherever I go.
—Jason.

Joy rushed through her, followed by a crashing wave of loss. He *had* cared something for her. Not only had he cared for her, but it had been strong enough to make him leave this gift for her.

Yet his feelings had not kept him from going.

She cast her eyes toward heaven. Why had God brought Jason to her to take him away again? Suddenly Charity knew with a faith that was unshakable that she and Jason were meant to be together. She knew it as she knew Papa and Mother were meant for one another. Love was like that: bestowed by God, it was meant to be accepted as the true gift it was.

So why, she cried silently, had Jason gone away? Why was this mysterious quest of his more important to him than what he felt for her? It was surely strong, even if he was not willing to see it as love.

She wanted to scream in frustration and hopeless longing. There was no way to keep him, and there was no living without him.

Suddenly a verse from the Bible leapt into her mind with startling clarity. *Wither thou goest, I will go.*

It was then that Charity knew what she had to do. If Jason wouldn't stay with her, she would have to go after him—she could not do anything else.

Of course, Jason wouldn't willingly take her. She would just have to convince him.

A sudden and inspired thought came to her. Jason was looking for Wayne Grisak. Charity just happened to know the name of the plantation to which the man was taking Lizzy. And perhaps—oh, most certainly—there was a possibility, she realized with a flash of hope, that Jason could be persuaded to help Lizzy escape and to bring her back to safety. He was a good man, gentle and kind. He would not be able to ignore her plight, especially with Charity there to persuade him.

All Charity had to do was follow Jason and make him see that he needed her. How difficult could it be when in truth he did feel something for her?

She had to go now, when she still had some hope of catching up to him.

In a matter of minutes, Charity was closing her bedroom door behind her. In one hand was a carpetbag with a blanket, a nightdress, clean underthings, and a comb. In the other hand was the hatbox containing the gift Jason had left for her.

She planned to raid the pantry for some provisions. Some bread, cheese, and leftover beef would do nicely. Aware of the fact that Jason was getting farther ahead with every moment, Charity gathered some food into a cloth.

Then, with a deep sense of sadness, she left the note she had written for her family on the kitchen table. In it she tried to explain her love for Jason, her certainty that he would help her to regain Lizzy's freedom, and a plea for them to refrain from coming after her. She would simply leave again if they did so. She'd ended by telling them how very much she loved them and hoped to be back with them soon. Charity knew that her mother and father would never physically force her to do anything, including staying on the farm. She only hoped that they would understand that she did indeed love them, even though she had done this mad thing. She didn't allow herself to think that they might not.

She slipped on her sturdy black boots and left the house without looking back.

Saddling a horse, she took a deep breath and headed in the direction she had seen Jason go.

The first hour was more than unpleasant. She had to prod Dan constantly to try to keep him moving at a gallop. Yet she did not falter. Jason was some minutes ahead of her and she had no idea of the pace he had set.

Finally, when her legs were weak from urging the old gelding on, Jason came into sight on the road ahead. Charity was so startled at the actual sight of him that it was a moment before she pulled on the reins to slow the animal she was riding, turning him into the shelter of the trees at the roadside just as Jason glanced around.

Breathing slowly and carefully, she told herself that she must have more care if she was to gain some distance from home. The farther they went, the more difficult it would be for Jason to take her back, in the event that he was not inclined to heed her reasons for going with him.

But she would not think about that possibility yet. She would find a way to convince him.

Completely resolved to see this through, she settled in to several hours of grueling effort and misery. Though not riding at a gallop, Jason set a brisk pace, and Charity was not used to riding for long distances.

She and her sisters did not ride for entertainment, and rarely went far from home without a wagon. Also, Dan was not a pleasure mount but a workhorse, more used to dragging a plow than carrying a young woman. Thus, as the hours wore on, Charity began to understand that riding was something that should be learned gradually. Yet she kept going, knowing that she could not lose sight of Jason—of her hope that they would be together.

The reason he would be so eager to travel so very far in the middle of the night she attributed to his need to catch up with Wayne Grisak. It was not very comforting to imagine that he could be so determined to put as many miles as possible between himself and the farm—and her.

When sometime around dawn Jason turned off the road into the forest, Charity almost sobbed with relief. Her relief was short-lived.

The ground in the forest was littered with fallen trees and other natural debris. It did nothing to improve Dan's irregular gait.

She kept her eyes peeled for Jason, caring about nothing so much as keeping sight of him in the trees ahead of her, which was sometimes difficult on the dark road. Suddenly though, she paused, frowning. One moment, Jason had been right there ahead of her, and now he wasn't.

Desperately she scanned the forest all around her. There was no sign of Jason, or of movement of any kind for that matter.

Disappointment washing through her, Charity shifted in the saddle, and the insides of her tights brushed the hard leather. She moaned aloud as agony shot through her sore muscles.

She tried to draw her legs up away from the saddle to ease them, but the insides of her thighs had become so raw that even the feel of her dress against her skin was excruciating. At the same time, she realized how very tired and heavy her arms had grown from holding the reins and fighting to keep Dan on the road. And that was not to mention her bottom. Gingerly she told herself that it was best to try not to think about any of these aches, including the unceasing flicker of discomfort which seemed to burn its way up her lower back.

Then, as a sigh escaped her, she asked herself why she couldn't think about how sore and tired she was. She'd lost sight of Jason. Suddenly she knew she'd had enough for one night. Charity was going to have a rest. If that meant telling Jason she was here, so be it. Surely now she would have to call out to him to find him.

She rode forward, her face set with determination. Jason had to be close by, he couldn't have just disappeared. She'd seen him only moments ago. She opened her mouth to call his name, "Ja—"

One minute she was on her horse, the next she felt herself roughly pulled up against a broad, hard chest.

Instinctively she began to struggle, gasping aloud. "Let go of me."

Jason spun her around and the thunderous look on his face was enough to make her cringe. He shook her as he growled through clenched teeth. "What the hell are you doing here?"

Charity's agonized body screamed at the rough treatment, but she drew herself up straight to glare back at him. "Thee should have known I wouldn't let thee go without me after I learned that the man thee might have some connection with had taken Lizzy."

With a grunt of rage he shook her again. "I damn well didn't know any such thing. Why do you have to be so blasted stubborn?"

This time Charity could not keep back a moan of anguish. Her muscles felt as stiff as boards.

Instantly Jason's face crumpled with concern. His hands loosened only a little, but his intent had clearly become protective. "What . . . what is it, Charity? Are you hurt?"

She tried a rueful smile, but none would come. She hurt in every part of her. The blood that had begun to rush back into her thighs and buttocks felt as if it were on fire. Slumping against him weakly, she gritted her teeth to stifle a moan. Her voice was hoarse as she replied, "I'm afraid I overestimated my horsemanship."

Understanding washed over Jason's face. His anger seemed to dissolve before her very eyes. Gently, he picked her up and held her to his strong chest. "You're right, I should have known you'd come after me. You're brave, and loyal, and you follow your heart."

In spite of the pain, which did in fact seem far less agonizing with his arms around her, Charity smiled against his warmth. Wasn't this just what she'd hoped for, that he would welcome her with open arms? Exhaustion and relief overwhelmed her. She closed her eyes. . . .

When Charity opened her eyes again, she saw a strange sight. Above her was a high ceiling covered with long rocky growths. Some of these reached almost to touch equally odd growths on the stone floor.

Her brow creased with confusion. Where was she? Where was Jason?

She could recall her arrival, Jason's anger, then tenderness. Her lips curved as she recalled the way he had held her.

After that, everything was a blank. Where she was and how long she had been there was a mystery.

There was a scraping noise to her left and Charity made a move to turn to her side. A white-hot surge of pain snaked through her muscles, and she gasped.

Jason's voice came from the left, and she assumed it was him that she had heard a moment ago. "Try moving very slowly. I can't guarantee it won't hurt, but you may be able to manage."

Even in her present state, she felt a thrill at hearing his voice. She was here and he was here. No physical pain could equal the pain she'd felt at thinking she'd never see him again. As long as they were together everything would be all right.

Smiling gingerly, Charity did as he suggested. He was right. The motion didn't hurt any less, but the pain came in smaller doses, that could be more easily absorbed.

"Where are we?" she asked as he came into view. Gingerly she leaned back against the stone wall, facing him.

Jason straightened from the small fire he had built. "In a cave about eight hours' ride from Helmsville."

Her rueful chuckle was followed by a groan, as Charity found even laughing painful. "I know well enough how long it took to get here, and I imagined it might be a cave. Is there something less obvious that thee might tell me?"

Jason went back to tending the pan he'd set over the flames. "I would prefer to keep any details to myself. It might keep you from tracking me again."

Her heart sank. So he meant to send her back. She told herself she could not truly be surprised, though his lack of emotion hurt after his tenderness the night before.

Yet she did not want him to know that. Clearly Jason was not going to admit to having any feelings for her. Well, so be it, she would not then admit hers, not for anything, but she was not going back without Lizzy. Charity raised her brows, casting a cool glance at him.

Casually Jason said, "I met an old peddler on my way to Helmsville. He told me about this cave and that it was a good place to stop over." He gestured around with his fork.

"Warm, dry, and all the animals have been driven out by previous travelers. What more could you ask for?"

Obviously he had decided not to press a confrontation at the moment. She would follow his lead, and wait before challenging him with her information about where Grisak was going. She spoke evenly, though she reminded herself to be wary as she cast another assessing glance about the cavern. "It's certainly the most impressive sight I've ever seen." From this side, Charity could see that the room was huge. Hundreds of the long columns of rock jutted from the ceiling and floor. I never knew there was anyplace like this. It's like make-believe in a story."

Jason shrugged, but his gaze was undeniably wondering. "Truer words were never spoken. I've seen many things in my life: the Acropolis, medieval castles, and seas that stretch on forever, but none were more beautiful."

For some reason his words left Charity feeling hurt. "There are so many things about thee I don't know."

Jason seemed to sense her mood, for he gave a rueful sigh. "Don't worry, Charity. For all I've seen and the people I've met, I've come to realize it's what's inside that counts. Not where you've been or who you know. Being with you—your family was one of best experiences of my life."

The statement mollified her not in the least, for she was infinitely aware of his use of the word *was*. While he might wish to avoid an argument for the moment, she could not do so any longer. "I thank thee for thy kind words, but thee may not feel that way for long."

He frowned. "What is that supposed to mean?"

"As you must realize, I have guessed that thee are looking for Wayne Grisak. I have some information that would be very helpful to thee in finding him."

Though she could tell that he did not wish her to see it, the words did jar him. "And what could you know?"

If she hadn't been so bent on her own ends, Charity would have been quite perturbed at his disdainful tone. As it was, she ignored it. Her own hopes to help Lizzy took precedence over his opinion. "I know where he is going."

"How could you?"

"Lizzy told me. Now," Charity said into the silence that her words had created. "I had best get up so we can be on our way." She put her arm beneath her and pushed herself up gently.

Jason waited for the laborious operation to be completed before he replied, making Charity look to him in surprise. "We are not going to be on our way. At least not the way you mean. You are going to tell me what you know and then I'm taking you home."

She started to shrug, then thought better of it, letting her tone speak for her. "I am not."

"Why should I believe you know anything?" he asked, studying her closely.

She took a quick breath, deciding to reveal a part of what she knew. "River Bend, South Carolina. But that is all you will find out for now. I will not tell thee the name of the plantation until we arrive." He scowled as she went on. "And if thee think that thee can get on without the rest of my information, there is just one other thing thee should consider. I'll simply come after thee again. I cannot let that man leave Lizzy with those wicked people."

Jason's expression was just as confident as hers. "Not when your father finds out, you won't. He'll lock you up till it's safe.

Charity smiled, her eyes narrowing. "Don't let thyself be too sure. Papa would never lock me up. It would completely go against his beliefs. He truly believes that each child of God must follow his or her own heart."

His jaw dropped open and he stared at her as if she'd grown fangs. "You're lying."

Her head came up and her nostrils flared. "I do not lie. Thee should not be so quick to judge others by thyself."

"Guilty," he conceded openly. "I have done that and many other things I'm not proud of, but as I have told you, there is something that I have to do no matter what else it costs me. I won't have anyone else jeopardize my success."

She shook her head. "What is it, Jason? Why won't thee just tell me? Is Wayne Grisak connected to thy wife's death? If he is, why don't thee tell the authorities and let them take care of it? Better yet, leave him to the Lord."

His jaw hardened as did his eyes, and she wanted to shrink away from the anger she saw there, but she refused to do so. "Leave him to the Lord? That bastard will die, and by my hand. He has condemned himself."

"Thee would not have that on thy hands."

"Stop right there, Charity. I know you. I know where you are going with this, what you think about life. There isn't any point in discussing this with you, now or ever. Your being here will not stop me. I can't allow you to hold me back. I owe it to Daphne."

She raised her head, her eyes directly on his as she felt the words sink into her soul. What a fool she had been not to realize the true extent of his plans. There had been clues: the depth of his rage, his sorrow over Daphne, his warnings to stay clear of him. Did she truly have any right to try to convince him now? Yet she could not deny her own pain and regret as she said, "Have no fear of that, Jason. I won't hinder thee, or ask thee any more questions, but thee aren't the only one who has a purpose to fulfill. I am going with thee, and I am going to help that woman to escape."

He scowled. "You will be surrounded by people in total opposition to your opinion of slavery. Do you really think you can accept that, saying nothing when you feel the way you do? You must, if you are to keep your word about not jeopardizing my purpose. I would not have you drawing attention to me or yourself."

Her lips tightened at the very thought of accepting such thinking. God help her, she knew in the depths of her soul that, hard as it might be to imagine ignoring the southerners' attitudes toward slavery, it would be far worse to imagine Jason killing a man. Praying that it would never happen, she nodded sharply, unwaveringly, as she faced him.

For a long moment, Jason only stared. Then, with an exasperated sigh, he dropped the fork he held into the pan, and put his hands to his face. "Heaven help me."

Chapter Seven

They ate breakfast in silence and when Jason swung away from her and began to saddle his horse, Charity felt a rush of relief that overshadowed her dread of what he might do in the future. She had won. But the stiff line of his back also told her that Jason was far from happy with her or the situation.

Shrugging, she moved gingerly to saddle her own horse. She would not have him do it for her, not after she had so fiercely assured him that she would be no hindrance to him.

Though Jason did not look around as she went about the task, which was far from simple due to the soreness of her body, she could feel the weight of his attention. She made no effort to acknowledge it. She was here to help Lizzy. What Jason thought was of no concern to her, not anymore. He had made his position more than clear.

Yet when she bent to lift the saddle onto her horse, she could not hide the wince she gave at the agony that stabbed through her muscles. Before she could even speak to stop him, Jason was beside her, taking the dratted saddle from her and tossing it onto the horse's back. She frowned. "I did not ask . . ."

He swung around in dismissal as he said, "I didn't say you did."

Charity knew from his closed expression that there was no point in arguing or even thanking him. Jason was not interested in anything she had to say. Whatever feelings he'd had for her were gone, killed by his need to find Wayne Grisak.

They began their journey with no other conversation between them.

As time wore on and Jason showed his displeasure by ignoring her, Charity began to feel some resentment herself. She tried not to, and she told herself that it served no purpose, that Jason could simply feel the way he did, but the feelings only increased, churning endlessly inside of her. She found herself watching the back of his head, wishing she had known just how unpleasant he could be from the beginning. Perhaps she would not have come.

Quickly she dismissed the thought. Lizzy needed her either way.

They stopped for the night near a small stream. Jason built a fire and made them a meal of canned beans and some bread from his saddlebags. He declined her stiff offer of assistance.

This only made Charity's resentment burn all the brighter. He was a singularly unpleasant man. She had no notion of what might have made her believe she was attracted to him.

She could not wait to have Lizzy safely on her way north again, and to be done with him. Yet even as she told herself these things, she found her gaze lingering on the glossy highlights in his hair as the firelight played over it. She could not help seeing the supple strength of his hands as he reached to place another log on the flames.

As if sensing her attention, Jason looked up. His gaze locked on hers for one infinite moment in which she ceased breathing. The hunger in that stare seemed to call out to some place deep within her. Then he turned away, continuing to eat his meal without any sign that he was even aware of her, and she knew that it had to have been her imagination, a trick of the firelight brought on by her own unwanted fascination with him.

Her cheeks heating with embarrassment, Charity set her food aside and sought her blanket. She did not care what he might think of her leaving the cleaning to him. She was just too tired, too confused to sit there for another moment.

The second day went by in much the same manner as the first, and the endless, emotionally painful days that followed that. They passed through towns, barely stopping or speaking to anyone else any more than they spoke to each other.

Jason paused only to make inquiries of those they chanced to meet. Each time it was the same. Had anyone seen a man and a young black girl? Always the answer was the same. No.

Charity was beginning to wonder if they were wrong about Grisak's having taken Lizzy directly south, if they had indeed followed the wrong path. Then, at last, on the evening of the third day, an answer came in the affirmative.

A farmer they passed had seen a man and a young girl answering to that description that very morning. The fellow had stopped to buy eggs, and the farmer had sold them gladly. He did not want anyone to think that he was a sympathizer, and so would give aid to anyone whose work it was to take slaves back to their rightful owners.

Charity was appalled at the man's attitude. She did not understand how anyone could have so little care for their fellow human beings. She had to force herself to remain impassive. She would not forget Jason's warning to keep her opinions of slavery quiet while they traveled though the south.

He did not wish to draw any attention to them that might be hinder his own agenda. Watching him as they rode on, seeing his barely leashed anticipation at finding that they were indeed right on the heels of his quarry, reminded her all too clearly that he would not allow anything to jeopardize his plans, whatever they may be.

While she resented his single-mindedness, there was also something sad about the grief that fed such a blazing fire of persistence.

Almost against her will, Charity felt a stirring of sympathy and yearning. If only Jason were not so driven by this quest. He might be able to find some happiness or peace if he would only see that it lay inside him.

Obviously he was not willing to do that. It seemed

there was nothing she could do about it—even if she tried.

That night when they stopped, Jason paused beside her and spoke offhandedly. "We will be in River Bend tomorrow."

"Tomorrow?" she whispered, running a tired hand through the dirty fringe of hair that had escaped from her bun. She was suddenly aware of the fact that she must certainly be a horrifying sight.

He seemed quite unaware of her discomfort. "We'll be getting a room. You can stay there after you tell me where Grisak is going."

Charity heard the resentment in his voice, but did not react to it. Jason had actually accepted her refusal to reveal the name of the plantation with good grace, not even mentioning it until this moment. She had no intention of waiting in a hotel room, but she kept that to herself for the moment, as Jason moved off into the forest to gather wood.

What she was more immediately concerned about was the fact that she could not go to a hotel for the first time in her life in such a state. She cast an unconscious glance toward the place where Jason had disappeared into the forest.

The fact that Jason seemed to have taken no note of her appearance in any way did not lessen her self-conciousness. Although she knew it was vain to worry over her appearance, she had also been raised to believe that cleanliness was next to Godliness. And she was far from being clean.

As was his custom, Jason had brought them to rest close to water.

She cast a yearning glance over the fast-moving stream. It would feel so good to wash. And not just her face and hands, but all over, including her hair.

Yet she did not wish to do so here so close to the road and in a place where she knew Jason would soon return.

Taking up her bag, Charity headed downstream. She would find a more secluded spot than this one.

Jason made no haste as he gathered an armload of wood. He was in no hurry to get back to camp, to face Charity. Even now he was too conscious of the memory of how his heart had turned over at the sheer exhaustion on her face as she'd viewed their new campsite.

His sympathy had been what had driven him to tell her that they would reach their destination the next day. He'd thought to comfort her with the notion that tomorrow night she could put her head down on a real pillow.

The fact that it was it by her own stubborn folly that she now found herself in such a position did not ease his sympathy. Nor did it change the underlying tenderness he felt toward her, no matter how desperately he told himself that it should.

Yet he'd found himself reminding her and, Heaven help him, perhaps himself that she was only with him because she held information he required. From the moment he'd capitulated, and allowed her to come along that first day, he'd been telling himself that it was only because of the information she held.

He did not allow himself to believe anything else, even when the knowledge that she lay just across the fire from him each night nearly drove him mad. He could not seem to stop himself from trying to make out her lovely form beneath the blanket in the warm glow of the fire, or listening for the gentle intake of her breath.

Even in sleep there was little respite. His dreams were haunted by images of the two of them kissing, holding one another.

He groaned with frustration and self-directed anger.

Looking down at the heavy armload of wood, Jason knew that he could not just stand there indefinitely. He had things to do before dark, which was quickly approaching. He had pressed onward until the last moment—as he had every day since this journey had begun.

He told himself it was because he must catch up to Grisak, but he could not deny that some part of him believed his nighttime demons would be eased if he were too tired to think. Shaking his head at his own foolishness, Jason stalked back toward camp. He walked out into the clearing and stopped, realizing immediately that Charity was not there. Frowning at the fact that she would go off without telling him, he quickly laid the wood near the spot he had prepared for the fire.

He knew she had not gone off to answer a call of nature, for he had discreetly allowed for that as soon as they stopped. Quickly he searched the ground, which was fairly soft this close to the creek, for clues. Then he saw it, a footprint, headed off to the east.

Why did she have to be so very difficult? There was no telling who or what she might run into. She therefore had no business going off alone.

Knowing he would not rest unless he made sure that she was all right, Jason headed after her with a heavy sigh. When he'd fist met her, Charity had seemed different, more malleable. Since the night she'd insisted on the following after him, he was seeing a completely new and much more headstrong side to her character.

He did not allow himself to believe that this new facet had only served to intrigue him as surely as it irritated him. He would have to be mad to admit it.

Angry at his own thoughts, he set off down the creek. She'd said she'd be no bother to him. He meant to remind her of that the moment he caught up with her.

Jason noted the fact that the water widened and slowed as he followed its bank as it crawled back away from the road. Other than that, he paid very little attention to the green vibrancy of the forest or the scamper of small animals in amongst its protective depths.

It wasn't until he was nearly upon her that he saw Charity. And what she was doing made him come to a dead halt.

His startled gaze took in the wild mane of hair that floated in the water around the back of her head, all that was visible above the surface of the water. Her clothing, obviously discarded in haste, lay in a pile on the bank.

Jason blinked, taking a hasty step backward as a shock of warning raced through his body. He needed to get away from here, from the unnamed danger of this situation—now, before she saw him.

As he stepped back, his weight came down on a twig that lay on the ground. The ensuing sound, however soft, was enough to make her turn.

Her eyes widened as she saw him, and she leapt up

with her hand over her gaping mouth. Against his will, his gaze slipped down, over her slender form clad in nothing more than her bloomers and shift. His own belly tightened as he saw the way the white cotton had become transparent in the water.

The fabric in fact seemed almost more tantalizing than nudity, for he found himself straining to see past the pale shadows it created on her creamy flesh. It clung to the curves of her hips and flat belly, the delicate angles of her shoulders, and the sweet fullness of her breasts. Their tips seemed to beckon him through that almost nonexistent veil, seeming to press more pertly against the fabric even as he watched.

Jason swallowed hard, finding it nearly impossible to do with such a lump in his throat, such a tightness in his belly. It was in fact hard to think of anything but the sudden and inescapable aching in his loins.

All this happened in an instant, as his gaze found hers. What he saw there, God help him, only made his body respond more urgently: Her blue eyes were not shocked and appalled, as he had expected. They were dark and filled with longing.

Even as he watched, she took her hand from her lips, which now seemed fuller and more tempting than a moment before. "Jason," she said. The word was an invitation, an invitation that she likely was not even aware of offering.

It was this that brought him to his senses. He closed his eyes, breathing heavily, knowing he had to stop this. "For God's sake, Charity, what are you doing?" When he looked again, he knew that both of them were far too aware of what the words really meant, but he went on, trying to distract them both with anger.

"You should know better than to come here like this. Anyone could have come upon you. Even a wild animal. Did you stop to think about that?"

For a moment as he spoke she seemed hurt and confused, then her lips twisted in chagrin and anger. She quickly moved to cover herself with her hands. "No."

Good, he thought, anger would be much easier to deal with than passion.

Yet he experienced a flash of chagrin himself as she went on coolly, "You said we would arrive in River Bend tomorrow and I . . . all I thought about was how dirty I felt." She lifted a self-conscious hand to run it through the tangled wetness of her hair, then hurriedly brought it down to cover herself again.

Now Jason frowned, more moved by her sudden self-consciousness than he cared to admit. He focused instead on what she had said. He should have thought of it himself. Unfortunately he had been far too occupied in forcing himself to think of Charity as little as possible to consider anything as ordinary as her need to bathe.

He was not made to feel any better about himself as she turned and waded toward the bank. It was all he could do to drag his gaze away from the curve of her left buttock, completely exposed to his view beneath the sodden cotton of her drawers. But he managed to do so, and found himself saying, "If you are not finished, I can wait for you." He added quickly, "That is, I will wait a little ways up the bank. So you can be . . . have some . . . privacy."

She did not look around at him as she hurriedly grabbed up her dress and held it in front of her. "No, I am finished."

His lips tightened at her tone, which continued to be uncharacteristically cold, but he said nothing. Quickly he turned his back while she got dressed with no small amount of struggle, due to her sodden state.

He clenched his fists at his sides. He didn't want to think about her sodden state, about the creamy loveliness of her body. . . .

With a grunt of exasperation he headed down the trail. Charity could find her own way back to camp.

Charity watched Jason's retreating back as she worked to pull her dress down over herself. She felt the heat in her face as she realized just how much of her must have been bared to Jason's gaze. The fact that she had reacted to the heat she found there was even more disturbing.

His immediate disgust made her want to throw herself upon the ground and cry. She resisted the urge, determined to find some semblance of self-respect and dignity in spite of her shame and anger.

Once she had managed to get her clothing on, ignoring the discomfort of it, she raked her fingers through her hair until she had brought some order to the tangled mass. Then she dug in her bag until she found a piece of string, which she tied around it. She did not even want to try to put the pins back in, the way her hands were shaking.

She stood then, glancing about to make sure she had not left anything, knowing as she did so that she was only dawdling. The thought of going back to the camp and Jason was dreadful.

Yet it was just what she must do.

Raising her head and taking a deep breath, Charity

moved in the direction of camp. On arriving, some of her determination flagged when she saw that Jason had gone about setting up for the evening as usual. Even now he sat beside the fire preparing the meal.

He nodded in her direction, but made no indication that he recalled what had just occurred back at the stream. It only contrasted far too sharply with her own disquiet.

Somewhat put out, she moved to drop her bag at the foot of the blanket he had laid out across the fire from his—as if nothing were the matter.

She had a burning urge to move it far from his and his dratted lack of emotion. She would not allow herself to do so.

His indifference made her determined to display the same emotion, no matter how difficult it might prove.

When he handed her the plate, she took it with a carefully polite thank-you. She was actually quite pleased that her voice did not betray her agitation.

Jason made no reply.

With an inward shrug, she made an effort to eat at least a portion of the food. Her efforts there were not as successful as she would have hoped but she tried to hide how much remained as she scraped it into the fire.

It should have pleased her, but for some reason did not, that Jason paid her no attention at all.

Turning her back on him, she went to her blanket. Although her clothes were still quite wet from putting them on over her sodden undergarments, she crawled inside. Then, even as she pulled the thin covering over her, a chill raced down her back. She gritted her teeth, determined to ignore the discomfort until it passed rather than face Jason for another moment.

* * *

Jason was very aware of Charity, more so than of anything or anyone before. Yet he knew that he must conquer the feelings that roiled inside him, erase the tormenting images that had followed him from the stream.

Still, his attention remained centered on her, his gaze tracing the delicate curve of her hip beneath her blanket, her long legs. Jason swiped a hand across his sweat-dampened brow and shifted restlessly on the log. He realized that this night, as every other night they had spent on the trail, would not afford him much sleep. Perhaps it was this close scrutiny, or perhaps it was another deeper kind of awareness that made him realize something was not right with her prone form.

She seemed to be shaking—perhaps crying.

Standing slowly, he tried not to make any noise that would waken her—in case he was mistaken—as he moved closer, around the edge of the fire. Yes, he could see clearly now. She was quivering from the top of her head to her feet.

Frowning with uncertainty, he hesitated. If she was crying, what would he say to her?

Yet he knew he had to say something. The notion of her being sad was far more painful than he would have imagined.

He moved quickly to kneel down beside her. "Charity." Her eyes were wide as she turned to face him.

"J-J-Jason?"

Immediately, he knew that she was not crying but shivering. Without thinking, he reached out and pulled her into his arms. She was soaked. No wonder she was cold. If he hadn't been so distracted by his thoughts, he would have recognized it sooner.

"No." Charity tried to push away from him even as she was taken by another wave of shivering.

He held her even closer. "Why are you lying here in these wet clothes?"

She looked up at him with huge blue eyes as she continued to shiver. Quickly he stood, drawing her to her feet. Picking her up, he carried her to the other side of the fire and set her down beside his own blanket. He took the wet one from around her and held it out as a screen. "Take off your things."

She hesitated, and he turned his head to look off into the forest before ordering, "Now!"

He heard the rub of wet fabric as she moved to obey. Even though it took her no time at all to remove the garments and take the dry blanket from the ground beside her, he was hard-pressed to keep his mind from straying to thoughts of the smooth creamy skin that had so tempted him earlier at the river.

Even though it was only moments before Charity said, "I am finished," Jason had to take a deep breath before turning to face her again, an action that did not help, for her blue eyes were filled with a telling sort of uncertainty as they came to rest on his.

Slowly he lowered the wet blanket to see that she now held the dry one clutched close about her.

Her gaze continued to hold his. "Thank thee."

He spoke around very dry lips. "You are welcome. But tell me please why you would go to bed wet like that?"

Her lashes swept down to hood her blue eyes. "Thee said I had to stay in camp, and I didn't want to. . . ."

Even as the words left her lips, a definite charge filled the air around them. She hadn't wanted to change with him nearby.

The night thickened and swelled with the weight of all the things that lay unsaid between them. All the feelings Jason was working so hard to suppress. The very same feelings he suspected she was feeling, a fact that only made his own more difficult to deal with. For here, alone with the darkness around them, it was getting harder and harder to recall why he must do so.

His tormented gaze met hers, saw heaviness in those lovely eyes as she whispered, "Jason."

The wet blanket fell to the ground and his arms were around her in an instant. He looked down at her upturned face, saw the way the firelight played over her beauty even as his lips found hers.

At the touch of his mouth, the world tilted all around her. Charity moaned as a sweet wave of warmth rose up in her belly. She raised her arms to clasp them around Jason's neck, wanting, needing to be closer.

Jason's arms tightened around her, molding her pliant form to his. Gently he urged her mouth to open beneath his, his blood heating as she eagerly complied. Her soft tongue parried as he slid his own over it, bringing his desire to even sharper life.

Charity groaned when his lips left hers, feeling bereft at the loss of that passionate contact. Yet she was immediately soothed when his hot mouth found her jaw, trailing scorching kisses down her throat, then on to the nape of her neck, where his touch brought shivers to her suddenly oh so sensitive flesh.

Jason opened his hands, running them up her slender back to her shoulders, then slowly down again, and with them came her covering. His mind reeled as his fingers traced the satiny softness of her, his breathing ragged.

When they reached her hips, he molded them reverently, his fingers lying along the upper curves of her bare bottom. He could feel his own manhood, hard and insistent against her belly, and when she pressed herself even closer, he gasped. Urgently he clasped her to him, feeling his desire pulse in reaction.

"Jason?" her voice was husky, full of uncertainty and promise all at the same time. He knew what she was asking, even if she did not. And it was this, the fact that she did not know, that stopped him.

He could not do this to her—would not.

Laying his forehead against hers, Jason clenched his teeth down hard. Desperately he drew on every ounce of willpower he possessed.

She squirmed against him, making his decision all the more difficult to follow. Gently but firmly he stilled her, holding her hips with determination now.

He drew back slightly, looking down at those hooded blue eyes, being careful not to allow his gaze to dip any farther, knowing that she was completely bared to him. "Be still, Charity, please be still." He was shocked at the depth of desperation and pleading in his voice, the raw need it revealed.

She looked up at him in confusion. "What is it, Jason? What have I done?"

He groaned. "You haven't done anything. It's me. I . . . can't do this."

Confusion quickly turned to embarrassment as her cheeks flushed a deep scarlet. She dropped her head to stare at the ground even as her hands came up to cover herself. Her shame made his heart ache, but he knew he could not say so, could not relent.

Not for either of their sakes. Charity was eventually returning to Wisconsin, where she belonged. And he was going home, back to Boston and his own life. There could be nothing between them, for he could no more remain in her world than she could ever fit into his.

He was not Jason Wade. It was nothing more than a disguise he had adopted to allow him access to Grisak's world. He was part of a social world that would understand Charity no more than she would them.

He would not do that to her, and anything less than an offer to share his life, an offer of marriage, was unthinkable. Charity was too good, too pure to use and discard.

Jason would not further scar his soul by taking what she would give without considering how much it would affect her.

When she pulled away from him to search for her discarded clothing, he caught a haunting glimpse of her, the delicate and lovely hollows and planes of her. Hastily he scooped up the blanket and tossed it to her. "Take this. I don't need it."

"But . . ." she began.

He did not wait to see if she complied, just strode off into the woods. What he'd said to her was true. The way he felt right now, Jason didn't know if he would ever be cold—or even a normal temperature—ever again.

The next morning Charity rose without Jason having woken her. She had barely slept the whole night, though she had feigned sleep from the moment she heard him come back to the fire a very long time after he left.

She said nothing to him as they readied for the road. There was nothing to say. Jason had made his feelings quite obvious by drawing away from her last night. Nothing could better illustrate the fact that he did not want her.

She could think of no other explanation. Surely he had only kissed her again because he could see how very much she wanted him to. When their kisses had escalated, he had not been able to go on.

Unfortunately, her feelings did not match his own. In spite of her hurt and shame, she wanted him still. Just the memory of his hot mouth, his knowing hands on her body, made her ache with longing.

Yet she would do anything to keep Jason from knowing this. All she had left was her pride, and she must not forsake that, no matter how difficult it proved to be.

Her feelings of unhappiness continued throughout the morning, and were not lessened by Jason's silence. It was as if the night before had never existed, and Charity was left with no other choice but to follow his lead, though it proved far more difficult than she would have imagined.

It was only when they came across a man pulling cart down the road that he seemed to show any signs of interest in what was going on around him. He asked the usual question. Had the fellow seen a man and a girl answering Grisak and Lizzy's description?

To Charity's amazement, the man nodded. "I seen them pass by me less than an hour ago."

Charity was quite aware of Jason's agitation as he

Thrill to the most sensual, adventure-filled Historical Romances on the market today…

FROM  LEISURE BOOKS

As a home subscriber to the Leisure Historical Romance Book Club, you'll enjoy the best in today's BRAND-NEW Historical Romance fiction. For over twenty-five years, Leisure Books has brought you the award-winning, high-quality authors you know and love to read. Each Leisure Historical Romance will sweep you away to a world of high adventure…and intimate romance. Discover for yourself all the passion and excitement millions of readers thrill to each and every month.

SAVE AT LEAST *$5.00* EACH TIME YOU BUY!

Each month, the Leisure Historical Romance Book Club brings you four brand-new titles from Leisure Books, America's foremost publisher of Historical Romances. EACH PACKAGE WILL SAVE YOU AT LEAST $5.00 FROM THE BOOKSTORE PRICE! And you'll never miss a new title with our convenient home delivery service.

Here's how we do it. Each package will carry a 10-DAY EXAMINATION privilege. At the end of that time, if you decide to keep your books, simply pay the low invoice price of $16.96 ($17.75 US in Canada), no shipping or handling charges added*. HOME DELIVERY IS ALWAYS FREE*. With today's top Historical Romance novels selling for $5.99 and higher, our price SAVES YOU AT LEAST $5.00 with each shipment.

AND YOUR FIRST FOUR-BOOK SHIPMENT IS TOTALLY FREE!

IT'S A BARGAIN YOU CAN'T BEAT! A Super $21.96 Value!

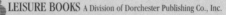 **LEISURE BOOKS** A Division of Dorchester Publishing Co., Inc.

GET YOUR 4 FREE* BOOKS NOW—
A $21.96 VALUE!

Mail the Free* Book
Certificate
Today!

---

4 FREE* BOOKS 🌸 A $21.96 VALUE

Free Books Certificate*

YES! I want to subscribe to the Leisure Historical Romance Book Club. Please send me my 4 FREE* BOOKS. Then each month I'll receive the four newest Leisure Historical Romance selections to Preview for 10 days. If I decide to keep them, I will pay the Special Member's Only discounted price of just $4.24 each, a total of $16.96 ($17.75 US in Canada). This is a SAVINGS OF AT LEAST $5.00 off the bookstore price. There are no shipping, handling, or other charges*. There is no minimum number of books I must buy and I may cancel the program at any time. In any case, the 4 FREE* BOOKS are mine to keep—A BIG $21.96 Value!

*In Canada, add $5.00 shipping and handling per order for first shipment. For all subsequent shipments to Canada, the cost of membership is $17.75 US, which includes $7.75 shipping and handling per month. [All payments must be made in US dollars]

Name _____

Address _____

City _____

State _____ Country _____ Zip _____

Telephone _____

Signature _____

If under 18, Parent or Guardian must sign. Terms, prices and conditions subject to change. Subscription subject to acceptance. Leisure Books reserves the right to reject any order or cancel any subscription.

(Tear Here and Mail Your FREE* Book Card Today!)

Get Four Books Totally
F R E E* —
A $21.96 Value!

(Tear Here and Mail Your FREE* Book Card Today!)

PLEASE RUSH
MY FOUR FREE*
BOOKS TO ME
RIGHT AWAY!

Leisure Historical Romance Book Club
P.O. Box 6613
Edison, NJ 08818-6613

nodded and rode on at a quickened pace.

Only after they had rounded several bends in the road did Jason slow to speak to her, his gaze hard. "Give me the name."

She should have expected this, Charity thought, but she frowned as she matched her pace to his. "Not unless thee allow me to go with thee."

Jason rode his mount close to hers, and she could see anger burning in his eyes. "That was not part of our deal. Are you changing your mind?"

She winced. "No, I'm not." She bit her lip. "I can tell thee that Ivy Plantation is not in the town itself, not according to what Lizzy told me. She said that it was on the west side of the city along a wide creek, possibly the very one we crossed a few minutes ago. We are only a very short distance behind them now. Thee would waste precious time in taking me somewhere before going there." She faced him earnestly. "I promise not to interfere with thee in any way. Please, Jason, I do not wish to be left alone."

He watched her closely for a long moment, then he swung around. "Come."

Without a word, she followed.

Chapter Eight

"Jason, look! It's him! It's Grisak and my poor Lizzy."

Charity's words sent a ripple of shock through Jason even as he raised his gaze from the thick brush around them. His eyes came to rest on the couple who stood on the steps of the elegant, white-columned mansion that lay just ahead of them through the trees. Rather than following the road to the house, they had moved alongside it, in order to stay out of sight.

Jason had been too occupied with his own unhappy thoughts to notice how close they were getting to the house. He had been concentrating on moving forward through the woodlands, on not thinking about Charity and how mixed-up she made him feel. He had to keep moving forward, remembering what mattered—what he had to do.

His pulse pounding, he raised a hand to halt her even as he pulled his own mount up short. He slipped to the ground, tying his horse to one of the trees, and silently moved closer. He felt Charity right behind him, but did not acknowledge her presence. He could not take his gaze from the man he had traveled so far to find.

He felt another wave of a disbelief and shock as he saw that Wayne Grisak was of medium height with neatly cut brown hair and a rather dapper-looking brown suit. His regular features were set in a placid expression. He looked like an ordinary man, more ordinary, in fact, than most.

How could this be him? How could such evil not show on the features, in the body?

Knowing that he had to come to terms with the innocuous appearance of this man he deemed a monster, Jason forced himself to look at the girl. She stood just a couple of paces behind him, her head down in a submissive attitude. Yet it was only as her terrified and hopeless gaze ran over the man's back that Jason saw the evidence he sought. For as she looked up, he could see the bruising along her cheek, the dark smudges beneath her lovely brown eyes.

Finally, in her frightened and bruised face, he recognized the signs of the monster that stood nearby.

Grisak was in fact capable of the most heinous of crimes. He had to remember what he'd seen and heard from the bastard's victims. Grizak had practically bragged to Tucker of his activities in Boston. And there was no excuse for the way he had treated his wife and children.

Even as he watched, the front door was opened by a tall elegantly dressed black man. As his gaze came to rest on Lizzy, his lips twisted before he quickly masked the expression, turning his attention to the white bounty hunter.

Grisak did not wait for him to speak. "I have business with your master."

He bowed politely. "The mastah ain't in, suh."

"Oh, is that right? Well maybe you should tell him that I got his darky here." He indicated Lizzy with an arrogant sweep of his hand. "Maybe he'll be in then?"

The black man kept his gaze down, his tone respectful in the face of the other's belligerence. "I'm sorry, suh, the master be away from home for a few days. He won't be back till the end of the week. The overseer, he be here, suh."

Grisak shook his head. "I don't want to talk to no overseer. This here girl was a heap o' trouble comin' down here and I don't mean to give her over without negotiatin' the reward just a little bit."

The other man remained respectfully impassive, although Jason did see the brief glance of sympathy he cast toward the girl. "Yes, suh."

With a grunt of frustration, Grisak said, "Well, I guess you're too damned dumb to get any more out of ya. You just tell your master to send me word at the Red Lady when he gets back."

Without waiting for a reply, Grisak swung around, shoving the girl down the steps in front of him. He then pushed her into his dilapidated wagon, where she huddled as far away from him as she could get. Grisak paid her no attention, getting up into the seat and flicking the reigns over the horse's back.

As the wagon moved closer, Jason's gaze fixed again on that face, that ordinary, deceptive face. Anger rolled through him that fate could have been so cruel as to give such a monster a human face.

Jason wasn't aware of the fact that he had started forward until Charity stopped him. "No, Jason, not here."

He turned to regard, her, searching her face through the haze of his own wretched thoughts as she said, "Thee don't want to approach him now, here, in this place. Thee would only be putting Lizzy—us—in danger."

Jason knew she was right, but the anger inside him was threatening to rise up—to overshadow his judgment. Calling upon inner reserves of reason, Jason nodded. "Yes, you're right. Not here."

He knew where Grisak would be.

He would force himself to wait just a little while longer for his revenge.

And at the back of his mind pressed another thought. For reasons he could not even begin to understand, he did not wish Charity to be present when he confronted the bastard.

Surely it was for her own sake, her belief in nonviolence. He had no care what she thought of him. Her seeing him as he truly was, a man driven and obsessed with hate, would be best for both of them.

Watching Wayne Grisak leave with Lizzy was one of the hardest things Charity had ever done, yet she knew she must do so. There was no hope of rescuing the girl here on the very land of the man who claimed her as his property. Yet as these thoughts rolled through her mind, she was equally distressed by Jason's strange and frightening behavior. She could feel the tension and rage that emanated from him. But his eyes were distant, cold, and eerily without emotion.

She continued to tell herself that he was only over-come at seeing the man he had come to find, that he would regain control of his emotions, get some hold over the rage that boiled inside him. They would rescue Lizzy. Any other thought was impossible.

In spite of her agitation at what had occurred at the plantation, Charity could not help being amazed by the River Bend. The lovely homes with their lush lawns and moss-draped trees seemed to go on and on from the moment they entered the outskirts of the city. She could feel Jason's brooding attention upon her as she stared at the lavishly gowned ladies with their lace parasols who strolled along upon the arms of dapperly dressed gentlemen in tall black hats. There were few folk in Helmsville who could rival such elegance, and here it seemed the model.

Self-consciously she ran a hand over her own plain gray skirt. Hurriedly she told herself that she was just being silly. Fine garments did not make a difference. The Lord well loved those who came to him without artifice. It was one of the cornerstones of her faith.

Yet she would have been less than honest with herself if she denied that a wayward part of her viewed those hooped skirts and frogged jackets with some degree of longing. Even so, as Jason led her on through the city, she followed him with her head held high.

Jason felt a growing urgency to find somewhere to leave Charity. He saw the way she watched everything around them, though he was in no state to try to fathom the many emotions that were passing over her lovely features. He did not wish to think about how she felt about anything. It only took his thoughts away from Grisak.

"Come," he told her, urging his horse down the thoroughfare more quickly than before. He would find the closest respectable hotel and leave her there.

Although he would have preferred to be closer to Grisak, he could not imagine taking Charity to the type of establishment he knew the man would frequent. Added to that, he did not wish Grisak to see and recognize him before he had a chance to surprise his enemy.

Before long they came to a three-story structure with a sign that proclaimed it to be the Royal Oak. Jason stopped before the gracious but slightly shabby hotel. It appeared as if it would cater to those with less than deep pockets, yet seemed respectable enough for Charity's sensibilities and safety.

He slipped from his horse even as he told her, "We will stop here."

She looked at the sign. "This is not the name of the hotel Wayne Grisak mentioned."

He frowned. "No, it is not. Did you really think I would take you there?"

She scowled back. "But I thought we would go there and get Lizzy."

He shook his head, realizing that he should have expected this. "No. We are not going there to rescue Lizzy. I told you that I have my own business with Grisak. If, and I mean if, it does not interfere with my plans, I will see what can be done for the girl. But you must realize that setting her free in these surroundings will be far from easy." He raised his dark brows high. "Now can we go inside, or do you wish to delay me longer?"

She took a quick breath, her slender nostrils flaring,

and raised her head high before turning to flounce up the steps. Jason could not fail to see the anger and outrage apparent in the stiffness of her back.

Jason felt a strange regret at having upset her, but he told himself his frankness was for the best. After the previous night, he no longer trusted himself to display any softer attitude.

They went inside, and Charity glanced about the lobby with its carpeted floor and high ceiling with barely concealed unease. As he signed the register, then followed the bellboy up to their rooms, Jason tried not to show any reaction to her nervousness.

Yet he could not help thinking that if things had been different, he could have allowed himself to tell her that she had nothing to be uneasy about, that she was equal to far grander surroundings than this. He could have watched her relax and enjoy each new experience, could have allowed her delight to make him see everything anew, could have anticipated showing her even more of the world that she had not experienced.

He could be going up these very stairs to a room they would share, a room where . . .

Harshly he dragged his thoughts away from that path.

He had finally caught up with Grisak only minutes ago, was so close to the end of his quest he could nearly taste the satisfaction of having it done, of being free. He would not be distracted by anything—including Charity Applegate.

The room the bellboy showed Charity to was, like the rest of the hotel, comfortable without being too grand, and had an aura of shabby gentility. It held a wrought-iron bed, a bureau, and a chair. The window was open and the lace curtains fluttered across the white chenille spread with a gentle caress.

The uniformed young man opened the door of the room directly next to it, telling them that it was Jason's. It was the twin of Charity's other than the green bedspread.

Fully aware that Charity had followed, and was watching him, Jason entered his room directly behind the bellboy. He went straight to the door that joined the two rooms and nodded when he found it locked. She stepped back and disappeared from sight.

With an odd sinking feeling in his stomach, Jason handed the boy a coin. "Thank you very much. We can manage from here."

With a touch to his cap, the lad disappeared.

He knew he was mad to do so, but he followed him out and went to the door of the other room, which remained open. Silently Jason watched Charity, who was sitting on the end of the bed beside her satchel, one hand clutching the handle as if it were a lifeline. Even as he watched, her gaze went to the locked door, her expression bleak.

Jason spoke without knowing he was going to do so. "Charity."

She turned to him, clearly trying to regulate her expression, though her voice was uncertain as she said, "There was no need to make such an issue of showing me the door was locked."

Jason returned her gaze without wavering. "I had to let you know that I . . . It's the only way, Charity. It's the way we both want it."

169

She looked down at the floor, then back at him, her lovely eyes blue as a rainy Monday. "Of course it is, but I felt . . . Thee had no need to remind me."

Shaking his head, Jason backed toward the door. "I was reminding myself."

Her eyes darkened on his. "Why must thee do so? Thee have made it perfectly clear that thee do not want me."

Jason felt the words slam into him. She could not be more wrong. But he would never tell her that, as he once had. The admission had only led to more problems.

Briefly he pinned her with his eyes, his expression hard, warning her that there could be no more discussion. "I'm going out. You get some rest. The bellboy pointed out the bathroom on the way up. You remember where it was?"

Charity stood. "Thee are going to Grisak. I want to come with thee."

His jaw tightened and he glared at her. "I've had about all I can take. You know I couldn't let you do that, even if I were inclined to involve you in my business here, which I am not."

"But Lizzy is *my* business. Thee know that is why I came. I have to take her home with me. If thee are not careful with Wayne Grisak, something will happen to her before I can set her free."

The furrow in his brow deepened. What she said was true, but Jason didn't want to stop to think about any of it, not now, not when he was so close to the end of his quest. Desperation made him harsh. "You will stay in this hotel and let me do what I have to. I mean it, Charity! Promise me!"

Clearly his determination registered, for she watched him in frustration for a moment before nodding with obvious reluctance. "I promise."

Relieved at her capitulation, Jason turned and left the room, closing the door firmly behind him.

Charity stared at the closed door for a full ten seconds without moving.

She wanted to think about anything besides Jason's having made such a point of checking the connecting door. She wanted even less to think about what she might have revealed with her own words. Her only hope was that he was too agitated about his need to see Grisak to consider what she'd said.

But her other pressing thought, that of Lizzy's safety, was even more painful.

She'd meant it when she told Jason she'd stay at the hotel. That is, she'd meant it in the instant she'd said it.

Yet Wayne Grisak was a very dangerous man, clearly capable of any ill her mind could conjure, not only as far as Lizzy was concerned, but also Jason.

Jason had admitted there was danger in what he was doing. How could she sit there patiently while he went off to face who knows what alone? While Lizzy was in the hands of that man?

The answer was simple. She couldn't.

She got up and hurried into the hall. Jason had not even reached the bottom step of the wide double staircase leading to the lobby when she reached the second-floor railing.

She stepped back as he glanced upward, a strange and indecisive expression on his face. But he didn't see her. Then, shaking his head, he went on. Trying to be as nonchalant as possible, Charity moved forward once more, stepping off the bottom stair just as Jason was going out the door.

Out in the street, she hung back as she followed him. More than one head turned for a second look at her Quaker dress, though curiosity soon turned to appreciation in the eyes of many of the men.

Not knowing what to make of this, Charity chose to ignore it. She had more important matters on her mind.

For several blocks she kept Jason well within her sights. When he turned a corner, she'd turn a corner, and there he'd be up ahead of her.

The fact that the neighborhood grew less respectable as they went along didn't disturb her, at least not overly much. She kept right on walking, continuing to ignore the increasingly interested glances that were cast her way.

She noted, though, that the few women she saw were dressed in gaudy fabrics, and leaned familiarly on the men who escorted them. They seemed to laugh with far more abandon than she had ever heard. Charity could see nothing to warrant such mirth. She wondered if they could be the . . . well . . . "soiled doves" she had once heard a traveling lady suffragette preacher call the women who made their living entertaining strange gentlemen.

When one red-faced gentleman lurched to a stop before her and tried to speak, she kept her eyes straight ahead and ignored him. She told herself she had nothing to be concerned about. Jason was well within shouting distance. All she had to do was call his name and he'd come running. Though he'd certainly be angry, he would not allow anyone to harm her.

Her determined self-confidence took a downward spiral as she rounded a corner expecting to see him there ahead of her, and found no sign of her protector.

Desperately she scanned the area. The street was lined with saloons, each bearing a gaudy sign with a ridiculous name such as Kitten's Den or Silver Slipper. The boardwalks here were teeming with life: gamblers, planters, cowboys, shopkeepers, and more mingled and shifted like sand in the wake of a receding wave.

There was no sign of Jason. Telling herself that he simply had to be there, she started forward again.

The crowd on the street made keeping her distance from everyone else somewhat difficult, and she had to work to keep from brushing up against them. Just as she was beginning to doubt the wisdom of going on, Charity felt a hand close around her arm.

She swung around and found herself gasping for air as a blast of foul breath hit her face.

Watery gray eyes peered into hers, and blackened teeth grinned from between heavy lips as the strange man leaned over her. Her accoster rubbed a pudgy hand over his beer-swollen belly. "Well, well, well. You're a tasty little morsel."

Revulsion fueled Charity's incensed response. "Get thy hand off of me."

"*Thy* hand?" The man ran his bleary gaze over her. "Your one o' them Quakers, ain't ya." His expression changed to irritation. "One o' them temperance preachers." He wagged a dirty finger in her face. "Don't think I don't know 'bout ya. You Quakers is just as quick to have a woman preacher as a man." He released her arm. "Well, you just go home. We don't need your kind around here. If I wanted to hear about the evils o' drink, I could go home to my wife."

Weak with relief at being released because of his assumption that she would preach against drinking, Charity put her hand over her heart and cast her eyes to heaven as she spoke aloud for anyone to hear. "Demon drink will steal thy soul. Repent and take up the Bible along with the banner of truth." In her enthusiasm, she completely ignored the fact that she had no Bible and no banner. Charity had not given temperance a great deal of thought in the past, but she was sure that this path would better serve the man before her than the one he was on.

Waving his hands in disgust, the man turned and disappeared into the crowd.

Charity continued on, more determined than ever to find Jason. Now, every time a man approached her, she simply and honestly warned him about the evils of liquor and he ran in the opposite direction. She hoped that God would understand her making use of his work for her own purposes.

She just had to find Jason. But not locating him on the boardwalk, she could only believe that he had gone inside one of these noisy establishments. She only wished she could find the Red Lady.

At last she saw it: the Red Lady Saloon. Her brow creased as she observed that the folk milling around near the entrance seemed even more rambunctious than those she had encountered thus far. Biting her lip, Charity realized that she was going to have to go inside; there was nothing to be gained by standing here in the street impersonating a lady preacher. Armed with sheer determination and her ingenious defense,

Charity took a deep breath and stepped across the threshold of the Red Lady Saloon. She told herself not to be so nervous. Red had always been her favorite color.

Once inside, Charity looked around with trepidation, yes, but also an undeniable curiosity. The room's focal point was a long bar with a mirror behind it. Several small, round tables were ringed by wooden chairs, most of which were occupied. On the walls were pictures of ladies in various stages of undress that made Charity blush with embarrassment as she cast a quick glance over them.

She decided to focus her attention on the clientele for her own modesty. Quickly she scanned the room, her gaze alighting on each man there for only as long as it took her to see that he was not the one she sought.

Just as she was coming to the conclusion that Jason was not here and she must certainly move on, Charity heard a woman scream.

Shocked, she spun around, searching for the source.

To her surprise, she noted that none of the other occupants of the bar seemed to have heard, for they went on drinking and talking without pause. The pitiful squeal came again, and she stood on tiptoe trying to see where the noise came from. When the screech came again, Charity finally pinpointed the direction.

Over in the corner, a chair had been tipped to rest on its back legs against the wall. A man was seated in the chair, a woman in his lap.

The man, a burly dark-haired fellow, was holding her securely. Even as Charity watched, he sank his teeth into the tender skin of her nape.

Rage boiled up in Charity's belly. After the way she

had been accosted outside, she was especially sensitive to the plight of this other woman.

Without pausing to think of her own safety, Charity ran across the room. She pushed the unsuspecting man back and, throwing her arms around the woman, she pulled her to her feet.

Charity's action jarred the leaning chair, and it tilted to the side. The startled occupant's eyes grew round as twin full moons. Helplessly, he reached out to claw at a thread of cigar smoke wafting by.

The chair hit the floor with a noisy crash.

A deafening silence followed, as the whole saloon stilled.

The rescued victim let out another screech of horror and threw herself on top of the fallen man. All the while she sobbed and called his name. "Maurice! Maurice!"

Maurice, who had obviously had the wind knocked out of him, was unable to do anything but grunt and wave his arms in the air.

"What have you done?" the woman cried, her red-painted lips twisted in a snarl as she turned on the Quaker.

Charity stared down at them in confusion. She held out her hands. "I was trying to help thee. I thought . . ."

The woman pushed back a strand of wildly frizzed black hair and glared her fury. "It looks like you didn't think. Maurice is my best customer."

Her eyes growing wide, Charity put her hand over her mouth and took a step backward. "Customer?" Realization dawned, and her voice lowered to a mere whisper. "I thought he was hurting thee."

"Like I said, you didn't think." Reaching out to take

Maurice's flailing arms, she helped him to a sitting position.

Charity's face flamed as she felt the attention of everyone else in the saloon on her back. But she hurried forward to help. "I'm so very sorry."

Both of them reached out to push Charity's hands away. "You should be. All you Quakers want to do is make trouble for other folks," the woman told her. "Why don't you just leave us alone?"

Jason pressed through the crowded thoroughfare with resolution. He knew he had been dawdling, had found himself standing still more than once, his thoughts not on the matter at hand, but on the memory of Charity's dejected face as he left her. He looked up, focusing on the scene in front of him, his eyes scanning the signs that lined the street. To his amazement and relief, the Red Lady lay just a couple of doors up and across the street from where he stood. He stepped out, dodging a galloping horse before reaching the other side.

He paused at the door, knowing he had to focus his thoughts, to recall what he was doing here, what lay ahead of him. In the beginning, he had thought to find Grisak and force a confession from him, feeling that this was the only way he could justify killing him. Jason no longer required a confession. He was sure, after all that he had learned, that Grisak was indeed guilty of the rape and murder of his wife. So why was he hesitating?

Perhaps it was because he was not sure how he would accomplish his purpose and get away without being arrested. He could not simply walk up to the man in a crowded saloon and shoot him. Not if he hoped to get away. And he had to get away. He could not leave Charity alone here so far from home. Nor could he disregard her hope that they would be able to free Lizzy.

These thoughts buzzed through his mind like a swarm of angry bees, and Jason shook his head. One thing at a time. First he must actually find the bastard, check out the lay of the land. He could only hope the rest of it would fall into place.

He pushed open the door. The first thing he noticed when he walked through the door was the silence.

Somewhat amazed at this unusual quiet, he paused, his gaze scanning the room. Everyone in the saloon had crowded into one back corner.

Then he heard the shrill, angry sound of a woman's voice making an unintelligible and angry comment.

There was a short pause, then an equally unintelligible reply followed.

The first voice came again. "You should be. All you Quakers want to do is make trouble for other folks. Why don't you just leave us alone?"

Closing his eyes in disbelief, Jason ran his hands over his face. Something, perhaps the sick feeling in the pit of his stomach, told him that he would find Charity at the center of the crowd.

He groaned. Why in the world had he trusted her?

No one even noticed him as he elbowed his way through the throng. They were too busy enjoying the spectacle that greeted Jason's weary eyes.

Seeing the scarlet-faced Charity, the overturned chair, the angry prostitute, and the even angrier man, who was now waving his arms and cursing in French, it wasn't difficult to fathom what had happened.

But as the two continued to rail at her, his chagrin was laced with a trace of protectiveness. Almost as a reflex, he put a hand on Charity's arm. As she turned to face him, Jason saw that her shock and undeniable relief at seeing him did not completely disguise the fact that she was very near laughter.

At first he was amazed at her amusement, but he swept another glance over the unhappy couple. It *was* quite a spectacle, but he couldn't allow Charity to see his own amusement.

It had been wrong of her to come into this place, to follow him. Especially after she had given him her word.

Good God, what would happen if Grisak were to come in? He could be anywhere in the building.

His voice was rougher than he intended as he whispered in her ear. "What are you doing here?"

Her expression became obstinate as she replied, "Looking for thee."

"You promised you'd stay at the hotel."

For a moment her gaze was truly regretful. "A lie for which I must answer to the Lord." Then her lips tightened with defiance. "But I felt thee . . . I mean Lizzy, needed me."

A gruff voice interrupted them. "Sir, is this your woman?"

Jason looked over to see a tall slender man with muttonchop sideburns standing at the inner circle of the crowd. At the same time, he became aware of the hostility directed toward them from the throng.

Another male voice called, "She's the very one what was preachin' about the evils o' drink outside."

The man with the sideburns turned on Charity with

frank revulsion. "I want you out of my place and I want you out now. And don't make the mistake of coming back, bitch."

Jason wasn't surprised by the man's vehemence. The last thing the owner of a drinking establishment needed around was a reformer. Yet Jason couldn't allow him to call Charity names. He swung around to face the man. "I think you'd better apologize to the lady."

The ends of the man's sideburns curved inward as he smiled. "I don't think so." His quick glance around the room made it clear he could do what he wanted. Jason was outnumbered.

Without pausing to consider the wisdom of his action, Jason let fly with his right fist. The tall man fairly flew backward, to land with his back against the bar. He was still for a moment, then groaned, shaking his head, clearly dazed.

Charity let out a squeak of surprise, then covered her mouth with her hands, her eyes huge, even as Jason realized that he had just burned a very important bridge. He would never be allowed to come back into this place.

There was a rumble of anger as many men's hands went to their gun belts. Jason stood tall, facing them all. "I didn't use a gun." He raised his fists. "Are you afraid to fight with these?"

The muttering grew louder.

A woman's voice rose over the din. "Wait!"

Every set of eyes, including Jason's, focused on a young blond woman in a cheap low-necked green dress. She was pointing a small pearl-handled gun toward the crowd, and watching Jason with unconcealed admiration. "This here fella's got the balls of a stud horse. There ain't a one of you would face a whole roomful of men just 'cause someone called your woman a bad name. I say he goes free."

By this time the man with the muttonchops had risen, his hand pressed to his jaw.

The prostitute smiled at him. "And what I say goes. Ain't that right, Hank?"

He eyed the woman for a moment, then nodded. "I guess he can go." Then he shook a finger of his free hand in warning. "But I don't want to see neither one of you in here again, or you won't be walking when you leave. You get my meaning?"

Jason nodded without taking his eyes from the other man. "You have made yourself abundantly clear."

He was somewhat shocked to see Charity rush over to the woman who had insisted they go free. She bent close, nodding as the other woman seemed to answer some query.

The other man spoke again, roughly. "Take her outta here."

Jason raised dark brows, facing his adversary with a deliberate lack of concern, though he was perturbed that Charity continued to press an already bad situation. "Charity," he said calmly, making her turn to him. She addressed one last comment to the other woman, put a brief hand on her shoulder, then ran to his side. He held out his arm as if he were simply requesting her company for a stroll in the park. "And now, my dear, if you're ready, we'll be leaving."

Without hesitation, Charity took his arm, holding on with both hands. Keeping his pace deliberately casual in spite of the fact that he was filled with frustration at knowing he could not set foot in here again, he led her from the saloon.

Chapter Nine

Charity nearly tripped over the hem of her skirt as Jason pulled her up the steps of their hotel, but she made no sound. More than one head turned to view their hurried progress through the lobby, but Jason didn't even slow down or acknowledge the stares in any way.

Though he hadn't seemed angry at the Red Lady, he hadn't said a word since they'd left, and the remote look on his face worried Charity more than a little. Up to now, Jason had accepted Charity's independence of action with fairly good grace.

She wondered if that was about to end.

Jason opened the door of her room and drew her none too gently inside. He then slammed the door and stood before it, his arms crossed over his chest. "Well?"

Experiencing a wave of intimidation in spite of herself, Charity backed up a few steps. Then, realizing she had done so, she tried for a casual shrug and feared she only managed to appear nervous. "Well, what?"

"What were you doing in that place?"

"I told thee." Deliberately she went to sit on the end of the bed. "I was looking for thee."

His eyes pinned her to the bed. "You promised me you would stay here."

Charity tried hard not to squirm. "I know. I am sorry I broke a promise—" She lifted her chin. "—but I'm not sorry I went to find thee."

His voice rose, each word a drumbeat. "Well, I am. Now I can't go back there. How can I find out about Grisak if I'm barred from the saloon he's in?"

Charity tried for a reasoning tone. "Surely they won't stay angry."

He moved closer, to stand in front of her, his legs wide apart, his hands on his lean hips. "I didn't see what happened there before I came, but I can easily guess. How did you come to dump that poor man on the floor?"

Her eyes focused on the bottom button of his blue shirt. "I thought he was hurting that woman. He was biting her neck—" She blushed deeply. "—and she was screaming."

Jason raked one hand through his dark hair. "Oh Lord, it's worse than I thought."

Charity looked away and swallowed back the lump that rose in her throat. It hurt to think that Jason was ashamed of her, especially after the way the angry woman had spoken, when Charity was only attempting to help her. Charity was not used to open prejudice. She had grown up in a community where there were many of the Quaker faith. Her people were generally accepted and tolerated by others in the area around Helmsville. Such open hostility due to her religion was new to her.

Her voice emerged as a whisper, and she didn't look at him. "I was only trying to help."

With a muttered oath, Jason put his hand to her chin and forced her to face him. "I'm to blame as much as anyone. No one asked me to hit the proprietor. We have ruined everything together."

Her eyes grew round. "But I do not know if all is ruined, Jason. I only had a moment before we were forced to leave, but I questioned the woman who came to our aid about Grisak. I found out that he is not there. He left Lizzy with the proprietor—who is a friend of his—as soon as he arrived. He will not be back for days."

He put his hands on her shoulders, his eyes searching. "Three days. Did she know where he had gone?"

Charity shook her head, wishing she could be of more help. "She did not say, and there was no more time to ask."

He threw back his head and sighed. "Damn. That was quick thinking on your part, Charity. It gives me three more days to plan." He bent to her, pressing a quick kiss to her cheek. Without thinking, Charity turned, so that her mouth came into contact with his. A spark flared up between their two mouths and she gasped. The next thing she knew, he was on the bed next to her, his arms drawing her close to the warmth of his body.

Charity didn't even hesitate. She melted against him like butter in sunshine, putting her arms up to his wide shoulders, loving the feel of him as she always had.

Charity sighed against his eager mouth, opening her lips wider, inviting him inside.

Jason drew a quick breath, pulling her closer as his tongue slipped into her mouth.

His obvious pleasure emboldened Charity to go further. She moved her hand down his muscular shoulder to the neck of his shirt, and slid her fingers inside to tangle them in the wiry mat of hair at the base of his throat.

That yearning, that now-familiar ache, was beginning to build in her lower belly.

Charity didn't know what she wanted. But she did know that only Jason could give it to her. Since the first time he'd kissed her in the barn, making her feel so good, she had longed for something just out of reach.

Her hands moved to encircle his neck, and when he lay back upon the bed, she went with him. His lean fingers slid down along her sides, molded her hips, and she moved closer to him, pressing herself along the length of his hard body.

Jason's head was whirling. He held the soft firm weight of her against him, wanting her closer and closer still, as his mouth melded with hers. His blood thrummed in a rhythm that summoned visions of her naked and eager beneath him. He rolled over her, never breaking the contact of their lips, his hands tracing the curves of her body even as his legs slipped between her parted ones.

Charity was infinitely aware of the path of Jason's hands. She held her breath, waiting, anxious, yet unbearably hopeful as they neared the swollen mounds of her breasts. When they closed over her, she cried out against his mouth, her nipples hard and aching under his sure touch. When his thumbs moved to circle those rigid tips, she felt a sweet pooling warmth between her legs and tried to move closer to him.

She gasped in frustration, for her clothing hampered these wonderful sensations. Jason seemed to understand her need, for he raised his leg higher, bringing it into contact with that place of honeyed longing. Yet strangely this only made her yearn for a more intimate touch.

She drew her mouth from his, pressed little kisses to the base of his throat. "Oh, Jason, love me. I want thee so much."

Her words drifted into the deep well of desire that swirled around him, made his every nerve quiver with longing for this woman. Jason shuddered, fighting desperately for breath, holding her soft cheek to his chest. He knew what she was asking, knew that he must try to find reason, for both their sakes. In giving in to the passion that urged him on, he would be betraying not only her, but himself.

His voice was hoarse as he strained to control his senses, which continued to vibrate with the power of her need in spite of his certainty that this was wrong. Frustration forced a reply of complete honesty from his dry lips. "Oh, Charity, you don't know how badly I want you, how much I need to lie here with you, forget everything in your softness."

It was as if a spark of sheer happiness was struck, and flared inside her eyes at his words. But the spark sputtered, then died as he continued, his tone heavy with sadness. "But I can't. Not because it wouldn't be right for me." He drew back to look into her eyes, compelling her to understand. "Because it wouldn't be right for you. Right now, you *think* you want this."

His body responded eagerly to the open yearning displayed in her eyes, and she made to speak, but he silenced her with a finger to her lips. His hoarse voice was as gentle as he could make it under the circumstances. "Afterwards, things are always different. Trust me, I know. Not that I could ever be sorry for having made love to you; as I said, the problem is not me. It's you. You've been brought up to believe certain things. Try to think about how you'd feel knowing you'd made love to me and us not married. How would you feel if your family found out? Right now you can return to the farm, face your parents openly, knowing you have nothing to be sorry for, that you haven't compromised your beliefs. If I was to give in to what I'm feeling, how I'm wanting you, that would all be changed."

Her eyes searching his face, Charity wanted to deny Jason's words. Every nerve in her body cried out to her in an agony of unadulterated need. She wanted him more than she'd ever believed possible, more than she'd ever wanted anything.

But she couldn't force herself to deny the truth of what he said. It was all too true. Her faith and beliefs were so much a part of her she'd never forgive herself for setting them aside, even if only momentarily. As far as facing her parents, Heaven help her, that part was also true. How could she ever look into her mother and father's eyes again?

What she was feeling was wrong. She had no right to want Jason so when he was not her husband.

Charity's gaze dropped, and her answer was filled with misery. "Thee are right. I know what I want to do with thee is something only for a husband and wife."

Suddenly, her brow wrinkled in thought, and she looked up into his handsome face, into those eyes, which were dark with desire for her. They were so dear, so beloved. She knew she could no longer convince herself that she did not love him. She loved him more than life itself. Perhaps her love was enough to build a future on. Perhaps.

Her tone was breathless with hope. "Why could we not *be* husband and wife? I want thee and thee want me. We could be married."

For a moment Jason could only stare at her, aghast at the idea. Had she lost her wits? Abruptly he pulled away and stood, looking down at her as he raked a hand through his hair. "We can't be married."

Her lovely face, which was still flushed from his kisses, registered confusion. "Why?"

He turned toward the window, unwilling to be swayed by the sight of her beauty, his own still-throbbing need. He could feel the muscles working in his jaw, no matter that he tried to control them. "It is impossible. We come from completely different worlds."

Her voice was filled with sadness. "Thee do not want me because I am a Quaker. Thee are ashamed of me, my ways, my dress?"

He looked at her again, his expression gentling. "I am not ashamed of you. But even if I felt free to marry again—which I don't and perhaps never will—your faith would be a factor. You don't know anything about me, or the way I live. You wouldn't be happy married to me."

He remembered how miserable Daphne had been, even though she had been born and raised in the same social circles as he had. Charity would wither like a plant without water. He had already driven one wife to her death with neglect. What would Charity say if she knew the truth about that?

Unaware of his thoughts, Charity's gaze was defiant, stubborn. "I want to be with thee, and that would keep me happy. It is all I want. Can thee not accept that? As long as we are together we would be happy." Her blue eyes grew damp. "Can thee say thee wants to walk away from me, from the way we feel?"

He raked a hand through his hair, shaking his head in confusion. "No, I can't say I do. Wanting you and not having you is sheer misery." He knelt to take her hands in his, trying to make her see sense. "But that's something I'm willing to live with. It's the decision I've made. You only think you want me, Charity. You don't even know me, not the real me. What you do know, you deny. I've told you what I intend to do when I see Grisak. I *will* kill him."

Her heart stopped, and he knew a wave of shockingly tender longing as Charity reached out and smoothed the hair back from his brow. "Thee hasn't done that yet, Jason. I cannot believe that thee will. Thee only think that revenge will bring thee peace. The answer to thy pain is inside thee, and thee will come to see this."

He caught her hand roughly, horrified at not only her words but his reaction to her touch. "You simply refuse to see the truth. Don't think I'm something I'm not."

"Who are thee trying to convince, me or thyself?" She paused, then added, "Do thee think that we can

189

spend the next days waiting alone here without touching one another again? I will think of nothing else."

He was amazed at her persistence and honesty. He reminded himself that the depth of desire that existed between them was indeed a hard-driving demon. "Marrying you so that I could have you would be selfish. Don't you see that? God help me, I want you so much I'd do almost anything to have you, Charity, but I can't give in to it. I'm trying to do what's right for you. I don't want to drag you down with me."

Her sad but reasoning gaze scanned the room and came back to him. "Here I am, Jason. I do not feel that thee have dragged me down. I do not wish to be where thee is not."

He stood, backing away from her. "You tempt me too much. If I married you, you'd grow to hate me. You wouldn't be happy in Boston. You don't know anything about me—my life. You'd be stuck in the city, away from your family and everything you know." He paused, taking a long breath.

Levelly, she returned his gaze. "As my husband, thee would be my family. Besides I will always feel that thee are my family now. I will never feel the things I feel for any other man. No matter what comes, I can never go back to the way it was before you came." She rose and, taking his hand, placed it over her breast so he could feel the beating of her heart. "Thee live here inside me now."

He let his hand rest there for a moment, feeling the life beating inside her—feeling for a brief moment the yearning inside himself.

Then he pulled away.

Disappointment swept over her, and before she could do more than call his name, Jason was gone.

Charity didn't want to give in to the despair that drove into her heart like a railroad spike. He'd rejected her love, the love she'd tried too hard to deny in herself, but no longer cöuld. He'd also rejected his own feelings which, though she knew they were nothing more than passion, were by his own admission more powerful than anything he'd felt before.

Jason went on and on about how much better off she'd be without him. Couldn't he see she couldn't even imagine being without him? Visions of such a future were unbearably bleak.

She considered going after him, but the thought of following him was gone as soon as it entered her mind. She couldn't fight Jason anymore. She was completely worn out from trying to make him see that they belonged together.

She was tired, alone, and lonely. She was also beginning to feel a certain amount of shame that she had so blatantly thrown herself at this man when he had rejected her time and again. Although honesty was ingrained in her, she could not help thinking that she must learn to hide her feelings enough to retain some self-respect. She drew her knees up around the knot of misery in her belly, unable to fathom how she would be able to make it through the next days.

She still had to find a way to rescue Lizzy, though she had no idea how she was to do this, especially in the face of Jason's determination to move forward with his own plans. The passage of time did not slow her spinning thoughts, and Charity grew weary with confusion and sorrow. Pressing her hot cheek to the softness of her pillow, she slept.

Morning sunlight, filtered though it was through the lace curtains, tickled Charity's eyelids.

Opening her eyes, she looked up at the unfamiliar pattern of the ceiling, confused for a moment. Then, with painful clarity, she remembered where she was, and last night's conversation with Jason.

Fleetingly, Charity knew a renewed sense of embarrassment. She had openly admitted her passion for Jason, had asked him to marry her, and been very decisively refused.

But she would not allow herself to hold onto her chagin. Charity had not been taught to dissemble and pretend. Her parents were open and honest about their caring for each other and their children.

There was no shame in the way she felt about Jason.

It was he who should feel embarrassed about the way he denied them a chance at happiness together.

Wondering if Jason had even returned to his room last night, Charity sat up and stared at the door between their rooms. There would be no use in trying it, even if she'd wished to do so. She knew it would be locked.

With a sigh, she ran her hands through her tangled hair, then down over her rumpled dress. It had already been dirty and wrinkled after traveling for days. The gown hadn't improved any from sleeping in it again.

Charity gave a start of surprise as a knock sounded at her door.

She stood, her smile unconsciously hopeful as she

hurried across the carpet in her bare feet. Had Jason come to make up?

Opening the door, she saw a young woman in a starched white cap and apron. The woman eyed Charity with ill-concealed curiosity.

Uneasy under the unusually close scrutiny, Charity asked, "Does thee have some need of me?"

Obviously remembering Charity was a paying guest in the hotel despite her outlandish dress and speech, the maid dipped in a curtsy. "No, ma'am. I mean, I was asked to take you to the bathing room."

"The bathing room?"

"Yes, Miss, a bath has been prepared for you."

Charity frowned. "I didn't request a bath."

The maid looked down the hall toward Jason's room, a small smile on her lips. "The gentleman did."

"Oh, I see," Charity followed her gaze. What was this woman smiling about? Jason? Whatever it was, she didn't much care for it.

Quickly she reminded herself that she had no right to feel proprietary about Jason. And what gave him the right to be deciding when she would have a bath? She stepped into the hall and started for his door. "I'll just speak with him for a moment first."

"Oh, you can't, miss. He's gone out."

"Gone out?" Obviously he meant to steer clear of her, and though that hurt, Charity could not be surprised. She could find no joy in this evidence that the passion he felt was not easily denied, though, for he was determined to do just that.

"Yes." The maid grinned at Charity in a way that made her feel there was something she didn't know.

She was pretty and blond, and she curtsied again. "If you'll just follow me, miss, so I can get back to my other duties . . ."

Now, Charity hesitated for no more than a second. She did not wish to cause the other woman any difficulty. If the bath was already poured, she might as well make use of it.

The bathing room was decorated in pale colors, pink walls and white trim. A settee in robin's-egg blue stood not far from a huge copper tub. On the settee was a pile of blue towels and a large white box.

"What is that?" Charity asked, pointing toward the package.

"Some things the gentleman sent," she answered.

Charity made no move toward the box. She had no intention of allowing this pretty blond to see how surprised she was at Jason's gift. Though she *was* curious about what he had sent.

The maid watched Charity with the same avid interest she had shown when Charity had opened her door. "Would you need some further assistance, miss?"

Again, feeling that there was something she knew, Charity shook her head, eager to see the woman go. She turned her attention to the tub. The maid nodded and left, giving one last smiling glance at that box.

As soon as she was gone, Charity hurried over to lift the lid. Parting the tissue paper on top, she saw some soft fabric. Reaching in, Charity took out the top garments, a fine lawn chemise and drawers. She had never worn anything so fine, and wondered if such garments would be considered sinful. She thought they must.

Beneath, and separated by a layer of tissue, were a dress and a pair of slippers. Sucking in a quick breath,

Charity pulled the dress from the package to hold it in front of herself. The tall mirror sent back her reflection clearly.

The dress was blue like the sky in winter, just the color it got when the weather was really cold. Surprised, she saw that it was just the color of her eyes.

With a sigh of longing, Charity laid the dress back in the box. How could she wear such a garment? It would certainly be considered too worldly.

Her eyes went back to her reflection in the mirror. Her old dress looked even worse than she had thought. No wonder the maid had stared at her. It was creased, dusty, and stained dark in several places. Even washed, it would not return to its former serviceability. Were she at home, her mother would certainly delegate it to the ragbag she used for making rugs.

Charity's gaze went back to the blue gown.

It might not be so very bad of her to wear the dress—since Jason had already bought it. It occurred to her then to wonder why Jason would be so thoughtful. Surely it was guilt. A poor reason, but that did not mean it would be right for her to throw this olive branch back in his face.

Her gaze went again to the blue dress. At least it was clean.

With a sigh that was half resolve, half sadness, Charity divested herself of her clothing and climbed into the tub. At home they had only a large metal washtub. This one was so deep that the warm water reached all the way to her shoulders. Feeling decadent, she leaned back and dipped her dirty hair into the water.

When her hair and every inch of skin had been thoroughly washed with the sweet-smelling bar of soap she found floating in the water, Charity reluctantly stepped from the tub.

It would be wrong of her to linger. The hotel likely had only one bathing chamber, and someone else must surely wish to indulge in the same joys.

Without allowing herself to think about what she was doing by donning such worldly clothing, Charity dressed. Only when she had done up the last button did she swing around and look at her reflection.

And stared.

For a moment she didn't recognize the girl in the mirror. She turned from side to side in the blue slippers, which were like none she had ever owned. They looked and felt unbelievably light and dainty on her feet. The blue dress hugged close to the supple curves of her body, and her golden hair hung in a glorious halo around her. With a sense of awe, she realized that she was indeed very pretty. Much prettier than the maid who had brought her to this room.

Immediately after the thought came to her, Charity felt guilty. It was wrong of her to compare herself to another that way, and wrong to care so about her looks.

Charity's gaze lit on her old black boots. They were certainly not as attractive as the slippers, but they were hers. There was no way she could convince herself she shouldn't wear them. They simply needed a good cleaning.

Putting the slippers back in the box, she set about cleaning her boots, feeling slightly less sinful once she had them on her feet.

It was true the plain and sturdy boots were completely at odds with the blue dress, but the gown covered all but the toes. Her gaze went again to her reflection in the mirror. She couldn't help wondering, if only for a minute, what Jason would say.

As if thinking of him had called him to her, Charity heard Jason's voice beyond the door of the bathing room. "Charity?"

For a moment, she didn't answer, feeling shy and unsure of herself in these unfamiliar clothes. She was also quite uncertain of how he would treat her after all that had passed between them the night before.

Her answer was hesitant. "Yes?"

"Are you ready?"

Ready? Charity wondered silently at his choice of words. To face him again? She took a deep breath and raised her head high, then put her hand to the knob and slowly opened the door.

Jason stood outside, facing her, his feet crossed at the ankles, his arm outstretched as he leaned against the casement. He looked so handsome in his clean blue shirt and dungarees that she nearly sighed as she took in his lean-jawed face, which was topped by a mop of freshly washed dark hair. She did not know what she had expected, but the instantaneous heat in his dark eyes with their heavy lashes surprised and—though she did not wish to admit it—secretly pleased her.

A low whistle escaped him and Charity blushed, her gaze dropping to the flower pattern of the hall carpet.

He took his arm from the doorway and stepped closer, his breath warm on her neck, but she could not bring herself to look at him, confused and uncertain as she was about what was going on. Taking her chin in his hand, Jason raised her eyes to face him, to see the appreciation in his gaze. " 'Is she worth keeping?

Why, she is a pearl, whose price hath launched a thousand ships and turn'd crown'd kings to merchants.' "

Charity's blush deepened and she tried to look away. "Thee shouldn't say such things."

Jason's smile was rueful as he bent to place a gentle kiss on her cheek. "I'm afraid I cannot take any credit, my dear. The words belong to William Shakespeare. I was just quoting what Troilus said of Helen on the day they were to be married."

He watched her closely as his meaning dawned on her and her blue eyes lit from within. "Married? Oh, Jason." Then she hesitated. "But thee said . . ."

He faced her searching gaze with unswerving directness. "I've been walking all night, thinking of you here. I want you so much I can't seem to think of anything else. I don't know how we can possibly make this work, but I can't fight it any longer." His gaze grew hot. "Do you understand me, Charity? I want you so much I can't even think straight. Are you sure that you want that, that you know what it means?"

Charity was embarrassed, but she didn't look away this time. She wanted Jason to know that what they were doing was right. What she felt for him was much more than just this intense wanting, but if that was what it was for Jason, so be it. Surely he would come to love her as she loved him. This great deep desire they felt had to be based on more than a physical reaction, even if he didn't yet know it. She held out her arms. "I know what it means."

His arms enfolded her, and for a brief moment she was surrounded by the scent of him—soap, new cotton, and his own manly musk. Then he released her to take her hand and pull her along after him.

She began to follow, then stopped short, pulling away from him to hurry to her room. She had retrieved her rose bonnet and was back in the hallway before he caught up to her. As soon as he saw her, his puzzled frown turned to a smile, and he kissed her soundly. "You are beautiful."

She blushed happily and they made their way down the stairs and out of the hotel without another word. His strides were quite long in his haste, and trying to keep up with him caused her boots to clump noisily behind him.

Jason stopped suddenly and turned to face her. His gaze traveled down the length of her to rest on her boots peeping from beneath the hem. He frowned as he studied her, his hands on his lean hips. "Didn't the slippers fit?"

Charity folded her hands before her, hoping no one would overhear their conversation. "Yes, they did." Then she raised her chin with stubborn pride. "But there was nothing wrong with my own boots that a good cleaning wouldn't fix." She raised her skirt to expose the offending footwear. "The dress I could accept. My own was damaged beyond saving, but I can at least wear my own shoes."

With a laugh, Jason grabbed her around the waist with both hands and swung her around before crushing her to his chest. "My little Quaker girl." He pulled back to smile down at her. "Don't ever change."

His expression was warm and intimate, and Charity was tempted to run her hands through his thick brown hair. But she resisted; this was not the place to give in to such longings. Her answer was a whispered, "I won't. Now put me down before someone comes."

Jason laughed again and placed a brief kiss on her mouth. He took her hand and continued on.

Charity felt like laughing herself. Never had she seen Jason so happy. It was as if in deciding to marry her he had, if only for this moment, allowed himself to feel good again. Not for the first time she wondered about the man he had been before the tragedy in his life.

Such wonderings could be worried over another day. Charity was going to enjoy these moments, no matter what came next.

"It wasn't easy," he said over his shoulder, "but I found a justice of the peace who will marry us without the usual waiting period." He shrugged and glanced back at her, his expression a bit apologetic. "I'm sorry, but I had to tell him that you were . . . well . . . that we were in a bit of a fix."

As what he meant dawned, Charity flushed scarlet. "But that is not true."

"I know, sweet, but once I'd decided to do it, I didn't want to wait for banns and licenses." He paused right there in the street, his hungry eyes devouring her. "I don't think I can wait even one more night."

Charity swallowed, feeling an answering tug of desire in the pit of her stomach. "It doesn't matter." Even as he started off again, she knew she should feel sorry for agreeing, but she couldn't. If given more time, Jason might change his mind again. And that she didn't want.

She told herself that the happiness he displayed was reason enough to disregard everything but their coming together.

The justice of the peace had his offices just a few blocks from the hotel. Along with the justice himself, there was his wife, Mrs. Evans, and another man who introduced himself as their son Brian. Mrs. Evans and her son would act as witnesses.

Charity tried not to be bothered by the sympathetic looks his wife kept casting in her direction. She kept her attention on the man at her side.

Jason made his vows with quiet determination. It was clear to Charity that once he made up his mind to do something, he did not waver.

As she made her own promises, Charity was committed to making this marriage what it should be: a lifelong promise to love and care for each other.

When the service was over, Jason led Charity out into the late-summer morning.

To Charity's surprise, nothing really looked any different than it had before. People strolled along the sidewalks, totally oblivious to the fact that she was now Mrs. Jason Wade. Then, on looking more closely, she was sure the birds chirped a bit louder and the flowers spread their petals just a little wider; the sky shone just a bit more brightly.

All in honor of the new Mrs. Jason Wade.

Chapter Ten

Charity knew that Jason wanted to kiss her. It was clear in the possessive way his gaze lingered about her lips.

Her answer was a shy smile.

As if her sudden shyness touched him, Jason took her hand and placed it on his arm. "Why don't we see a bit of River Bend?"

She pressed his arm close against her side, grateful for his understanding. Now that they were actually married, she hardly knew what to do or say. All she could think of was going back to their room and easing the ever-present ache inside her, but she could not say that. Could she? Instead, she answered softly, "That would be very nice."

They strolled along the boardwalk in silence, Charity wondering if Jason was as aware of her as she was of him. After his admission about why he was marrying her, he suddenly seemed somewhat reticent, his attentions almost deliberately casual.

She did her best to concentrate on where they were going. The walk ran along the front of a row of shops. Judging from the goods displayed in the windows, they were far too expensive for close consideration.

Yet, in spite of that, she found her gaze lingering on a flash of scarlet in a dress shop window. Looking more closely, Charity saw that she had been attracted to a red petticoat which was displayed beneath the discreetly raised skirt of a dressmaker's mannequin.

She looked up into Jason's amused gaze. "Very pretty." He grinned. "And very worldly."

She raised her chin. "It's simply the color I like. I would never wear such a thing."

He bowed. "Of course not." Without another word he went into the shop, leaving her standing on the stoop. Crossing her arms over her chest, Charity stood there, telling herself that he would come out again if she did not follow him.

And he did, only a moment later.

He held out his arm, and she said, "What were thee doing? Thee did not buy that?"

Jason smiled and placed her fingers on his arm as he started off. "Why would I buy something like that for someone who would never wear it?"

Realizing by his expression that she would get no more out of him, Charity went with him. They continued to stroll about for some time, and Charity was very careful not to admire anything. She was not even accustomed to the notion of being Mrs. Jason Wade.

She did not wish for him to think she expected him to purchase useless trinkets for her.

She was not sure what would come now, other than rescuing Lizzy. She knew so little of Jason, but for reasons unknown to her, she felt that her thoughts would best be left for another day. This day, her wedding day, would be free from the concerns of an uncertain future.

After a time, Jason asked her if she was hungry, and Charity realized that she had not eaten. Although she was not hungry she nodded, thinking that he must be.

They went to the hotel, where a meal had been prepared for them. The same pretty blond maid who had shown Charity to her bath served it, her smile even wider than before. Now Charity knew why she had seemed to know something. Clearly Jason had told the hotel of his plans to marry.

Throughout the meal, which she barely tasted, Charity was completely aware of Jason. He seemed to do very little better than she as far as eating was concerned, pushing the roast chicken, beautifully cooked potatoes, and vegetables around on his plate.

Each time she reached for her glass, or the salt, or her bread, their hands seemed to come into contact. His knee seemed to find hers beneath the table with each shift of his body.

Charity's senses cried out with each brush of flesh upon flesh. All she could think about was the coming night, for surely they could not . . . not in the middle of the day.

Yet Jason seemed to have a different notion. For just when she thought she must surely scream from her desire to be alone with him, Jason suggested they go upstairs.

She blushed, glancing at him and away. "In the middle of the afternoon?"

He took a deep breath, not meeting her gaze. "Not if you don't want to."

Holding her own breath, Charity nodded quickly. "I will . . . I mean, I did not know if it was proper."

He took her hand, smiling gently. "Whatever we want is proper, now."

She avoided the gazes of the hotel guest in the lobby as they moved through it and up the stairs. She would not concern herself with what anyone else thought. All that mattered now was herself and Jason.

When he opened the door of her room, the first thing she noticed was the splash of scarlet draped across the chair. It was the petticoat from the shop window, and along with it was a matching corset.

Charity swung around. "Jason, thee should not have bought it."

He looked at her seriously. "You are my wife, Charity. You must become accustomed to the idea that I am in a position to buy you many pretty things. Anything, in fact, that you desire."

She was reminded anew of how little she knew this man. Yet he was her spouse. "My husband." She was not oblivious to the huskiness of her voice.

She watched as his gaze darkened in reaction to her words. "Yes."

His eyes asked a question, revealing the passion he had kept at bay over the past hours with her. Charity answered it by raising her lips.

Jason did not disappoint her. His lips met hers with

a fierceness that took her breath away, even as his arms closed around her. Charity reveled in the strength of those arms, the warmth of his hard masculine chest as she raised her hands to steady herself, her head spinning in reaction to his kisses.

How her gown came to fall forward on her shoulders she did not know. She only realized that her clothing, which had so hampered their caresses before, would now be disposed of, and with little effort on her part. Even as she flushed at seeing her bosom come into view, she felt a thrill of anticipation.

She looked up and into Jason's hungry gaze. Slowly, deliberately, he slid the gown down over her arms, his gaze dropping to the fullness of her breasts, which seemed to swell beneath the thin fabric of her chemise. Without thinking, suddenly shy in spite of her desire for him, Charity moved to cover herself with her arms.

Jason reached out to put his hands over hers. "Don't hide yourself from me, Charity. You are lovely, more lovely even than my memory of how you looked that day at the river. You are the most beautiful thing I have ever seen."

She flushed, but not from embarrassment, allowing the dress to slip down her body to the floor as she whispered, "Jason."

He reached for her then, kissing her even more deeply, more passionately, until she felt as if the world had tilted, and she didn't ever want it to right itself again. He picked her up in his arms, and she held tightly to him, pressing herself to him as she kissed him back with a wild and joyous abandon.

Jason was on fire. Her reactions to him left him weak with longing, eager to give vent to this burning need. But he was determined to take his time, to give as much pleasure as he would receive. And he was as certain that he would receive pleasure like none he had ever known, as he was that the sun would rise the next day. Her eager responses, the heat of her kisses told him so.

With trembling hands, he laid her back on the bed, his gaze taking in the flush along her delicate cheekbones, her temptingly parted lips, her heavily lidded blue eyes. He kissed her once more, then straightened to remove his own clothing, aware of her gaze upon him. He felt a spiral of desire that raced through him to settle in his belly, as her gaze fixed on his buckle, and she wetted her swollen lips.

Jason swallowed hard, closing his own eyes as he dropped his pants to the floor, knowing he could not control his reaction to her gaze. Quickly he moved above Charity, his hands trailing over her. Now the chemise that had seemed such little covering was suddenly too great a restriction for his questing fingers.

Charity felt this last barrier fall away with no regret. She wanted this man, wanted to be a part of him. She held out her arms, urging him back to her. When Jason came into them, leaning down and putting his lips to the turgid tip of her breast, she cried out. Her body arched on the bed, and a shaft of indescribable yearning raced down through her body to settle at the joining of her thighs.

He continued to suckle her until she was near faint with the fury of need that made her pulse pound and her body quiver. She held his shoulders, glorying in the play of his hard muscles beneath her fingers.

She was so beautiful, more lovely than any mere

mortal should be, her skin so soft and smooth that he knew a feeling of reverence as his fingers moved over her. He drank in the sight of her, admiring each perfect curve and plane, reveling in the fact that she did not shy from him in the light.

Jason was on fire, the eagerness of her touch making him groan with need. He'd waited so long to be with her, to touch her like this without restraint, but he wanted so desperately to hold back, to give her full pleasure from this joining.

Then, to his utter amazement, he heard her hoarsely whisper, "Please, Jason, I need to . . . I am on fire."

Joy washed through him, joy and relief, for he was ready too. His desire was driven by all the weeks of wanting and denying himself.

Jason raised up above her, ready to give himself to the desire that knew no bounds. As he rose over Charity, reaching out to part her silken thighs, he enjoyed the naked passion on her face, knowing it matched his own. But when she looked into his eyes—her own having deepened to indigo—and whispered, "I love thee," he felt a jolt of something strange and awesome. It tore through him, leaving a wide and gaping hole in his heart.

Tenderness like none he had ever felt in his life poured through. Just as suddenly, his touch changed, gentled.

Charity felt the change, was aware of the new sweetness in his kiss as he returned to her mouth, felt a sweet flickering of something new and fragilely wonderful within herself. And wanted him all the more.

When she reached up to urge him on, he stilled her hands with a gentle touch. "No, not so fast, let me savor you. I want to remember this moment for the rest of my life."

His eyes held hers and she did not look away, the passion for a moment almost secondary as the two prepared to join their flesh in this most intimate of acts. He read the knowledge in her face as surely as he felt it in himself, slipping inside with a sense of wonder and reverence that was nearly shattering in its intensity.

Then she closed her eyes, arching her body to meet him, and the passion rose up to overwhelm him. His body urged him on, riding the wave of ecstasy with a will and delight of its own, crashing back to earth with wide-eyed wonder, Charity stilled beneath him.

As the ripples of pleasure eased, Jason was filled with a peace he had never known, nor even hoped for. Never in his life had he thought that the joining of flesh could bring such feelings as he had just known.

Charity looked up at him, her blue eyes filled with joy and so many emotions he did not wish to acknowledge, for they would make him responsible for her happiness. He had failed so miserably at making Daphne happy, how could he ever hope to succeed with Charity, who was so foreign to all he knew?

Driven by some need that he could not explain to himself, Jason began to talk. "Daphne was not happy, you know, even from the beginning. That was what led her to Grisak's path. She was working in her brother Michael's clinic, helping those less fortunate than herself. It would not have happened if I had given her a reason to make a home for the two of us. I did not. I went my own way, not caring about anything but my law practice. It is *my fault* she died. She was helping the woman who had just miscarried Grisak's baby when he raped and murdered her. It is up to me to make him pay for that misdeed. It is all I can give her."

Charity swallowed hard, her heart aching for him and for the girl who had endured such a horrible fate. "I am sure she would not expect murder of thee."

Turning away from the lovely and vulnerable sight of her, he sat up in bed, self-hatred washing through him. Daphne would never have shared a moment such as the one he had just shared with Charity. She certainly had not done so with him. Though he had tried to please her, she had never enjoyed their marital relations, obviously sensing his own ambiguous feelings toward her.

Charity spoke so softly that he could barely hear her. "Thee must have loved Daphne a great deal."

He could say nothing. Guilt at his true feelings bound his tongue. He stood and began to dress.

Her voice gave him pause. "It is all right, Jason. I know that what thee feel for me is not the same, but surely we can build something from what we have."

Jason did not turn around, wanting too desperately to tell her how tempted he was to just take her and leave this place right now. To try and salvage some peace, to rest in the joy and tenderness he had found in her arms.

He could not. He said instead, "I can't have any peace until her murder is avenged. Not with you or anyone else, not for a moment."

He strode toward the door, ignoring her cry. If he looked back now, he would never leave her side again.

Carefully, Jason let himself into her room, wishing that the hours since he'd left had healed the breach between them. Yet he knew that they had not, that nothing could.

It was impossible. Everything he knew of Wayne Grisak told him that the man must die. No matter how upset Charity got, Jason had a moral obligation not only to avenge Daphne, but to stop the monster from defiling anyone else.

In the light of the room's lamp, Jason's gaze moved over his wife's sleeping body, outlined under the quilt. He moved across the room to look down at her. Her face was flushed, and her lashes were spiky and dark against her cheeks.

She'd been crying.

Compassion for her rose up in an all-encompassing wave. He reached out and touched one hand to her soft cheek.

Even in her sleep, Charity rubbed her cheek against him, gentle and welcoming, as always. She raised one arm above her head and sighed, her firm breasts outlined beneath the thin coverlet.

Desire tightened his body. But he made himself step back. He knew if he woke her, said he was sorry, that he had rethought everything and changed his mind, she would welcome him with her goodness, her love, and yes, her passion.

He could not do that, didn't deserve the gifts she offered, not until he had honored the memory of the wife he had unable to love.

And honor her he would, this very night. Being banned from the Red Lady, Jason had realized that he would have to find some other method to watch for Grisak's return. He'd paid one of the street urchins who loitered about the district to keep an eye out for the bounty hunter. Tonight he'd had unexpected news. Grisak had returned to the hotel hours ago, while Jason was enjoying the day with his bride.

The boy had also reported on the condition of the slave, Lizzy. Jason had not asked how he had attained the information, for the boy had been far from concerned when he'd said, "That slave girl cain't be doin' too well without any food or water—and they ain't givin' her any."

The words only made him more determined to kill his enemy.

There would be no more stolen hours to feel guilty about. He would not touch Charity again until he had rid the world of Wayne Grisak.

Only then would he be free to think about his life with Charity. Though he could not name his feelings for her, he knew that he could not imagine a future without the Quaker beauty beside him. Because of that, he would have to be more careful than ever before. He must kill Wayne Grisak cleanly, without leaving a trace of his presence behind. He could not risk being caught and put on trial.

Charity deserved better than being widowed or married to a convict.

All he needed to do was keep his head. If everything worked out the way he planned, they would be gone from here by late tomorrow night. Gone and free to start a life together.

That is, if Charity was ever able to understand why he had to do this. And the very fact that he felt this desire to move on, to have a life with her, made him all the more determined to see his plan through.

* * *

Charity opened her eyes, seeing Jason there by the window. As if sensing the fact that she had woken, he spoke softly. "I have had word that Grisak is back. I'm going after him tonight."

Her eyes widened and she felt the shock of his revelation roll through her as she sought desperately for some words that would make him change his mind. His fixed expression told her none would suffice, yet she was compelled to ask, "Jason, thee can't mean to go through with this?"

He looked away from her, his jaw tight, refusing to answer.

She rose, taking the coverlet with her, feeling strangely uncomfortable in his presence in spite of all that had passed between them that very afternoon. Holding it close about her, Charity went to the window, lifting the curtain to peer out into the busy street. How could she make him understand that killing Wayne Grisak could never be right, no matter the circumstances?

She turned to face him, unable to do anything but beg. "Please, Jason, please don't do this."

He glanced at her as he went to the wardrobe and removed his saddlebag, but he made no effort to reply. He took a black shirt out of the bag, then removed the rumpled one he was wearing, the one she had been so eager for him to shed earlier.

But she couldn't think about that now. She must make him see that he would be gaining nothing by going through with this. It certainly would not bring his wife back, nor would it ease the pain inside him.

"Please, Jason, just let it go. We can go to that place, take Lizzy, and go home. Today. It could all be over today."

Jason refused to face her as he buttoned his shirt. "Listen, Charity. Letting Wayne Grisak live would be wrong. We aren't dealing with a man who is a little naughty." His tone was cold as winter. "He is evil personified. He doesn't care about anyone or anything but himself. Think about it." His hands shook. "What kind of man would rape and kill a defenseless woman? What kind of man leaves his wife and children to starve at a remote cabin? Who? One who leaves a slave bound, hand and foot, in one of the rooms in the Red Lady without any food or water. An animal would get better treatment."

Charity put her hands over her ears so she couldn't hear any more. Lizzy, bound hand and foot without any food or water? She didn't ask how Jason knew this. She was too horrified at his lack of action. How could he carry on about killing Grisak when he could have already rescued Lizzy?

As if sensing her agitation, Jason swung around to face her. Sadness and regret darkened his eyes when he saw her horrified expression.

"How could thee leave her there?" He came to her, reaching out to clasp her hands and bring them down to her sides.

"No," she cried. "Don't touch me!"

"Charity, Charity," he whispered, putting his arms around her to hold her close. "Forgive me. I'm sorry. I shouldn't have told you. I only want you to understand why the bastard has to die."

She remained stiff in his embrace. "I will *never*

understand. Not when thee believe it's more important to kill a man than to save someone in need. Thee do not seem to understand that there are others like him, that you cannot fix the world by killing."

Slowly his hands dropped to his sides. "I'll make sure there is one less man to cause hurt."

She refused to look at him, crossing her arms and turning her back to him. "Thee will change nothing, for thyself or anyone else. Thee cannot bring your Daphne back with murder."

He walked across the room and took his hat off the hook by the door. He stopped, his hand on the latch. "I want you to be ready when I get back. Have everything packed, because we'll have to leave in a hurry. If I don't come back tonight . . . there is enough money in my saddlebags for you to take the train home to Wisconsin."

If he didn't come back! What was he talking about? Angry as she was, Charity simply couldn't think of what would happen if he didn't come back. She reached out to him. "Jason?"

He didn't turn around. "Remember what I said, be ready."

Then he was gone.

A moment passed in silence, then suddenly Charity knew that she must go and try to see Lizzy freed before Jason could destroy any hope of that with his mad determination to kill. But how? She had been told that she could not return to the Red Lady. She had no notion of how Jason meant to do so.

She bit her lip as her gaze came to rest on the puddle of red silk in the chair. It reminded her of the flashy garments she had seen the women wearing that other

215

night. In it she would look quite unlike the Quaker girl who had caused such difficulty.

Perhaps it was divine intervention that had prompted Jason to buy her the petticoat. She dropped the coverlet to the floor. There was no time to waste.

A short time later, Charity took one last look in the mirror. For at least the tenth time, she adjusted the ruffle along the bottom of the red petticoat in order to keep from thinking about the way her bosom spilled from the top of the matching corset. She frowned, her gaze drawn back there. There was just entirely too much of her exposed. It didn't help to focus on her hair: she had it arranged in a loose bun on top of her head like the woman she had seen in the Red Lady saloon. The long curls that hung down seemed to draw attention to her bare neck and shoulders, and Charity felt decidedly uncomfortable about what the men who she would encounter might think—especially after having just made love with Jason. She now understood all too clearly what lay behind those lecherous glances.

What on earth would Mother say?

Charity turned away from her reflection and took a deep breath. She knew it was now or never. If she didn't go right now, what little courage she had mustered would be gone.

Picking up her traveling cloak from where she had laid it across the foot of the bed, she drew it around herself.

Taking one last look around the room, Charity knew it was time to go. Standing there would not make it any easier to do what she had to do.

Due to the late hour, there was no one besides the night clerk in the lobby. He was reading a paper and barely looked up as she passed through the dimly lit room to the outside. Now all she had to do was remember how to get to the Red Lady. It all looked very different traveling in the dark.

Charity decided to let the Lord guide her.

The fact that she soon found her way to the area of the city she sought gave her hope that she was doing the right thing. The streets were lined with men and, of course, flashily dressed women. Now that Charity knew precisely what they did for a living, she had trouble looking directly into their faces. It was hard for her to imagine anyone doing with a complete stranger what she and Jason had just done.

Resolutely, she squared her shoulders. It would be impossible for her to carry out her mission if she didn't take hold of herself, try to fit in. Hesitantly, she allowed the front of her cloak to gape open, and she tried to look as if she were enjoying the tiny-sounding music coming from inside the saloons.

She wanted to appear as if she belonged, but she could not forget where she was going and why. She hurried on, hoping she would be able to not only locate Lizzy, but find a way to set her free.

A short time later, Charity was standing outside the Red Lady. The noise from inside was nearly deafening. Even as she hesitated at the bottom of the step, a man came flying through the swinging doors to land at her feet.

He stood up, swearing and shaking his fists, but then drunkenly shuffled off down the street.

217

Slowly, Charity climbed the steps. She could only hope she had not gotten herself in for more than she'd bargained for.

As soon as the thought entered her mind, she straightened and took a deep breath. Someone had to help Lizzy, and she was the only one who was willing to do it.

She pushed her way through the swinging doors.

If she'd thought the place sounded bad from outside, she was even more horrified to see what was going on inside. Clearly the proprietor had a disdain for fighting only when it involved him personally. There were several altercations going on at that particular moment, and no one seemed to be taking any note. Briefly, she wondered what the man who'd been thrown out had done.

Her question was answered when the huge man behind the bar—Hank, if she recalled correctly— grabbed a patron by the shirt collar. Roughly he lifted him off the ground. "No more money?"

He passed Charity without even a glance, then heaved the customer out as if he weighed no more than a bag of goose feathers.

On his way back, he stopped and stared at Charity. "You the new girl Mildred was tellin' me about?"

She nodded, gulping back fear at her own temerity. Yet if she did not allow him to think she was this woman, he would surely throw her out as well.

He jabbed a finger at her cloak. "You better take that off."

Charity shrugged off the cloak and draped it over her arm. Immediately she felt a desire to cover her bare shoulders and bosom with her hands, but she forced herself to keep them down.

He nodded with approval and grinned without warmth as he went on, "Just remember, don't try to cheat me out of my cut. You go upstairs, I'll see ya." He pointed to his own massive chest. "I get fifty percent. You got that?"

Looking down at the filth-covered floor, she nodded.

"Good." He turned to disappear into the chaos.

Suddenly Charity realized she couldn't let him go. He seemed to be the only person in the whole establishment who wasn't drunk or well on the way. "Excuse me?"

He swung around to face her with a scowl. "Yeah?"

"Uh . . . I was wondering. Do you know a man named Grisak, Wayne Grisak?"

He put his huge hands on his hips, peering down at her. "Now ain't that funny. He sure is popular tonight. You got an *appointment*?" He smirked at his words.

"Uh, yes." She tried for a seductive smile. "I was told to go on up to his room."

He pointed above. "Is he back already? Humph. It's the door at the very end of the hall."

She practically ran up the stairs and then down the long hall. All the while fear rode hard on her heels, along with the shock of being told exactly where to find Grisak—and please God, Lizzy. She paused then, rubbing her hands against her skirt. What was she to say if he *was* there? She could only pray that he would not be.

Not allowing herself to hesitate a moment longer, Charity moved on. When she got to the right door, she lifted her hand. Her knock sounded loudly in spite of the noise from below. The door opened.

It was him. She could see nothing in the darkened room behind him.

Her heart sank even as his watery brown gaze raked over her. "Well, what have we here?"

Reacting out of desperation, Charity said, "M-Mildred sent me up."

Wayne Grisak smiled. "Good old Mildred." He reached for her and pulled her inside the darkened room. He let go of her hand to cross the floor and light the coal oil lamp on the bureau.

It was all Charity could do to keep from gasping aloud when she saw Lizzy lying on the floor. A heavy rope ran from her bound hands and feet to the metal bed frame. She barely raised her head as Charity came in, revealing the fact that this was probably not the first time Grisak had had a woman in his room.

Gulping back nausea, Charity kept her face averted from the other girl as she pulled out the chair and arranged her cloak over the back, then sat down. She did not want Lizzy to inadvertently give her away before she could think of what to do. Deliberately, she laced her hands together in her lap to hide their shaking.

She watched as Wayne Grisak reached for a bottle, which sat on the table beside the bed, and slopped some of the contents into his glass. "Care for a drink?" His voice was slightly slurred, and Charity realized he was somewhat inebriated.

Perhaps there was a way to use that. She spoke as calmly as possible, knowing she had to have time to figure out just how it could be done. "Uh, yes. I would, th-thank you. But there isn't another glass." She smiled, and raised her hands as if unsure as to how to solve the problem.

He watched the way her breasts surged upward with the motion. "You can have mine."

Her nose wrinkled in distaste at the thought of putting her mouth where his had been. "Oh, but I . . ." She halted herself, realizing that she was not playing her part very well. Stalling, she moistened her dry lips with her tongue.

Unexpectedly, his smile widened. "Never mind, I'll get you a clean one. Looks like you're gonna be worth it." With that, he got up and went to the bureau.

Heaven help me, she prayed as she took the proffered mug. *Please let me get out of this alive. And Lizzy too. And please keep Jason, wherever he is, away until we're safely gone.*

Grisak took his seat again with the same leering grin. He reached for the bottle and poured a liberal amount of liquor in the clean glass she held out. "Just remember, you owe me somethin' real special."

She nodded. Then, as he watched her expectantly, she raised the glass to her lips. The sweet, almost oily smell made her hesitate. Smiling with forced confidence, she took a sip. The fluid was like liquid fire in her mouth, burning a wide path down her throat. Unable to stop herself, she opened her mouth and gulped air.

"Thought so." He leaned close to her. "I don't know what you're doin' here, sugar, but you ain't no whore." He grabbed a handful of her hair. "You got some man waitin' downstairs who's gonna bust in here and shoot me for takin' his woman?"

Charity was completely taken by surprise. Her shock added the ring of authenticity as she answered him. "No, I don't know what th . . . you are taking about."

"Lady, you ain't no whore," he repeated.

She knew she would have to think quickly or all would be lost. "You've guessed right. I'm not. I mean I wasn't, but my sister—she's real sick and I had to have a way to take care of her. I've only done this a few times. I don't have any choice."

Well, wasn't Lizzy her sister in a sense? Her gaze went to the other girl and found her dark eyes upon her. Clearly Lizzy saw through her disguise. Though the girl's gaze was fearful and questioning, she said nothing.

Gratefully, Charity quickly turned back to Grisak. The man looked into her eyes for a long time, scowling. "I don't know. There's somethin' familiar about you."

Her heart stopped, then started again with a sickening thud. God, she couldn't let him guess. She had to bluff it out. Unblinking, she stared back at him. "If you don't want me, then let me go on my way. I have to earn some money tonight."

"Oh, I want you." His eyes raked her, the lust in them making her feel dirty. She wanted to cover herself, but she forced herself to remain impassive. He released her and drained his glass. "Come on."

Grisak rose and shot the bolt on the door home. He swung around and clasped Charity in his arms, drawing her close to his sour, sweaty body. "Now, let's get to it."

Using her elbows for leverage, Charity leaned away from him. She couldn't stop the scarlet blush that stained her face as she indicated Lizzy with a nod of her head. "We aren't going to do it in front of *her*?"

Grisak shrugged, trying to pull her closer. "Her, she don't count for nothin'. She's no more than an animal."

Charity's blue eyes widened as she held him back, a disgusted rage rising up inside her. It was everything she could do to fight her growing hatred, and remember that she had to play her part. "Can we have another drink first?"

He shrugged and dragged her back to the table, sloshing more of the awful liquor into the glasses. Charity barely managed to sip hers as he downed two full shots.

Without preamble, he reached for her again. He laughed harshly at her involuntary resistance. "You shy, girly?" he asked, bending to nuzzle her neck.

"I . . . why . . . uh, yes. I quess I am." Was she mistaken, or had he slurred a bit more as he spoke?

He didn't raise his sweaty face from her throat. "Like I said, don't pay the darky no mind. If she so much as looks at us I'll blow her head off."

The next thing Charity felt was his teeth as they nipped the soft skin of her neck. She cried out without thinking, pushing away from him with all her might. Having caught him by surprise, she stood back, frowning as she raised her hand to rub the sore spot. "That hurt!"

Seeing the suddenly icy determination in his eyes, she knew she could push him no further. "I think this has gone just about far enough." He took a threatening step toward her. "You know what you came up here fer. Let's don't play any more games."

Horrified, she stepped back. He lunged forward and his arms closed around her. Charity cried out in panic.

"It's too late for that." He held her close with one arm while he put his other hand on the back of her hair and held her still. He lowered his full lips to hers.

Terror gripped her as a primitive wave of self-preservation swept through her trembling body. As his lips closed on hers, Charity bit down hard.

With a growl of rage he cursed, then lifted her, tossing her onto the bed like a rag doll. Her head banged against the headboard and for a moment she was dazed.

Before her mind even cleared, she lunged from the bed, catching him off guard. But he caught her, spinning her around as he put himself between her and her avenue of escape.

His gaze measured her for a long moment as he took in her hair, which had tumbled down in the struggle. Suddenly he grinned, looking over at her with cruel amusement. "I got it. I don't know what you're doin' here, but I do know who you are. You're one of them Applegate girls. You Quaker girls was always too good for the likes of me, prancin' around with that purty blond hair and them blue eyes." He smiled as he undid his pants. "You come for the darky, didn't you?" He didn't even glance at Lizzy. "Well, you ain't gonna get her, but yer gonna get somethin' else. We're gonna have us a real good time tonight."

She jumped up, trying to dodge around him, but he caught her easily. "You're just makin' this more fun for me," he told her.

Rage overwhelmed her and she pounded his chest with her fists. "Don't touch me."

He laughed and tossed her head back on the bed.

Her frustration and fear erupted in a stifled scream.

Chapter Eleven

Sitting across the street from the Red Lady, Jason was worried. He couldn't allow himself to think about what would happen to Charity if he was caught.

He wouldn't be, not if he was smart. Grisak had to go to bed sometime, and Jason's spy had told him to which room he would be going. Jason would simply watch and wait.

He couldn't tell how much time had passed before he saw the light go on in Grisak's room, but the moment brought a rush of both adrenaline and regret. The regret he refused to examine. The adrenaline he understood. Gun tucked in the waistband of his pants, Jason crept up the back stairs and inside the establishment. He moved quietly down the hall.

He hoped Grisak hadn't locked his door.

At that moment Jason heard a woman scream. It was a cry of desperation that pierced him to the quick.

There was something about the pitch and sound that reminded him of Charity—and the shriek was coming from inside Grisak's room.

Jason didn't take any more time to think. He hit the door with the full force of his body, sending it crashing into the room. He landed on top of it, slightly shaken from the impact, and it was a moment before he could stand.

When he rose to his feet, his gaze went to the bed, where a woman in a red satin petticoat lay amongst a tangle of pillows and blond hair. Her legs were bare to the knee and the tight corset that matched her skirt left little of her figure to the imagination.

"Charity!"

Awkwardly, Charity raised herself up on her elbow, her golden hair tumbling around her, her blue eyes enormous and beguiling in her distress. "Thank the Lord thee have come."

That was all she had to say? What in the hell was she doing here? He wanted to throttle her, and to comfort her, and most of all he wanted to kiss her.

Recovering more quickly than he would have imagined possible, she scrambled to the edge of the bed and reached out to take a knife from the table. "We've got to hurry."

Dazed, Jason watched as she ran around the end of the bed and began to fumble with the rope that bound Lizzy to the end of the frame.

At the edge of his consciousness Jason could now hear the sound of excited shouts coming from the floor below. Obviously the noise of the door crashing in had been heard by the occupants of the bar. He realized there was very little time.

Grisak was *there*—under the fallen door. He took the gun he'd bought from his waistband. The moment he'd been waiting for had finally come. There was a clatter of footsteps on the stairs.

He turned to his wife. "Get out of here, Charity. I have to finish this."

Charity seemed not to have heard him. She continued to saw at the rope.

"Charity!"

Finally she looked at him, not pausing in her efforts to release Lizzy, though it was taking what seemed to be a very long time to cut through the rope. "I can't go without her. Thee have to decide, Jason. Save a life or take one."

He glanced toward the door and then back at the slave girl, who stared up at him with desperation. The noise had reached the top of the stairs. He saw that Charity was halfway through the rope.

With a last wretched glance toward Grisak's frame, which protruded from beneath the door, Jason realized he had to help her. He grabbed the knife from Charity's trembling hand and sliced through the rope cleanly.

Immediately Charity dragged Lizzy to her feet and toward the window. "We'll have to go out this way."

Lizzy did not hesitate. She pulled up the window and crawled through.

Charity followed her, turning as she swung her leg over the ledge. "Jason?"

It had all happened so quickly. Jason could hear the noise in the hall now. With no more time to consider, Jason did what his heart told him to.

He pushed his wife through the window and followed after her.

The ledge was narrow, but he didn't stop moving as he hurried after Charity. Up ahead of them he could see Lizzy as she climbed a ladder that led to the roof. Jason cursed aloud at the certainty that they would be trapped up there. Yet there didn't seem to be anyplace else to go.

Turning to look behind them as he climbed up the ladder, Jason saw Hank, the proprietor and bartender. If the man's expression was anything to go by, he was bent on murder.

Now that Jason had helped Charity release a slave, he was not only a nuisance, but also a criminal.

As he gained the roof, Jason looked down. His pursuers hadn't quite reached the bottom of the ladder, which was attached at the top by ropes. Jason made short work of cutting them.

He pushed the ladder over and it tumbled down the side of the building to the ground.

Hank shouted an obscenity and shook his fist, and Jason waved in return.

Charity appeared at his side. "That was good thinking, Jason. Now, come with me. Lizzy and I have an idea."

Without a word, Jason followed. Charity led him to the other edge of the flat roof. He could see that another building ran directly alongside it.

Taking his hand, Charity smiled. "We're going to jump."

"Are you crazy?" Jason cried, then felt ridiculous for having asked. Of course she was. Why else would they be standing on top of a three-story building with an escaped slave, with a horde of angry drunks trying to get to them, and no way down.

She closed her eyes, then looked at him as if he were a bothersome child. "They know where we are, and it won't take long for them to figure out some way to get up here. What do thee think they're going to do to us? Good heavens, Jason—to Lizzy. We have to get away from here."

Jason couldn't argue with that, but they would be jumping down one story and across several feet. He tried to reason with her. "Would it be better to be caught with our legs broken? Because you must realize that's what will happen." He pointed to Lizzy. "Look at her. She can't make it. She's too weak."

Lizzy spoke up. "I can make it. I can't go back to that man, nor to River Bend. They's sure to kill me this time."

The determination in her eyes was so real, Jason didn't doubt her for a moment. But he couldn't let Charity risk herself this way, even to save Lizzy's life—or his own for that matter. He was sure the southerners would let Charity go if he took the blame.

He turned to explain this to her, and cried out in panic. "Charity, no!"

It was too late.

While Jason had been thinking, Charity had moved back on the roof, closing her eyes for a brief moment as she gathered herself. Then, with a deep breath, she ran toward the edge, leapt, and flew through the air. She landed with a painful thump, the wind knocked out of her.

The next thing she knew, both Jason and Lizzy were there beside her. Jason seemed to be favoring his right leg a little, but other than that he appeared to be well—well enough to lecture her even as he extended his hand.

"You shouldn't—"

She grabbed his hand and pulled herself to her feet. "We don't have time for this now." To her chagrin, she discovered that walking was slightly painful. She had hurt herself a bit, but she wouldn't let Jason know.

As quickly as she could, Charity moved to the other side of this building and looked down. Coming along the street was a wagonload of hay.

She raised grateful eyes toward heaven.

She then turned to Jason and Lizzy with an irrepressible grin. "Our deliverance has arrived."

The two of them came to stand on either side of her, Lizzy with an expression of hope, Jason with a look of apprehension.

Taking their two hands in hers, she waited till the wagon was directly below them, then shouted, "Jump!"

"Well, now what?" Jason's smile was anything but pleasant.

Charity's brows arched, and she tilted her nose at a haughty angle. "I don't know why thee must be so unpleasant." She gestured at the woods around them. "We were able to ride the hay wagon right out of River Bend." Her gaze held his. "Thee chose the right thing when the time came. We are all well."

She pointed toward Lizzy, where the girl lay upon Charity's cloak. The act of escaping had completely exhausted her in her weakened condition. "Lizzy is free, Jason. Can thee not rejoice in that?"

He sighed. His sense of elation at their escape was beginning to fade in the face of their present predicament, that of being stranded outside the city with no money and no transportation. He also knew a growing regret that he had failed Daphne again—he had not been able to avenge her.

He forced himself to answer Charity's question. "Of course I am glad that she's free. I just don't see my actions the same way you do. There had to have been some way I could have . . . if I had only wanted to badly enough."

He stopped, knowing there was no point in discussing this with her. She wouldn't understand the guilt he felt each time he touched her, knowing that he owed his first wife something. Grisak's death had been all he had to offer, and he'd failed to accomplish it.

Instead of explaining, he ticked off their more immediate problems on his fingers. "We have no transportation. We're in trouble with the law—or soon will be. Lizzy is malnourished and weak, and we have no way of feeding her or getting her home." His gaze raked her. "You have no clothing." Even as he said this, Jason knew a tug of desire. She was so beautiful to him right now, in a wild wind-tousled way that made him wish he could take her into the woods and kiss the breath out of her. But he could not do that.

Even as these thoughts passed through his mind, Charity flushed and folded her arms across her chest. Unexpected tenderness tightened his chest at her embarrassment, but he forced himself to go on. "Although I had little else of value in my saddlebags, they did contain my money."

Charity's mouth widened in a sudden smile. "Thee shouldn't be so hasty, Jason." With that she stood and raised the hem of the red petticoat. She reached underneath, fumbled about, and drew out a handful of bills. "I hid this in the pocket of my underdrawers."

With a cry of elation, Jason jumped up and raised her in his arms, swinging her around and then kissing her cheek loudly. "You beautiful, wonderful woman!" He set her down and turned to Lizzy, who had sat up to stare at the two of them with wide dark eyes. "Did any man ever have a more clever wife?"

Lizzy grinned weakly. "No, I don't see as how they could."

Charity felt herself blush with pleasure at his praise. She looked up at her husband with uncertain eyes.

Jason had said very little during their escape from the hotel. After they had managed to get out of the city, then off the wagon without mishap, he had only seemed to grow more morose by the minute.

Yet while Jason seemed to be upset by what had happened, and though she did feel badly about leaving Old Dan, Charity could barely contain her happiness that they had saved Lizzie.

And Jason had helped. When the choice had been presented to him—to kill or assure Lizzie's escape— Jason had decided to do the only thing a really good man could. He had forgotten his hatred for the sake of someone else. Someone who was a complete stranger to him.

Charity wasn't truly surprised. Deep within herself she'd known how he would choose all along. How else could she love him as deeply as she did?

Late the next evening, Jason watched as Charity spread their blankets over the pile of fresh hay. She was wearing a light cotton dress that he had taken, along with blankets and other items, from the wash hanging behind a farmhouse. All the things were well washed and not particularly fine, but he had left several times over enough money in their place to buy new ones.

He had also taken food. Lizzy was still weak, though the meals she'd eaten had left her feeling strong enough to go into the woods by herself while Charity made their beds. Jason was glad of her improving health, especially after the time they had spent together since her rescue. She was a bright girl, and apparently a good friend to Charity. They'd gotten to know each other during Lizzy's short stay at the Applegates' farm.

Jason was now nearly as determined as Charity to get her safely out of the south. In the morning, he planned to go into the next town to buy a horse and wagon. In it, the three of them would make the journey back to the Applegate farm.

After that, well, Jason didn't allow himself to think that far ahead.

As Charity reached down to smoothe the top blanket, his eyes lingered on her trim waist and the gentle swell of her hips. This was his wife.

Not since the day of their wedding had he even been alone with her.

As if sensing the direction of his thoughts, Charity straightened and turned to face him. Her gaze dropped to the ground, and when she spoke, her voice was barely audible. "It's ready."

Jason looked at her, seeing the welcome he would find in her arms. Jason knew that Lizzy would be returning at any time, but that was not what held him back.

He hadn't been able to resolve the fact that he had

not been able to do what he should have for Daphne.
How he would learn to live with his decision, he did
not know.

What right had he to take this loving and passionate
woman in his arms when Daphne would never know
passion? What right had he to lose himself in Charity's
love when Daphne had never known it? She had never
received anything from him but grief.

Stiffly he stood, putting his hands in his pockets.
"I . . . I think I'll keep watch for a while." He turned to
leave, unwilling to acknowledge the hurt that colored
Charity's expression.

She stared after him for a long moment, her chest
tight as she wondered why Jason could not seem to
share her happiness in the way things had turned out.
Surely, she told herself, he would come around.

Hearing a soft sound behind her, she turned, wondering if he had come back to her.

It was Lizzy. Charity tried for a cheery smile.
"Come and lie down. Thee will need thy rest for
tomorrow."

Lizzy moved to the blanket, lowering her small
graceful form gingerly. "I am right sore." She sighed,
her large brown eyes luminous as she smiled at
Charity. "But I can travel for sure. There ain't anything that could keep me down here where that man
could . . ."

Charity found herself asking the question that had
prodded at the back of her mind since learning that
Lizzy had been taken. "He didn't . . ."

Lizzy shook her head vigorously. "No, he didn't
touch me. You heard him. I'm just an animal to him."
Charity heard the bitterness in her voice, and nodded.

She took a deep breath and let it out slowly. "He won't ever come near thee again. Jason and I will see to that."

Lizzy nodded, her gaze holding Charity's. "He's a good man, your Jason. It ain't for me to tell you what to do, Charity, but you say I am yer friend. I heard what you said. Still, I got to say that you'd best take him as he is and not try to go changin' him. He ain't like you and yer family, but he's better than most. So that's what I got to say. Just take him as he is and you'll never be sorry."

Charity shook her head. "There are things thee don't know, things that Jason cannot forgive himself for."

Lizzy smiled softly. "When a woman loves a man, he can begin to see himself through her eyes. It might take a little time, but it happens. A woman just has to remember to look on her man with love, to accept him how he is."

There was nothing Charity could say to her words. Jason was the one who stood between them—not her.

Jason could not help knowing that they were a strange sight to meet Elija Applegate's eyes as they rode into the yard. Jason was not surprised to see him stop still in shock where he stood in the open barn door.

He, Lizzy, and Charity were mounted on two of the mangiest looking horses he'd ever had the misfortune to see. The women rode on the larger of the pair, an old mare that appeared as if each step might be her last. Jason rode atop a sway-backed gelding, whose gait jarred him with each step.

Jason knew their fatigue would be obvious in their drooping shoulders and lagging pace.

As he watched, Charity sat up straighter, shading her eyes against the glare of the setting sun. Her other hand was raised high in greeting, and he heard the joy in the one word she called out. "Papa!"

Elija's pitchfork fell to the ground and he raced across the yard.

Charity slipped from the saddle and ran toward him, her happiness clearly giving her renewed vitality. Her father held out his arms and she threw herself into them.

"Charity." Jason's heart swelled as Elija held her close. They spun around, the dust under their feet seeming to dance with their joy at being together again.

"Oh Papa, Papa."

The kitchen door banged against the side of the house. The next thing he knew, her mother had joined Charity and her father. Crying and laughing at the same time, she hugged them both. "Daughter, thee have come home to us."

Charity pulled away from them to look back at himself and Lizzy. "Do thee see, Mother and Father? We have brought Lizzy back safe."

Her parents turned to face them and he saw the uncertainty mixed with their obvious happiness at seeing Lizzy. Jason rode forward slowly, his gaze now on Charity's suddenly anxious face. She did not speak until he had brought the horse to a halt and slipped to the ground beside her.

She faced her parents with a deep breath. "Mother, Father, I have something to tell thee." She linked her arm through his. "Jason and I are married."

The ensuing silence was deafening.

When Jason felt that he might explode with tension, Elija held out his arms. "Welcome, son."

He embraced the other man briefly, feeling Mary Applegate's gaze upon him. He met it directly as she spoke. "Well, I can't say that this comes as a surprise to me. I hope thee know what a fine woman thee have got."

Jason only had time for a sharp uncomfortable nod before the other sisters, who had obviously overheard, broke into their own excited congratulations. As they rushed to hug their sister, he was overwhelmed by the knowledge that he did indeed know what he had, but he could not help knowing too that he was far from deserving.

It was clear that Mary tried to make supper that night something of a celebratory feast. It was not only a celebration of Jason and Charity's wedding, but also of Lizzy's freedom.

Elija shook his head in wonder. "I still don't see how thee managed to travel so far without being asked for papers for Lizzy."

Charity and Jason exchanged glances. She looked away hurriedly. Jason was quite aware of the tension that had risen up between them in the last several days, and he had been grateful for Lizzy's presence, for he was unwilling to do anything that might diminish that distance.

He listened as she spoke softly. "Jason thought of that. When we were close to any sign of people, I rode the other horse and Lizzy walked beside us. Also, Jason was prepared—just in case someone asked us to prove she was our slave. Jason is a lawyer. He knew what to say."

Mary said, "A lawyer?"

He shrugged, trying to sound unconcerned. "Yes, I never had a reason to mention it to any of you. Thanks to my profession, I had a rudimentary understanding of the ins and outs of the slave laws."

Jason realized it was time he shared some of the truth about himself, yet it was difficult to admit the extent of his lies to these people who had taken him in and been so kind to him, people who had lost their precious daughter to him. He cleared his throat.

"I . . . uh . . . There is something I have to say. I thank you all for welcoming me into your family so heartily from the beginning, even before we . . . Charity and I were married." He could feel his wife's attention on him, but focused instead on the faces of her family. "I didn't know how much I had missed you until we saw you again. It was like coming home."

There were sympathetic smiles even from Mary, and he paused, unsure of how to continue. "There is something you have to know. From the information that I am a lawyer you must realize that I accepted Elija's offer of a job under false pretenses. I . . . well, I came to Helmsville looking for someone. That someone was Wayne Grisak. I was trying to discover if, as I suspected, he had been the one who murdered a member of my family. My wife Daphne."

There was a stunned silence, then Mary, who was sitting next to Jason, covered his hand with hers. "I am so sorry for your loss, my son."

Jason had to clear his throat at the well of emotion her words of compassion evoked. "Please. I need to finish. This is so hard for me to say."

Charity caught and held her husband's gaze. "Do thee want me to finish?"

Empathically Jason shook his head. "It's my doing. I'll do the telling." He took a deep breath. "It was my intent to kill him. Without trial or verdict, I was quite willing to put him to death. That is why I came here, why I went after him when he took Lizzy to South Carolina. It was only because of Charity's determination to come after me and save her friend that I did not do so."

Elija held his hands together in an attitude of prayer. "But thee did not take his life, my boy. In the end thee did what was right."

Jason turned to Elija. "And by letting him live I have created even greater chaos. I am deeply sorry, but I have put your family in a very difficult position. Charity tells me that he recognized her on the night that we rescued Lizzy."

Mary nodded thoughtfully. "Then it is a very good thing that Louisa has gone to her parents with the children."

Jason spoke with conviction. "Yes, that is very fortunate for her sake. Because, after recognizing Charity, he will likely come looking for us here. He is not a man who would take our actions against him lightly."

Elija's expression was grave as he put his palms down on the table. "That is very likely true, but we will have to wait and see what comes. Thee did the right thing in helping Lizzy. She must go into hiding at another house now that ours is not safe. I will take her to Levi tonight, and from there she will go directly to Canada. As to thy quarrel with Wayne Grisak, what he does is on his own head. Thee did not harm him, no matter thy original intentions. Thee have nothing to blame thyself for."

"You can't just sit back and hope he doesn't come."

"We will not harm anyone, even to save ourselves. It is the heart of our religious teachings."

Mary spoke up softly. "Live by the sword, die by the sword."

Jason's jaw grew hard. "It won't be Grisak who dies by the sword in this case. He won't hesitate for a moment to—I will not allow him to hurt any of you." He pushed himself away from the table. "Tell them, Charity."

She only stared at him, her eyes damp with tears.

With a muttered curse, Jason stood and stormed out of the house, slamming the door behind him.

Looking at the dearly beloved faces around her, Charity said, "He will do what is right. He did so last time. He chose to save a life rather than take one." Though her words were hopeful, Charity was not so sure as she pretended. This time the question might be very different. What would Jason choose when it was his life in jeopardy? Deep in her heart she was not at all sure.

She was not sure she even knew what she wanted him to do. Lizzy's words of advice kept running through her mind, making her wonder if Jason could feel her disapproval of his way of thinking.

For a moment, as she looked at her father's face, she wondered if Jason would really be so very wrong if he did act to protect them. Was it right to allow a man like Grisak to harm others who had done him no wrong?

She gave herself a mental shake, but her confusion

remained. Things that had once seemed black and white had shaded to gray.

She was aware of a strong sense of loyalty to Jason. Which was only reasonable, wasn't it? For he was, after all, her husband. At the same time, another part of her could not deny that Jason had been behaving very oddly since the night they had escaped from Grisak's hotel room. Not once since then had he even intimated that he would like to be close to her.

Charity tried to tell herself it was because they had not been alone. But deep inside her dwelled the certainty that something was definitely wrong, that the once fiery connection between them seemed to have disappeared. The very idea that Jason might not want her physically anymore was devastating. Not only because she was aware of the fact that he had married her for that very reason, but because she was equally aware of her own still fierce desire for him.

Charity gave a silent groan. Heaven help her, she was so confused she didn't know what to think. Her loyalties had been thrown into complete confusion and all because of a man who had wanted to lie with her enough to marry her, then turned his back on that passion.

Murmuring that she was very tired now, she bolted from the kitchen and up to her room, which her mother had prepared for her and Jason. Would he be sharing it with her?

As the door closed behind her, Charity could not help noticing the special touches that her mother and sisters had added to the room. A vase of late-blooming wildflowers sat on the dresser. The bed had been newly made and turned down to show crisp white sheets.

Recognizing the delicate embroidery on the edge of the sheet and pillow slips, Charity knew that they had come from her hope chest.

The sight of these familiar items brought a rush of tears to her eyes. She had hoped and dreamed of so much when she'd stitched them. Now she wasn't sure what the future held for her, didn't know what being Jason's wife would mean.

They had not spoken of their future. Surely they must do so at some point.

Again she wondered what would happen if Jason didn't come to her? How was she to face him, her family?

She brushed her hair back from her forehead and realized how very tired she was. Not wanting to think anymore, Charity undressed and slipped into a clean linen nightdress. It felt good to be wearing her own things again.

She took her brush from the dresser and sat on the end of the bed. Leaning her head forward, she began to brush the heavy mass from underneath.

When the door opened, she started, her hair falling in a heavy silken curtain around her face.

Jason stood framed in the opening. "Charity?"

She knew not what he asked, nor what he wanted her to say. "I . . ." She took a deep breath and began again, trying to sound self-assured. "Please, do not just stand in the doorway. I am thy wife. Come in."

His face creasing in a troubled frown, he moved inside, closing the door behind him. He was so tall standing there inside her room, so very masculine, so handsome with those unfathomable dark eyes of his. She recalled her thoughts on that day he had stood next to her as she held Louisa's baby. That experience seemed a lifetime ago. She had been a girl then, with a girl's thoughts. Now she was a woman, married to this man who, though his values were so different from her own, had come to earn her respect and love without even trying.

Suddenly, she knew a sensation of awareness so acute that goose bumps raised along her flesh. But she also knew a feeling of unease. Why had he come? Surely not for loving, not with that strained expression upon his face.

Taking her hand, he drew her to the bed, pushing her down gently. Still, without saying anything, he seated himself next to her and took a deep breath.

Charity wanted to ask what this was about, but she could not, fearful that what he had come to say might hurt.

"Charity," he began finally. "There are some things that simply must be said." She watched him closely, her heart thundering as he went on. "I don't think that I can . . ."

She could not hide the tears in her eyes. "Thee does not want me anymore."

His gaze grew round with a shock that could not be feigned. "Good God, how could you even think such a thing?"

Her heart soared. "Then you *do* still want me?"

He swallowed, closing his eyes as he visibly fought for control. "More than anything."

This admission, though reluctant, was all the encouragement she required. All else could be settled by love. His face was so very handsome in the candlelight, his eyes so very dark, and she loved him so deeply. She reached up to run a tender hand through his dark hair and found it wet.

He groaned at that touch, obviously distracted as he answered her unspoken question. "I went to bathe in the creek."

Her mind was filled with a sudden vision of him wet and naked. Blushing, she looked down—and inadvertently saw the state of his arousal.

She looked away, then, shocked and unmistakably thrilled at this evidence of his growing desire. She made no effort to resist him as he reached for her hair brush. "Let me."

She was surprised at his request, but willing to let him take the lead. Gently he plied the brush, making her think of those strong hands on other parts of her body. The strands clung to his fingers as if attracted by some magical force.

Her eyelids grew heavy, but not with fatigue. She felt a growing tension, one that was always present when Jason was near. She had fought it each moment since their wedding night, yet it had never been vanquished. It had only lain dormant, close beneath the surface of her consciousness, ready to flare up with the least encouragement.

Charity turned toward him, knowing her longing would be displayed in her eyes. As his gaze met hers and held, she took the brush from Jason's hand and laid it on the night table.

His eyes never left her face. "Charity, this is not why I came here tonight. There are things that must be said. Promises I can't make—"

"Shh." She placed her fingers over his lips. "Thee don't have to promise anything. Let's forget everything else this one night. I want thee and thee want me. For now let that be enough."

He reached up to press her fingers more firmly to his lips, closing his eyes as he kissed them. "Oh, Charity, if you only knew how much I've wanted you, how much I need your goodness and strength."

"As I need thee."

He watched her as he lowered her hand to his knee, and he reached out with the other to trace the lace edging of her high-necked gown.

She found herself caught by his gaze as he brought up his hands and loosened her top button, then the second, and the third. As his fingers brushed against the swell of her breasts, her lids drooped closed, her lips parted.

His mouth closed on hers and she lost all ability to think. She could only feel, wrapping her arms around his neck in an effort to get closer. His hot, wet kisses fanned her desire, awakening the slumbering wanton inside her. Her head fell back, and his lips trailed rapture down the sensitive flesh of her throat before he held her away from him gently. Then, slowly, his trembling hands parted her nightgown and he sighed as flesh met flesh.

Charity shuddered at the heat in her husband's gaze. Wanting nothing more than to please him and be pleased by him, she leaned backward on her hands, offering herself to his lips.

He accepted her gift with reverence, pressing his mouth to one breast's pink tip and then the other. Her breath caught and she fell backward upon the bed, holding his head to her as he paid homage to the tender mounds.

"Come to me," she whispered, her voice husky with passion. Jason moved up, meeting her eager lips.

The heat in her belly was a fast-burning fire, leaping higher as it grew. Her arms twined around his neck and she raked his thick, silky hair with her fingers.

It wasn't enough. Charity wanted more and she pressed closer to him, sobbing in frustration. "Gently," he whispered against her skin. "Go gently. Let me pleasure you."

Putting her hands on his face, she raised him to look into his eyes. After all these days of wanting, Charity had no need of more coaxing. She was ready now, eager for the joining of her flesh to his.

Deliberately, holding his gaze, Charity reached down and grasped the front of his shirt. With a jerk, she parted the buttons from the fabric, and his chest lay exposed to her questing fingers. "I've waited long enough."

His reaction to her hunger was instantaneous and intense, rippling through him in a tide of liquid flame. He could no longer forestall his own need. Jason stood, his hands quaking as he opened his pants. He slid them off, taking his socks with them. His shirt dropped to the floor.

Then he was above her, his body merging with hers. The sheer sweet gladness of their joining caused Charity to cry out in ecstasy, and she rose up to meet him fully with each powerful thrust of his hips.

The sensations built, roiling inside her, bringing her every nerve to shattering life. And then she tensed, arching under him as her pleasure exploded in a shower of clear white light.

His mouth stifled her cries as he too arched in

release. He was left shaken and weak with tenderness and wonder, holding her until the ripples subsided.

Only when she lay still did he shift until she was cradled in his arms. They lay quietly. Jason found himself strangely unwilling to speak. Once again, this simple act had become something more fulfilling, more moving, because he had shared it with Charity.

When he felt her move to lean over him, he, with disturbing reluctance, opened his eyes.

He saw that she was smiling, a deliciously wicked grin. "Now it is my turn to love thee." She leaned over to flick his left nipple with her tongue.

He was surprised when his body reacted so immediately to the stimulus, especially in the face of his own confused thoughts and feelings. He'd come here to tell her that he could never be what she and her family expected of him, that she must accept that, if they were to go on at all. He wanted her to be the one to make the choice.

Her painful assumption that he had lost his desire for her had driven all thoughts of asking her to reconsider their marriage from his mind.

Clearly unaware of his thoughts, Charity chuckled as she noted his response, and she pressed her mouth to his.

For a moment, Jason had to acknowledge a degree of surprise at her abandon. Then he asked himself why. Obviously, no one had ever told her it was wrong to give in to one's feelings. The same code of honesty that made her speak her mind without hesitation, freed her of inhibition as far as physical pleasure was concerned.

He could not allow her to make love to him this way again, not until he had made himself clear about who and what he was willing to be. No matter how force-fully his body urged him to do otherwise.

"Charity . . ."he began. Then a completely unex-pected and horrifying sound rang out through the open window: gunfire.

Chapter Twelve

Jason leapt from the bed. He was dragging on his discarded pants even as Charity sat up to stare at him with wide, confused blue eyes.

"What is it?" she asked, holding her hand to her throat. He didn't meet Charity's gaze as he reached under the edge of the bed and took out his saddlebag.

His reply was curt even to his own ears. "Gunshots." With that one word she knew what he did. Wayne Grisak had come.

Charity looked to the window as another shot sounded, then back at Jason. Her gaze widened further as Jason removed his gun from his saddlebag. "Where did thee get that?"

He set it on the dresser as he pulled on a clean shirt. "I bought it that night in River Bend. You knew I had gone to the Red Lady to kill Grisak. How did you think I meant to do that?"

"Thee didn't say anything."

He looked at her then, his eyes devoid of expression. "Knowing your feelings, what could I have said?"

She shook her head in confusion. "I don't know. But surely thee understand that *this* is wrong." She motioned to the weapon.

He turned his back on her, picking up the gun and checking it for bullets. It was loaded. "I warned you, Charity. I can't let him hurt you or anyone in your family. It's my fault he's here. It's my responsibility to protect you all." He went to the door, then paused, his voice so soft she could barely hear him. "Even if you hate me for it."

He left without another word, knowing there was no point in arguing with her. Neither of them was willing to budge on this. Neither of them could.

When Jason entered the kitchen, Elija was already there. His gaze went directly to the gun in Jason's hand, his eyes registering sadness and pity.

They stood like that in silence as Wayne Grisak's voice rose from outside. "Come on out, Applegate, or I'll come in after you."

Jason was aware of Charity entering the kitchen as Elija put his hand on Jason's arm. "Son, thee cannot harm this man."

He felt the weight of Charity's misery as he gave Elija a long look. "What do you think is going to happen here? Do you imagine that we can all just go to bed and ignore him? Do you think he's going to go away?"

Elija shook his head, his expression unwavering. "Thee cannot do this, not in order to protect us. Our lives are no more important than his."

Desperately, in spite of the fact that he knew she felt the same way as her father, Jason turned to fix pleading eyes on his wife. "Tell him, Charity. You've seen what Grisak can do. Tell your father that this monster will kill you all without compunction—as he did Daphne and likely many others. His life is a cheap price to pay in order to protect good, loving people like you and your family."

Charity felt her heart thundering in her chest, and she knew that in some part of her, Jason's words rang true. Her father *was* a good man, her mother and sisters innocent of any crime against this undoubtedly cruel man. Yet was her father not right? Was it not the Lord's place and no other's to decide who lived and who died?

At that moment, her mother came into the room. Charity looked to her for guidance. But Mary Applegate said nothing. Her hand clutched the neck of her robe close to her as she went to stand beside her husband.

Charity focused on each face in turn, unable to make sense of her own confused thoughts and feelings.

Finally, Jason turned away from her, holding his head high. Charity, loving him as she did, could feel his pain. In her aching heart she wished above anything that she could change that. Still, she said nothing.

Shaking Elija's hand from his arm, Jason went to the back door and jerked it open. He stepped out into the night, closing it softly behind him.

Suddenly she wanted to call Jason back and tell him she would stick by him no matter what he had to do.

It was too late.

Charity ran to the window, peering out into the moon-drenched yard. Grisak sat on his horse, his posture relaxed as he leaned his forearms on the saddle horn. He hooted with pleasure as Jason stepped from the shadow of the house.

"Well now," he bellowed. "Who are you? Them Quakers hire you to protect 'em? Guess they must figure it ain't no sin, long as they don't do the dirty work themselves." He laughed rancorously, his attitude making it clear how little he feared Jason.

In spite of the danger and what had just passed between them, Charity felt her heart flutter with love and pride as Jason spoke up, his voice even and sure. "Why don't you just ride on out of here before anybody gets hurt?"

Grisak raised one hand. In it was his pistol. He used the barrel to tip his hat back on his head. "Now, why should I do that?"

"Just do it."

Nonchalantly, Grisak waved the gun. "You gonna see that I do?"

Jason didn't back down. "If need be." He took a step closer, and Grisak finally seemed to see Jason's gun, as the moonlight glinted off the barrel.

Grisak's tone grew hard, and Charity felt her blood freeze in her veins. "I don't think you ought to be pointin' that thing, Quaker-lover. Just get on out of my way and let me finish my business. You can say you done yer job by tellin' me to go. If yer lucky I won't hold none of this against you."

Charity shivered as steel rang out in Jason's voice. "Killing you wouldn't be a job. You've caused enough pain in my life that it would be a pleasure."

Grisak frowned, that deceptively mild face of his taking on a thoughtful expression. "I don't even know you, fella."

Jason nodded, "Oh, you know me all right, but it's through my wife. She was a friend of Angie Monahan's. And I know that you killed her."

Grisak's face registered shock, but he quickly suppressed it. "You got the wrong man."

Jason smiled coldly. "I've got the right man, all right. The only reason I haven't already killed you is the love I bear the people in this house. I want you to remember that the Quakers you disdain so easily are all that's keeping your mangy butt alive right now."

Grisak scowled. "Now that's about all the sass I'm takin' off you. I gave you your chance, you shoulda took it." He leveled the barrel of the gun.

At that moment, Charity's mind had only one thought—one purpose. Jason must live. As she jerked open the door, she began to pray. "Oh Lord, please protect Jason. I cannot go on without him."

She ran out into the yard.

Her desperate eyes searched for and found Jason. He stood directly in Grisak's sights. Without stopping to think, she ran to block him.

Grisak laughed aloud. "Well, if it ain't the little Quaker whore. You are gonna be sorry you made a fool of me." His gun swiveled to aim at Charity.

Fear swept through her in a blinding wave, but she did not move. Then suddenly, the sound of several shots exploded nearby. So dazed was she by the volume, that she could not tell from which direction they had come.

The shots rang in her ears for what seemed an eternity. The next thing she was aware of was Jason's voice calling her name. Charity spun around to see him moving toward her. "Dear God, Charity, are you hurt?"

253

Even as he asked, she realized that miraculously no bullets had struck her.

He reached her, his hands moving over her with frantic haste. His eyes were wells of fear. "Are you all right?"

"I'm fine," she answered quickly.

Yet Jason did not relax his search of her person. His anxious words told her why. "Men have been shot and not even been aware of it, because they were in shock." He paused then, his hand on her sleeve. "Dear God."

Charity reached to feel the same spot and felt that there was a ragged tear in her sleeve.

He spoke the words that seared her mind. "My God, he nearly shot you."

She faced him directly, even as she forced back a hard gulp. "There is no blood," she responded. "I am fine."

At the same time, she looked over his shoulder, noting that Grisak's horse was no longer standing where it had been. It was galloping down the road toward Helmsville.

Jason swung around to follow the path of her gaze. To her utter amazement, he raised his pistol and began running after him.

Horror tinged her voice as she cried, "No, Jason. Let him go. I am all right. We all are." But even as she said it, she wondered if her words would bear any weight. She'd heard the rage and pain in Jason's voice as he told Grisak that he knew he had killed his wife.

It seemed as if her screams reached him, because he stopped dead on the very spot where Grisak had sat atop his horse only moments ago. After what seemed a very long time, his arm lowered, and his pistol dropped to the ground.

Charity ran to him.

She threw her arms around her her husband as she reached him, holding him to her in relief, only now realizing how close both of them had come to death. He was enraged, and lost in grief over his first wife, but he was warm and real and so very much alive. She sobbed out loud. "Thank God. Thank God, thee are all right."

Jason held her too tightly, but she reveled in it, hearing the desperation in his tone when he finally spoke. "You ran in front of me." He shook her. "Don't ever do anything like that again."

Before Charity could reply, Elija interrupted from beside them. He had come outside. "Are thee all right, Jason? Is . . . was Wayne Grisak hurt?"

Jason looked at him over Charity's head. "I don't know, he rode away." His jaw tightened, as did his arms. "He shot first. I had to protect Charity."

At that moment, Charity was no more capable of knowing who was in the right than she had been before. A part of her agreed with her father and the teachings she had followed her whole life. The other part, the one that was aware of the strength of Jason's arms around her, her inexpressible joy, understood that he'd had to shoot back. For, in the instant when Grisak had fired, might she not have done the same thing to save Jason's dearly beloved life?

Jason held on to Charity tightly, so glad that she was alive, safe in his arms. In that instant when he'd thought he might lose her, his mind had been swept into a dark and terrifying void. He'd had to shoot back.

255

Even now as he held her in his arms, he felt such sweet relief, and he wondered what would happen now. How would her family react to this?

Not wanting to see what he knew would be there, but unable to stop himself, he looked into Elija's troubled eyes.

He turned back to Charity. His wife's eyes searched his with confusion and sadness.

Taking a deep breath, he took his arms from around Charity and bent to pick up his gun. Some ways away on the ground, in the silvery moonlight, a dark patch was evident on the dusty ground. He moved to the patch and peered down, testing it with his fingers.

"What is wrong?" Charity asked.

He didn't look at her. "It's blood. But it isn't mine or yours. It has to be Grisak's."

Grimly, Elija turned to his wife, who stood in the open door of the kitchen. "We must find him. See if he is in need of aid."

Even as she nodded, Jason grimaced, knowing he was only offering out of respect for Elija. "I'll help."

Elija made no reply.

After some searching, they found a trail that they could follow even by the light of their torches. It led toward the creek.

Jason searched just as diligently as any of the Applegates, even though he could not really find it in him to be sorry—even if the bastard was dead. He did it because he couldn't do anything else in the face of their concern.

Jason found Grisak's blood-soaked horse standing in the stream. Wading out to bring it to shore, Jason saw Grisak's body floating in the water beside it.

256

Calling up to the others on the bank, Jason said, "Don't come any closer. He's dead."

The silence that followed was deafening. Unable to face Charity, he looked to Elija. Yes, he'd known what to expect, yet as Elija's gaze slipped away from his, he felt as if a stone had taken the place of his heart. This man—one whom he had come to respect more than any words could ever express—could no longer look him in the face.

He turned to Charity. Her agonized expression told him all he needed to know.

What else could he have expected? He had done the one thing he knew she could not forgive. He had taken a life.

He realized that there was no going back to the relationship he had once known with these people, with Charity. He was silent as he pulled Grisak's body up from the water and draped it over his gelding.

Slowly, he then led it to the bank. Charity stood there watching him and he knew that he had to say something, to tell her what he was feeling, for the sadness in her gaze made his heart ache.

"You were right all along," he admitted. "Killing him hasn't solved a damn thing. It's only made things worse. But I would do it again to keep him from killing you. I couldn't do anything else after bringing him here and putting you all in danger.

"It didn't bring Daphne back, it only destroyed your . . ." But he couldn't finish, couldn't bring himself to say that he knew she didn't love him anymore.

Without knowing that he was going to do so, he reached for her and she flinched. Agony shot through him, even as her gaze widened with horror at her own reaction.

She reached toward him. "Jason, I did not mean . . ."

He shook his head, refusing her pity. God, she couldn't even bear his touch. Knowing that he was going to have to face how much her distaste hurt, but unable to do so now in front of the others, he squared his shoulders.

"I am going to take him into town and arrange for him to be buried. When I get back, I will get my things. I am going back to Boston. I'll leave it for you to decide what you want to do."

Charity watched Jason get on his horse and ride away through a fog of misery. She'd feared that what had taken place this night had only opened new wounds for him rather than healing old ones. But having him say it aloud sent a pain through her that was nearly unbearable.

The last thing she'd wanted was for him to see her misery. When he'd reached out to her in regret, admitting that in spite of his gladness that he had saved her own life, he was still as unhappy over his first wife's death as he had ever been, she'd been unable to bear the pain of it.

Now, Jason's hurt reaction to her flinching away from him would haunt her till the end of her days. Though she'd tried to explain, he was too miserable to even listen, too caught up in the pain of his past.

Charity wanted to cry out at the unfairness of it all.

She wanted Jason to love *her*, to want to be with *her*, to let go of his grief. Yet it was horribly obvious that he could not. The fact that he'd left it up to her to decide whether or not to go home to Boston with him was evidence of that.

How could she not go with him? He was her husband.

Unable to face the sad gazes of her family for another moment, Charity turned and ran. She didn't stop until she had reached her room.

Yet even there she knew no respite from the sorrow that tore at her.

She had no idea how much time had passed when the door opened. Her mother stood there, her gaze filled with sympathy.

Charity whispered, "Thee heard what he said to me?"

She nodded. "I did."

"What should I do?"

"What do thee want to do?"

She looked down at her hands. "I do not know. I love him, but he is still in love with *her*. How can I compete with the memory of a love so dear to him?"

Her mother moved forward and raised Charity's chin with her soft hand. "There is no need to compete with her, Charity. Each love is as dear as another."

"He doesn't love me."

"That I have no answer for. I do know that I saw the way he looked at thee when he came to the farm. There is something there. Perhaps he only needs time to put his grief behind him."

Charity did not wish to tell her mother of the passion that existed between herself and Jason. She could not. But the memory of it decided her. If Jason had been drawn to her so strongly, perhaps there was something more, something he did not yet realize.

Charity spoke softly. "He is my husband. What future is there for me if I do not try? I will never have children, a home of my own . . ."

Her mother nodded in agreement, albeit regretfully. "It is as I thought. In thy heart, thee are not yet ready to let it be done between you. Thee know that Papa and I would always wish for thee to follow the dictates of thy heart—even if it means thee will go from us."

Charity heard the catch in her mother's voice and knew a new sorrow, but it was one she had to be prepared to face. It was only right that a wife leave her family to make a new life with her husband. Even if she was not sure that Jason really wished to begin a life with her, she had made this choice. She would see it through.

Her mother rose. "Just remember, daughter, that our door will always be open to thee if thy heart makes a change." With that she was gone.

Jason made no comment on the fact that she was packed and ready to leave when he returned. Charity did not know what to say, so she said only, "I am thy wife. My duty and my place is with thee." Although she could hear in her voice the fear that he would refuse her, he simply nodded stiffly and turned to gather his own belongings.

Her family took them into town the next afternoon. After a strained and tearful goodbye, and still without exchanging more words than necessity dictated, Jason and Charity boarded the eastbound train.

As the days passed in travel, she realized that deciding to go with her husband might prove even more difficult than she had imagined. Although Jason was extremely courteous, treating her gently and respectfully, he made no move to touch her other than in the way he might an old maid aunt.

Telling herself that this should not surprise her, given the state of his feelings, Charity none the less grew more and more withdrawn herself. Although she was uncertain about meeting his family, about whom she knew nothing, she was almost relieved when they at last drew into the station in Boston. Any distraction that would take attention away from this painful wall of reserve was welcome.

Though she caught glimpses of the city through the window of the carriage he had hired to take them to meet his parents, she had little thought for it. She was just too aware of the tension in his lean body, his obvious distraction. Perhaps, she told herself hopefully, things would improve once they were in their own home, where they could begin to make a life together. She imagined herself doing all the things her mother did, cooking, cleaning their home, Jason coming home after working in his law office.

It was not until they stepped from the carriage that the first bits of reality began to penetrate the dense fog shrouding her mind. Looking up at the dwelling before them, her fingers tightened on Jason's formally extended arm.

Jason had told her of course that his background was completely different from hers. But never in her remotest imaginings had Charity guessed at the truth.

The house, if one chose to put such a common name to a dwelling that was so clearly a mansion, was built from seasoned red brick. It was three stories high and hung with trailing ivy. The many windows were made of lead-paned glass, and the curving drive led to a street lined with perfectly groomed weeping willows.

The complete picture was one of permanence and gracious elegance. Wealth.

What would these people think of her? Charity ran a self-conscious hand over the skirt of her best dress, the one she wore to meeting. She felt a definite yearning for the blue gown she had been married in, which had unfortunately been left behind in Carolina.

She stopped and took a deep breath. For the first time in days, Jason seemed to take note of her. His hand tightened on hers and he smiled encouragingly, though she could see the strain around his mouth and eyes.

She did not have time to consider his reaction more than briefly. Not letting go of her hand, Jason led her up the steps to the front door. Even before he could knock, it was opened by a tall, gray-haired, and impeccably groomed man dressed in perfectly tailored pants and a cutaway coat.

The man didn't smile, but there was a true warmth in his eyes as he greeted Jason. "Mister Jason. It is good to see you again."

Jason answered distractedly, but she could feel his genuine liking for this man. "Thank you, Soames. It is good to see you." He paused, his body filling with tension again. "Are my parents in?"

Charity wondered at Jason's demeanor. She really knew so little of his life, had been too wrapped up in her own misery to think of what things would be like in Boston.

"Mr. and Mrs. Trenton are in the drawing room." Soames stepped back and motioned them inside.

"Trenton?" Charity whispered.

Jason leaned close. "Yes, Charity. I'm sorry I hadn't thought to tell you. My name is Jason Wade Trenton. I wasn't using it because it had been in the papers at the time of Daphne's death. I thought Grisak might recognize it. Your real name is Mrs. Jason Wade Trenton."

She barely had time to absorb this as they entered the foyer. Charity stopped still, unable to prevent herself from gaping in awe.

The ceiling was high above them, the stairs to the upper levels open to the foyer below. Charity had never seen marble, but she had read many books. Pink marble covered the floor. Along the walls were high-backed chairs with red brocade cushions. A large round table sat in the center of the entry, a huge bouquet of fresh flowers reflecting in its highly polished surface.

"Charity," Jason whispered gently. They moved forward after the man named Soames. Then, surprisingly, Jason seemed to hang back as the man went to a set of sliding oak doors and slipped inside.

Charity looked to him in question, but he would not meet her questioning gaze. When Soames returned to the door and nodded for them to come in, Charity felt a brief pressure as he gave her hand a quick squeeze.

Studying his rigid profile, she wondered who he was attempting to comfort, her or himself.

The drawing room was long and narrow. As they moved through it, Charity had an impression of plush carpets and gilt-edged paintings.

At the end of the room, a woman sat on a settee covered in yellow silk. Across from her was a tall, slim dark-haired man with a considerable amount of gray around his temples. They rose as she and Jason came closer, their expressions mirroring both surprise and caution.

Even as Charity watched, the woman folded one hand around a watch suspended on a chain around her neck. The gesture betrayed a certain nervousness on the woman's part that brought an instant sympathy from Charity. But her regal bearing discouraged any show of it. If she hadn't known this woman's relationship to her husband, Charity might have guessed. She was tall, almost as tall as Jason, and she had his dark auburn-streaked hair, though hers was arranged in elegant fashion. Her eyes were gray-black and studied Charity with hauteur. She wore a black silk gown with a high collar trimmed in lace. It rustled as she took a step toward them. "Jason."

Charity couldn't tell if it was a statement or a question.

Jason stopped a few paces short of actually meeting her. "Mother." Formally, he nodded, as if greeting a stranger. She was aware of a certain vulnerability in her husband, and she wondered at this relationship which was so different from her relationship with her own mother.

The man spoke less formally, though he did not move forward. "Jason, it is so good to have you back."

"Thank you, father." Jason cast him an almost yearning glance that made Charity's heart turn over in her breast.

The man did not seem to notice. He watched as his wife sent a pointed glance toward Charity.

Jason stiffened visibly. "Allow me to introduce my

wife, Charity. Charity, my mother and father, Mr. and Mrs. Robert Trenton."

There was absolutely no mistaking the shock on his mother's face, or on his father's.

For a moment, Jason appeared almost amused. Then he sobered, casting Charity a glance of reassurance, even as his mother gasped. "Your wife?"

Charity felt a rising sense of indignation. She could understand some surprise now that she knew of Jason's circumstances and the enormous difference in their material status. But Charity had never been treated so rudely, and she was not about to take this lying down.

She held out her hand. Her voice was pleasant, although there was no hint of docility in it. "I am pleased to make thy acquaintance."

Her hand was not taken and she drew it back. "Thy acquaintance?" the older woman murmured. Charity felt herself being studied from the top of her gold hair, which she had braided and wound around her head in a simple style, to the tips of her black boots.

Protectively, Jason put his arm around Charity's slender shoulders. "Charity is of the Quaker faith."

His mother frowned.

Charity's back stiffened as she told herself that she would not let this woman intimidate her. At the same time she wondered how she was ever going to warm to Jason's mother. The matron was so cool even to her own son whom she had not seen for quite some time.

She was overwhelmed by longing for her own mother, her father, her sisters. She wondered what they were doing at this very moment, if they were missing her.

Quickly she chided herself. Charity had chosen this life in choosing to marry Jason. He had tried to warn her and she had thought that nothing mattered except her love for him.

It was up to her to see this through, to give her new life the best she could. Frances Trenton was her husband's mother and therefore hers. Surely she could make peace with the woman. With a little work and patience, a miracle was possible.

Miracles just had to be possible; it would take nothing short of a miracle to heal her and Jason's relationship.

Telling herself that there was nothing to be gained in thinking about this now, Charity forced herself to attend as Mrs. Trenton turned to Jason. "You must realize how great a surprise this is. I would . . . perhaps it would be best if we spoke to you alone."

Jason shook his head. "There is nothing you cannot say in front of my wife."

Charity was pleased and grateful for his defense. Clearly it was a sign, however slight, that he was not completely indifferent to her. Yet he didn't need to leap to her aid when there might have been no real insult intended.

With the thought of making an eventual peace with this woman in mind, Charity said, "It is all right, Jason. I am sure that our news has come as a great surprise. I am not offended by thy mother's wish to speak with thee in privacy."

"That is very kind of you, my dear," Jason's father told her. He turned to his wife. "Isn't it, Frances?"

Frances Trenton looked at her closely. "Why yes, of course. Thank you." But there was little more warmth in her voice than before. She went to pull the cord that hung against the wall.

Soames opened the door instantly.

"Please take, Mrs. . . . . Trenton to the library." As he nodded, showing no surprise at Charity being addressed as Mrs. Trenton, Jason's mother added, "See that she is served some refreshment."

Charity followed him out with her head held high.

Jason watched her go with regret. Yet he knew that it would likely be best for him to face his parents alone. At first.

His mother spoke as soon as the drawing room door had closed behind them. "How could you have gotten remarried without informing us?"

He shrugged, not caring for her high-handed manner. "I took Charity down to the justice of the peace. He asked some questions. We both said I do."

His father shook his head. "Very amusing, Jason. What your mother is asking is, who is this girl and how did you meet her?"

Jason sighed. "She is—was—Charity Applegate of Helmsville, Wisconsin. I met her while I was looking for Wayne Grisak, whom I have killed—just in case you were wanting to know about that."

"Well, I'm glad that you can now put all that behind you," his father said. "Come back to the firm. And speaking of the firm—" He stood, looking at his pocket watch. "—I have an important meeting in fifteen minutes. I really must go." He turned to Jason. "Please tell your bride that I am very sorry and that I wish you both my heartfelt congratulations. I will certainly see you at dinner."

Jason watched his father leave with a sense of familiarity and disappointment. He had always seemed to put work first, leaving Jason to face countless unpleasant situations with his mother.

"You say you met her while you were searching for that horrible man?" His mother went back to the subject most important to her. "What sort of family is she from?"

Jason looked away from her, remembering the farm, the hard but satisfying work, the peace and happiness of Charity's family. "The very best sort of family, mother." He faced her levelly. "If you ask me, she's made a very poor bargain in trading them for me."

His mother threw up her hands. "That is utterly ridiculous. I have seen her hair, her clothing. She's completely unsuitable."

He faced her squarely. "You are not to change one thing about her."

She returned his look in full measure. "If she does not change, she will never be accepted amongst your peers. Is that what you want for her?"

Jason flinched. "No."

"Then I suggest you allow Charity to decide herself what she will and will not change. It is her only hope of ever adjusting to life here. I will have your things taken upstairs."

He hesitated. "I have not told Charity that I live here. I believe she thinks we have only come by for a visit."

"Why would she assume that?"

"Because I told her so when I hired the carriage. It is my intention for us to find a home where we can have some privacy." He did not say that he was attempting to keep his communication with Charity as brief as possible, that she had come to Boston with him because it was her duty.

His mother interrupted his thoughts. "You will continue to live here as you always have." When he looked at her, she faced him squarely. "Let me speak plainly, son. Unless you remain in this house where I may teach her all that she must know to become a part of society, to be accepted, you will no longer be able to count on the support of your father and me. As your wife appears now she would be turned away from every decent home in Boston."

Jason stood. "Well, the gloves are off then, are they mother? So be it. Keep your money and the firm. I am not concerned with what Boston society or the rest of the Trentons think of me."

His mother waved a dismissive hand. "Please, son, no histrionics. Do try to think about something other than your pride here. What about your children? I am assuming that you will have children. Would you deny them their birthright simply to save your pride?"

His mother continued sharply. "Jason, think about the girl as well. She may be a bit reluctant at first, but she will adjust, son. She wouldn't want anything but the best for her children."

He watched her closely, feeling as if he were being squeezed into a trap. "If Charity agrees," Jason answered slowly.

His mother cast him another long look but said nothing.

Jason spoke softly to himself. "I only pray that she can find some happiness here."

How could Charity ever be happy here?

Jason went on to answer her questions and explain

what had happened while he had been gone as honestly as he could, knowing she would relay everything to his father. He included the circumstances of the death of Wayne Grisak.

She showed little reaction to Grisak's death, other than to say that she was glad all that was behind him now.

He did not tell his mother of the specifics surrounding their marriage. She would never understand the passion that had driven the two of them to make such a disastrous choice without heeding the consequences; the passion that had bound them to one another with an overwhelming intensity; the passion he had taken such joy in.

That passion had died in his wife the night he had killed Wayne Grisak.

Chapter Thirteen

The library was as impressive as the rest of the house. Wall to floor shelving was lined with leather-bound books. An enormous oak desk sat before the windows, and a lush dark green carpet muffled her footsteps as she moved to sit in one of the two green-and-beige-striped chairs.

When Charity said, "Thank you," Soames bowed and left, closing the door silently behind him.

Sometime later, there was a knock at the door.

Again it was the butler. His deep voice was respectful and formal. "Madame requests Mrs. Trenton's presence in the drawing room."

She nodded hurriedly and placed the fragile china cup she was holding back down on the tray the curious-faced maid had brought. "I'll be right there."

She smiled. These moments alone had given her time to think. Jason's wealth had caught her off guard, but she was determined to go on as she would normally. "Please, thee must call me Charity. I am a Quaker and we do not use titles."

He nodded. "Most respectfully I must beg your indulgence. I cannot do that, madam. I am the butler and you are the master's wife."

Charity sighed. Obviously she was going to have to be patient with more than Jason's mother.

As Soames led her back to the drawing room, she prayed she had done the right thing in leaving Jason to speak with his parents alone. Hopefully the three of them had reasoned things out and his parents now wished to greet their new daughter as they should.

Any dissension between herself and Jason's mother would only bring further strain to her and Jason's relationship. With this thought in mind, Charity smiled warmly when she made her way through the long room.

That smile faltered slightly when she saw that Jason's face was an expressionless mask. Hesitantly, Charity came to a halt before them. When Jason met her gaze and smiled at her as if in encouragement, she told herself she was being far too apprehensive. She listened carefully to what he had to say.

"Charity, my father has asked that you excuse him, and that I inform you that he had to return to the firm for a few hours. He offers us his congratulations on our marriage and will render them in person this evening."

He paused before going on, nodding toward his mother. "I have explained the fact that we were not in a position to inform Mother of our marriage previous to its occurrence and she too is very happy to welcome you, both of us, to stay here."

Charity could not hide her surprise at this last part. "Does thee mean we are to live here in this house?"

For a brief moment, Charity thought she sensed a hint of strain in his face before he nodded slowly. "It has been my home all my life. But it is your decision."

Charity bit her lip. His now closed expression gave away nothing. Her intention to make peace with his mother had been made before she realized that they would be expected to live in her home—her domain. A part of her wanted to tell Jason that she would much rather they found some small space, however humble, to call their own.

How would his mother react when she realized the tension between Jason and his wife? How was Charity ever to ease it beneath the other woman's watchful eyes?

Her thoughts were interrupted by Frances Trenton's voice. "Please . . . dear. You must not even consider living elsewhere. This is Jason's home. It has been for his entire life. As our only offspring, he will inherit the house, the firm, my father's business interests, the trust funds, everything when we die. It is not only his heritage, but his children's." Her hand swept the elegant chamber. "It was where he brought his first bride. We want you to feel welcome here—as she did."

Charity saw the look of sadness that passed though Jason's eyes before he was able to disguise it. Of course he had lived here with Daphne.

Realizing this only made her decision more difficult. How could she live here in the house he had shared with the woman he could not forget?

"Please, Charity . . . dear. You would make Jason's father and I very happy."

How could she refuse to stay in the face of his

mother's pleading? Charity felt as if she were a wild bird trapped in a golden cage that was beautiful, but a cage nonetheless.

She had no one to blame for this situation but herself. Jason had tried to tell her that marrying him, becoming a part of his world, would be more difficult than she imagined. He had been honest in that. Was she so faint of heart that she could not accept the consequences of her own actions?

The silence stretched on for what seemed an eternity.

At last she answered. "I thank thee for welcoming me into thy home. I cannot turn away from such kindness."

Frances Trenton smiled. "Well, it's settled then."

Charity looked to her husband, trying to gauge his reactions to what was happening. His gaze was dark with doubt and sadness as he watched his mother, who moved to pull the servant's cord. "Soames will get your things."

Still Jason said nothing. Clearly he was so miserable that it made no difference to him where they lived. In spite of this, Charity was very glad of Jason's presence as she followed Soames up the stairs. The house was so unexpectedly grand, Jason's mother so very different from her own.

She was infinitely conscious of the fact that Jason's mother had looked at her one carpetbag with disapproval. Her quick smile and assurances that a dressmaker would be called in the very next day were not as reassuring as Charity thought they were meant to be.

She was realizing more clearly by the moment that her whole life was changing at the speed of a shooting star. She cast a glance over her shoulder at Jason. He was the reason she was doing this, and she would not forget that. Surely hardship was worth it if she could be with him, love him enough that he began to feel the same toward her.

Soames stopped before a wide, dark wood door. It was identical to many others lining the hallway. He opened it and waited for her to precede him. Charity did so.

She heard Jason tell the butler, "That will be all for now, Soames. I know the way to my own room."

Charity told herself not to show any surprise that she would not be sharing a room with him. She must grow accustomed to the way things were done here.

Jason stood out in the hall as she glanced about the large chamber, which, with its tall windows and lush carpet, was as elegant as the rest of the house. Something, a tension that went beyond even what he had shown of late, made her look at him more closely. Even as she watched, he wiped a bead of sweat from his upper lip. She glanced about her again. The pale yellow bedcovering and draperies, the delicate cherry wood furnishings and daffodil-patterned wallpaper, all told of the fact that this was a woman's chamber.

Her heart hammering in her chest, she whispered, "This was Daphne's room." How difficult it must be for him to see any other woman here.

He nodded, unable to even look at her, the tautness of his tall lean form giving away his grief. Sadness tore at her heart as she said, "There is no need for thee to come to me here. I do not want thee to—"

Jason blanched as he broke in. "There is no reason to go on. I understand."

But did he understand, did he know that when he was ready to love again, she hoped to fill that empty space inside him? Before she could give in to the temptation to tell him just that, he was gone.

Which was just as well, she told herself. It would not help to push him. Jason could only come to her when his heart was free, and that was the only way she truly wanted him.

Yet it was with regret and misery that she heard the next door open, then close with a heavy finality.

Jason was fully conscious of the closed door between his room and Charity's, as he had been each of the six long days they had been in Boston. He knew that she would be downstairs in the drawing room before dinner, but he felt her presence behind that door, thought of the crisp white pillow where she would lay her head, the white sheets that touched her body each night.

Forcefully he splashed cool water from the basin over his face and head. He could not allow himself to think about that, especially when she had been so very clear in letting him know that she did not want . . .

God, how could she feel any differently?

Jason knew how she felt about his having killed Grisak. He also had a sneaking suspicion that she was not happy here in Boston, though she had managed to put a brave face on things. How could she feel anything but unhappy? How could she do anything but resent wearing the clothing his mother had chosen for her, and the formality of her existence in this house?

He thought every day of his mother's threats to disown him. Each day he considered leaving, but his mother's assurances that Charity would adjust, that his children—if he ever had any—deserved the best he could give them, kept him from it.

He knew how seriously Charity took her marriage vows, how badly she wished to try to adjust to this life, even as Jason felt himself resenting it more than he ever had. More times than he could even count, he thought of the Applegate farm, the peaceful life there. But he could not take her back. He'd burned that bridge by killing Grisak.

All he could do was treat Charity with the respect and consideration she deserved. Even if she couldn't bear his touch anymore.

He smoothed an unsteady hand over his clean hair and put on his jacket before going down to dinner. Arriving in anything less than immaculate condition would be even more unforgivable than coming late.

He wondered as he went if his father would be attending the meal. When Jason had explained to him that he could not work the obsessive hours he once had, his father had said nothing. He'd shown none of the outrage Jason had expected upon finding out that Jason had taken the law into his own hands and killed Grisak. He'd said nothing more than that he was very glad that Jason himself had not been hurt. His father had seemed, in fact, somewhat more reticent and thoughtful from that first day when Charity and Jason had arrived in Boston.

Although Jason wondered about this, he was glad. He did not mean to leave Charity to her own devices as he had Daphne. He'd left Daphne alone because he hadn't cared enough. His every instinct was to avoid Charity because he cared *too* much, but he did not.

In spite of the fact that it nearly drove him mad to be near her, he attended meals. He sat in the drawing room listening to his mother's talk of her friends and the parties they would soon hold. Parties Charity would be expected to attend. Charity seemed to be doing her utmost to show anticipation at the thought of wearing the many gowns his mother had chosen for her when they arrived from the dressmakers.

Knowing how she felt about expensive garments, Jason had listened to his mother informing her the first morning at breakfast that she was to be ready to go to the dressmaker's after the meal.

Jason had felt a rush of indignation on her behalf as she'd risen to make ready. He'd gone after her, saying, "You don't have to do everything Mother tells you to, Charity. You are allowed some time to adapt."

Charity had looked up at him, her gaze searching. "I do not mind, Jason. I am thy wife by my own choice. Thee did try to tell me when I spoke to thee of marriage. I would not listen to thee. It is my responsibility to adapt to thy life. Thy mother is trying to be kind in her own way and believes she is helping me."

Jason knew Charity was right. Frances Trenton could only think in terms of appearances, and he felt a growing pity for her. He was also aware that Charity's patience might very well be leading her to compromise her own beliefs, which would only leave her brokenhearted in the end.

He felt the stiffness in his shoulders as he went down to where the family always gathered in the drawing room before dinner.

When Jason entered the chamber, his gaze went immediately to Charity. He found himself sucking in a silent breath of wonder as he did each time he saw her. He took in her sweetly flushed cheeks, framed by hair swept up in a style that was both becoming and elegant at the same time. Obviously the new gowns had begun to arrive, for the one she wore was quite unlike the ones he had seen her in previously. The high, delicately laced neckline of the lavender silk gown brushed against the lovely line of her jaw.

She was beautiful, so beautiful that it made his heart ache to look at her, and he felt that familiar stirring in his body. What he would give to see welcome in her eyes—rather than that uneasy resignation—could not be measured.

Slowly Jason took a seat across from her, knowing he must accept what was.

His mother interrupted his thoughts. "Good evening, Jason. Is Charity's new gown not becoming?"

His wife flushed and looked down. He felt a rush of regret, and when she looked up at him, Jason found himself speaking to her with a wishfulness that surprised even him. "You are the loveliest thing I have ever seen."

She flushed again, and this time he saw an expression that he dared not recognize in those blue eyes, for he knew it could be no more than a trick of the light. His yearning, kept at bay by only the force of his will, rose up inside him, making him wish he could go over to her and pick her up in his arms and . . .

Only when his father cleared his throat, saying, "How is that Newman case coming along?" did Jason remember the other occupants of the room.

Jason knew a renewed sense of guilt along with an overwhelming sense of frustration toward his parents and the life into which he had been born. For if it had been different, if he had been different, Charity could have loved him.

"Well, Jason." His mother spoke again, calling all eyes to her. "I have a surprise for you tonight. Michael Morton came around this afternoon to see you. He said that you had sent him a note saying you would like to speak with him, and he was so anxious to see you that he simply could not wait. It completely slipped his mind that you would be working. I knew you would be so sorry to have missed him, and so I invited him to come for dinner. We had not heard from him since shortly after you left to . . ." She smiled and waved an elegant hand. "Well, that is all best forgotten, isn't it? At any rate, I thought it only right that we introduce him to your new bride."

Michael? Dear Heavens, how could he face him here in front of Charity? Daphne's brother would want to question him about Grisak.

As he looked to Charity, she did something she had not done since the night they had made love, the night he had killed Grisak. She smiled at him shyly. "I would be so happy to meet one of thy friends, Jason."

His chest tightened with longing, and he spoke through tight lips. "Michael is . . . was Daphne's brother."

"Oh . . ." Her smile faded and she watched him closely. "Then I shall be especially happy to meet him, as he is family to you."

Jason felt a swelling gratitude at her kindness, in spite of the fact that hearing Michael was Daphne's brother obviously made her somewhat uncomfortable.

Before he could begin to form a reply, Soames announced, "Michael Morton."

Charity looked toward the door with both dread and curiosity. What would this man be like, and what would meeting him tell her about the woman Jason had loved—the woman her husband could not let go of.

The man who stepped into the room was not as she had expected at all. He was dressed for dinner, as the Trenton family was, but his manner of walking, the smile that came to his handsome face with its regular features, were relaxed and genuinely friendly. She found herself warming to this man, the brother of her husband's lost love, instantaneously.

He greeted Jason's parents first, the first person in Charity's experience to show no hint of tension at addressing them—including Jason himself. Then he turned to her husband, this time holding out his hand even as Jason stood to take it. "How good it is to see you again."

Jason shook that hand tightly, obviously moved at seeing Daphne's brother once again. "You too, Michael. It feels like a long time."

Michael answered, "Too long. I almost didn't believe it when I received your card."

Jason nodded. "Yes, I'm back. . . . I wanted to see you . . . to talk about what happened while I was gone." Michael Morton watched him. "Wayne Grisak is dead—though he never confessed to killing Daphne before he died."

Michael's face creased with sadness at his sister's name even as he reacted to what Jason had said. "Then why would you—"

Jason stopped him with a raised hand, seemingly

uncomfortable. It was not surprising to Charity, considering his still unresolved grief over Daphne's death. "It's a very long story that I will tell you sometime if you wish to know the details. I will say, though, that I believe he was indeed responsible for her death and many other evil deeds. The world will not miss one such as he." His bitterness was obvious.

"I will accept your word on this and know nothing but relief for the death of the man who treated Daphne so cruelly. He deserved to die."

Before Michael could say more, Jason swung around, gesturing toward Charity and startling her out of her painful thoughts. "Michael, there is something I must do before we go any further. Allow me to introduce you to my new wife, Charity."

Michael looked at her with amazement in his brown eyes, even as Charity tried to summon a suitably happy expression. "Your wife? I had no idea."

Jason spoke with forced casualness. "We haven't announced our marriage yet. I'm trying to give Charity a bit of time to grow accustomed to me before I introduce her to the rest of Boston."

Charity felt even more uncertain of herself at this stiff explanation. She could only imagine how Daphne's brother must feel about Jason's returning with a new bride. She took a deep breath holding her head high. Yet she immediately realized that he seemed far from upset to learn of their marriage.

Michael bowed. "My most heartfelt congratulations, Jason. To you and Charity."

She found herself smiling in return. "I thank thee for thy kind words."

His brows rose. "Do I detect that you are of the Quaker persuasion?"

She found herself holding her breath now, thinking of Jason's parents' reactions to her faith. "I am."

His smile widened. "Fine folk, the ones I have met, living with respectable values in spite of society's disapproval."

Charity felt herself flush with pride and happiness. Here, at least, was one man in Boston who approved of her faith—her way of seeing the world. She spoke from her heart. "How very kind of thee to say that. I *have* felt somewhat out of place." Unconsciously, her gaze went to Jason. She found him watching her, his gaze dark with emotions she could not even begin to read.

The rest of the evening passed in torment for Jason. He had not seen his wife so happy since arriving in Boston. Michael was not the least bit intimidated by his parents. They indulged what they termed his eccentricities due to the fact that he was the only heir to one of the best-known and most respected families in the city. Michael chatted easily and effortlessly with them and had obviously charmed Charity.

The more easily his wife smiled, the freer her laughter became, the more Jason wanted her. He thought again of that shy smile, of the look of yearning he'd thought he'd seen in her eyes for that one brief moment when he'd first come into the drawing room. Could she be ready to forgive him? His heart thudded with longing.

What would she say if he acted on the growing need inside him? Would she feel obligated to perform this wifely duty as well, even if she did not want him? If she did, would he take what she offered?

Looking at her, seeing the life he had admired from the very first moment, he was not sure he could deny himself. It was with some discomfort that he looked up from his study of her lovely profile to find Michael watching him very closely.

Charity glanced toward the connecting door for the fifth time in as many seconds. Was Jason in his room?

It had been a strange evening, one she was still attempting to sort out, and it had been from the moment he'd entered the dining room. There had been a touch of vulnerability in his gaze—the same loneliness that had drawn her to him from the beginning.

It amazed and thrilled her to know that that man still existed beneath the starched white shirts and conservative suits. The man that was *her* Jason.

If she could have some hope that he might come to love her, it would be so much easier for her to act the part she had taken on, to live with his mother's efforts to make her an acceptable wife for him.

It had been so very difficult for him to speak of Daphne to Michael Morton. She was afraid of her own sense of expectation, afraid to hope.

So faintly that it was barely audible, she heard a knock at the door that connected her room to Jason's. In that instant, her heartbeat quickened to a deafening throb in her chest.

She stood, her fingers clutching at the soft fabric of her white-lined robe.

Slowly, the door opened.

Jason stood there for a long moment, his eyes

unreadable in the shadows that rose beyond the gas light. A dark green satin robe covered him from neck to toe. Her heart fluttered. His square-shouldered stance betrayed a barely leashed masculinity that made her incredibly aware of her own femininity, made her want to reach out and smooth her hands over the exposed skin at his throat.

The silence became thick as honey as neither of them spoke, their eyes saying more than their mouths ever could.

Then Jason stepped back into his room, holding out his hand and calling her name.

She ran to him, closing that door behind her as she went into his arms.

She could not question his presence. Her every thought—every breath—was filled with the sight and feel of Jason as his strong arms closed around her. He drew her close to the hard length of his body. It was so strangely foreign and unlike her own, yet so familiar.

It was as if the desire of all women, the need to complete and be completed moved within her. Or perhaps it was the overwhelming power of her love for this man.

She drew back slightly and her eyes met his, which had darkened to slate, seeing the passion that he could not disguise. She felt a rush of elation. She, Charity, had wrung this reaction from him.

Feeling an answering thrill within herself, she lifted her mouth, inviting his kiss.

Jason could not, did not wish to deny the invitation of her mouth. He had come here, driven by the need that seemed far more powerful than his will, knowing that he might be turned away, yet having to take that chance. He dipped his head and claimed her lips as his arms closed around her again. When her soft tongue prodded at his mouth he opened to her, his mind whirling, his body hardening in an instant.

How could he have forgotten how open she was in her loving, how welcoming? How had he denied himself this pleasure?

Determinedly he pulled himself back from that knife's edge of passion. Slowly his tongue met hers, sliding along that tender length with deliberate intent. He didn't mean to allow her all the advances. He too meant to give delight, to see her react to his caresses with passion.

His hands traced the curve of her back, sliding lower to grip her hips for a long moment, before molding the lovely curve of her bottom. He pulled her more closely against him, reveling in the fact that she gasped and held his shoulders tightly as he did so.

Obviously Charity too felt this deep and overwhelming need. He kissed her again, sucking at her bottom lip and chuckling softly in the back of his throat when she moaned with pleasure.

Charity was on fire. With each kiss the ache in her lower belly grew thicker, more delicious, more compelling. She pressed herself more closely to him and gasped as he reached down to grasp her hips, pressing her more closely against the hardness of his desire. She reveled not only in the feel of those strong, sure hands on her flesh, but also in the fact that in his hardness lay the end to her torment, the culmination of all her too-long-ignored desire.

Her fingers twined in the front of his robe, tugging urgently, and Jason knew what she wanted. Just the thought of her eagerness made his desire that much stronger. He had to close his eyes for a moment, to take a deep breath and gain control of himself. But in some part of himself, he knew that what was happening was beyond his control. He had become a creature of pleasure, taking and giving without conscious thought.

He wanted to be bare—free to feel and enjoy the woman in his arms with every inch of his heated flesh.

Quickly he drew away, but only far and long enough to shrug out of his robe. The moment he tossed it aside, he was taking her back in his arms, but Charity resisted him, stepping back so that she could see him.

Jason's chest tightened, his breathing becoming ragged as her hot gaze slid over his flesh.

He was so male, so powerful and lean, his skin golden in the light of the candles. Before looking upon this man, she would never have believed that a man's body could be so unbelievably beautiful in its nakedness. Her breath caught and her gaze found his without shame, telling him wordlessly how moved she was by the sight of him.

Made strangely humbled even as he was excited by her examination, Jason pulled her back into his arms.

He kissed her—kissed her so thoroughly and so deeply that the world tilted and her blood sang with wanting. When his freed manhood pulsed against her belly, Charity felt an answering reaction in her core, was aware of the swollen need of her own flesh. She clasped her hands to his hips, holding him tightly to her as he had done to her only moments ago.

He gasped in reaction, and she smiled a secret breathless smile of satisfaction and undeniable hunger.

Though she knew it was not love he felt for her, she

287

wanted Jason to feel the way *she* felt. She wanted him to lose control of himself and his reactions, as she did each time he touched her.

She was determined that it would be her and not Jason who took command of their lovemaking. With this thought in mind, she stepped back from him, catching and holding his gaze as she, with deliberate intent, reached up to slowly trace a hand over the skin of his chest. It was so different from her own flesh, so smooth and supple, but unmistakably male. She paused, her fingers teasingly on the tips of his small male nipples.

Charity's tongue came out to wet her lips as he gasped, his mouth opening as his breath quickened. How good it was to know that she could bring this reaction in him.

When he reached out for her, she shook her head, her voice an unrecognizable utterance of both passion and assurance. "No, not yet."

She moved to place her mouth where her hands had been. Her tongue tasted the salt of sweat on his skin and she sighed. His nipples puckered beneath her tongue and she smiled.

His hoarse murmuring of her name only served to drive her on, to further embolden her. Without pausing to consider, she dipped her head lower, trailing her lips over his abdomen and down. Deliberately she nuzzled the dark hair just below his navel, pressing gentle kisses on his quivering stomach. She could hear his breathing become more ragged with each movement of her lips.

Reveling in the knowledge that this man was hers, her husband, his body belonging to her as hers did to him, she reached down and closed her hand gently over the hardness of him.

Jason's knees buckled and he moved to stop her, but she would not be denied. This moment was hers to command.

She slipped her mouth over the throbbing tip of him, meaning only to kiss that eager flesh. But his gasp of her name told her that she was pleasuring him, driving him beyond himself—as his touch had done to her. She found herself acting on pure instinct, her tongue flicking out to taste him as her lips closed more fully on him.

Jason was drowning, his mind and body awhirl with the sensations she was calling from the depths of his soul. She, Charity, was the center of all desire, all pleasure, all joy. Wave after wave of sweet delight rippled through him with her every motion.

Yet even as his pleasure mounted, from some distant place inside came the knowledge that he must find the will to stop her. He would soon find release, and that he did not want.

More than anything he had ever wanted in his life, he wished to pleasure her. He wanted to see the passion in her that he was now experiencing, to know the rapture of bringing her to culmination.

With a great force of will he pulled away, hearing the rasping sound of his own voice. "No more, Charity. You don't know what you're doing to me."

His hands reached to part her robe, and he slipped them inside. He had to close his eyes on his own reactions to the feel of her soft and luminous skin.

When Jason's hands closed over her aching breasts, Charity gasped aloud. Her nipples hardened under his

289

gentle thumbs and she moaned at the increasing pressure of longing between her thighs. She was afire, her need for him like a hot river that rushed through and over her in an inescapable wave.

"Please, I can't wait any longer."

Hearing her hoarsely whispered plea, Jason drew her up to hold her against his body, taking deep gulps of air as he rested his hot forehead against her wildly tangled hair. When she wriggled against him, her own breathing quick and harsh, he knew that his control had reached its end. Calling on the last shreds of his will in order to keep himself from taking her right there on the floor, he lifted her in his arms and carried her to his bed.

As he positioned himself over her, Charity opened to him.

His body merged with hers as it had been meant to do from the beginning of time. Without thought, their bodies found a rhythm that was as perfect and natural as the joining of their flesh.

Charity no longer thought of making Jason lose himself: she *was* Jason. They were merging into a rapturous oneness that seemed to preclude their ever having been separate entities. His sighs, his pleasure, his breath were hers, and hers his as she rode higher and higher on the hot driving ache of desire.

The sensations built and built until she felt as if she were poised on the summit of all pleasure, her head thrown back in abandon as she hovered on the peak of inexplicable delight. Yet it was only when she felt the shudders of completion that rippled through Jason that she tumbled from the summit, falling into a place where there was only ecstasy.

Jason cried out as his body stiffened and waves of pleasure rolled over him. When finally he was released from those powerful convulsions of pleasure, he sagged above Charity, his mind and body still pulsing with desire.

Weakly, Jason rolled to lie beside her on the tangled coverlet.

She turned to him, her face alight. "Oh, if it can only be like this sometimes, the rest will not be so hard to bear. I only wish that there was some way I could ease the pain of thy lost love."

The words slammed into him with the force of a speeding train. He sat up, knowing he had to tell her the truth. "My God, Charity, don't feel sorry for *me*. You have it all wrong. I haven't grieved for Daphne because I loved her, but because I didn't."

She sat up, pulling the coverlet along as she moved away from him. "What are thee talking about?"

He raised his head, "I never loved her. I married her because she was pleasant, beautiful, and my parents wanted it."

"Why would thee marry just to please them?"

"Because it didn't make any difference to me whom I married and I thought their choice was as good as any." He looked at her closely. "Don't you see, Charity, in the long run it really didn't matter. I chose you and made a mess of that by killing Grisak."

She took a deep breath, her expression impossible to read as she faced him. "I have not held that against thee. Although thy actions went against the beliefs my family taught me, and I was somewhat confused about what I felt at first, I was under the impression that thee

291

had acted out of grief for Daphne, out of love, the love thee bore her. I even felt that if it had been thee who he'd shot at and I had a gun in my own hand—" She looked down. "I have been taught that there is no nobler purpose than love."

Jason could only stare at her in stunned revelation. Yet even as hope soared within him, it as quickly dropped like a stone when she went on. "But now I learn that thee did it all not out of love, but out of hatred—and not even hatred of Grisak, but hatred of thyself! How, Jason, can thee ever love anyone, if thee feel such hatred for thyself?"

He shook his head, his mind reeling. "I can never forgive myself for the things I have done, keeping you here when I suspected how unhappy you were. Yet my mother was so determined that we live here. She'd threatened to disown me, and said that you would want to stay for our children's sake. How could I ask you or any children we might have to give up my family's wealth to save my pride?"

Charity's voice was very quiet when she replied. "Thee stayed here in order to provide me and our children with *wealth*?" He could tell the next words were not easy for her. "Although I must admit, if I am to be completely honest, that I have not entirely disliked some of the pretty clothes and things, they are not so admired that I would choose, even for a moment, the formality and coldness of this life above my old one."

He shook his head. "I knew you would not care, Charity. It was for our children, and I did hope that you might come to forgive me eventually, that we might actually have children. They would be deserving of the very best."

She stood, moving toward the door that connected their rooms, pausing as she reached it. She took a deep breath, her eyes hollow with regret. "I have tried so hard to please thee, Jason—accepting thy mother's word on all things, thinking that I might make thee love me if I became the wife thee wanted. But none of this was even what thee wanted. Yet thee could not tell me that—all because of some notion thee have that the children we might have would require anything but thy love. We have both suffered for it."

She opened the door. "Thee thought thee must revenge Daphne to be whole, or suffer unhappiness to secure thy children's future in order to be a good father. Thee alone would have been enough if thee could have but seen it. I tell thee that thee were all I ever wanted.

"Thee gave nothing because thee did not know that the gift was thyself. Thee cannot be whole until thee see that thee have nothing but love to give, Jason, and I am no longer willing to live without it." She closed the door very softly behind her.

Staring at the closed door, Jason felt an ache in his chest that nearly took his breath away.

He could not deny anything she had said. Yet for someone who could not love, he felt suspiciously as if his heart were breaking.

Chapter Fourteen

Charity rose the next morning with one horrifyingly painful certainty in her mind. She had to leave Boston and it had to be today.

No longer could she wait and hope that Jason would someday come to love her. He did not even wish to see that it was he who kept them apart.

Quickly she dressed in the plainest of the gowns that had been made for her. She packed her carpetbag with the bare minimum of items that would be needed for the journey back to Wisconsin.

She then sat down at the delicate cherry wood desk and sighed as she took out paper and pen. How could she ever explain to Jason? She could not.

In the end she wrote very simply.

Jason:
Please forgive me for not understanding when

*thee tried to tell me that we were too different. I
am sorry for everything.
Charity.*

Not allowing herself to think about the sorrow that
hovered at the edge of her determination, she left the
note on her bedside table.

With that done, she took some of the money Jason
had insisted on alloting her from her top drawer. She
took only what she felt would be necessary to get home.

Home. The word tugged at her heart, for she did not
know if anywhere away from Jason would ever feel
like home again.

Immediately she reminded herself that Jason did not
feel that way about her, would never feel that way
about her. She could not continue to live with a man
who could not give anything of himself. She knew that
she must get on with her plan. She must leave before
he returned from work. And the next thing she
required was transportation to the train station.

Without bothering to think about what she was
doing, Charity left her bedroom and made her way to
the kitchen.

She had never been there, and so was not sure of the
reception she would get, but she intended to get to the
train station—and she was not going to ask Jason's
mother for assistance.

Hesitantly, fearing that the servants might not give
her aid without permission from Mrs. Trenton, she
pushed open the swinging door. Her eyes took in the
huge room with amazement. She could only think that
her mother would be in awe of this vast chamber with
its gleaming tile floor and high ceiling. The counter

tops and ovens were large enough to accommodate cooking for twenty, rather than the few who lived in this home.

She breathed in the warm air, which was sweet with the scent of baking bread and hickory-smoked bacon. She felt a new rise of homesickness. Then she told herself that she would be back there soon, though the thought was not as comforting as she wanted it to be.

At first, no one took any notice of her presence as she stepped inside and allowed the door to swing closed behind her. A tiny lady in a huge white apron that dwarfed her diminutive figure was directing the maids, Liza and Alice. They chatted amiably while arranging cutlery and dishes upon a silver tray.

Charity could only assume that this was for Mrs. Trenton, who always had tea in her room before coming down to breakfast. Seeing this reminded her that she could not linger.

Her gaze went to Mr. Soames, who sat at the table, his sleeves rolled up, smoking a cigar while he read the paper. A steaming cup of tea sat close at hand. She had never seen him look so relaxed, so approachable.

This kitchen, Charity realized, was the place in the Trenton home where she would have felt the most comfortable. Yet it was not the proper place for Jason's wife.

The thought made her all the more certain that she was doing the right thing in leaving. "Excuse me," she said softly.

Mr. Soames looked up, setting his paper aside as soon as he saw her. His exclamation of, "Mrs. Trenton," brought the attention of the others who spun around to look at her with surprise.

Charity spoke hesitantly. "I . . . excuse me. I didn't mean to interrupt."

Mr. Soames stood. "You aren't interrupting anything, Mrs. Trenton." He turned to the tiny woman in the white apron. "Is she, Mrs. Soames?"

Charity hadn't even known he was married. It was a further indication that she did not belong here to hear the servants calling one another by such formal address. She longed all the more for the easy familiarity of her parents' home.

Clearly unaware of her thoughts, Mrs. Soames smiled kindly. "No, not a thing. Would you care for a cup of tea, miss?"

That kindness did little to ease her longing as she replied, "No, thank you." She turned back to the tall man, who was shrugging into the coat he had retrieved from the back of his chair. "Mr. Soames, I was wondering if I might get a ride to the train station."

His brows rose. "A ride to the train station, madam?"

"Yes."

He watched her too closely. "Would Mr. Jason be accompanying you, madam?"

"No."

Again she felt his eyes upon her, and she attempted a casual demeanor. Charity wondered if he would have to ask Jason's mother for permission. Well, so be it. She had hoped to avoid a confrontation with her mother-in-law, but she would face her if she must.

To her relief, he nodded. "I shall have the carriage readied and brought around, madam."

She tried not to sound too anxious as she said, "Please, do not be too long."

His expression did not change. "I'll tell Wilson not to be above half an hour." He left with a formal bow.

Mrs. Soames turned to Alice. "You take the tea up to your mistress."

She then swung back to Charity. "Are you sure you would not care for a cup of tea yourself, while you wait, madam?"

Realizing that it would give her something to occupy her time, Charity said, "If it wouldn't be too much trouble."

"Of course it wouldn't be any trouble." She turned to the other girl. "Please, take a pot of tea into the dining room for . . ."

Charity stopped her. "No, I will not cause thee such inconvenience. I would prefer to have it here, if thee don't mind. And could someone collect my bag and coat from my room, please?"

Mrs. Soames nodded quickly. "As you wish, madam. Please, come and sit down at the table."

Mrs. Soames brought the tea and sat it in front of Charity, then turned to Liza. "You may go now and bring the lady's things down to the front hall."

When she was gone, Mrs. Soames waited nearby. "There now. You just have a bit of tea and it will warm you to go out this morning."

The words reminded her that it was October. She had only met Jason some three months ago. Who would have believed that her life could have changed so greatly in such a short time?

And changed it had, though she would go home and live out the rest of her days alone, married but not married. She bent over her tea, unwilling to let this woman, however kind she seemed, see her sorrow.

She was grateful that the cook made no more small talk, going about her work quietly, giving Charity a thick slice of fresh bread and jam on a china plate without comment. Though she did not feel hungry, Charity felt she should try to eat, and managed to swallow a few bites. She was only able to take a bit before Wilson, the coachman who had driven her and Jason's mother when they had gone to purchase her new clothing, appeared in the kitchen doorway.

"The carriage is ready, madam."

The moment had arrived. Slowly she stood. "Thank you, Mrs. Soames, for your courtesy."

The cook's expression was gently searching, and Charity felt another wave of sadness that there could not have been more moments of kindness in this house. "You are very welcome, madam."

Charity pushed that sadness away, following the coachman out of the kitchen.

At the front door of the house, she paused as Wilson opened it for her. "Where is Mr. Soames? I wished to thank him."

He shrugged, his expression telling her that he did not question the butler's actions. "Mr. Soames has gone on an errand, madam."

Charity nodded, stepping through the door. She would delay the inevitable no longer.

Jason woke with a throbbing in his head that made his stomach roll. He sat up, knocking the empty whiskey bottle to the floor.

His bleary gaze went straight to that of his assistant,

who sputtered. "Mr. Trenton, I wasn't expecting you to . . . I was just going to put the Jefferies brief on your desk."

Jason grimaced. Of course he hadn't been expecting him to be here. He'd not slept on the leather settee in the office since returning with Charity, and before that it had only been because he had stayed to work until he couldn't keep his eyes open any longer. He certainly had never gotten drunk in the office.

That was exactly what he had done when he'd left Charity last night. He'd come to the office and gotten so drunk that he could forget—for a little while at least—how much of a mess he'd made of their lives.

He had no intention of telling the assistant, Theodore Hudson, any of this. He faced this very efficient and neatly dressed man as if there were nothing in the least bit unusual about his being there. "Ted, would you mind getting me some coffee?" He held out his hand. "I'll get started reading that brief."

Ted handed it to him and left the office without another word.

With a grimace, Jason tucked the empty whiskey bottle under the settee and slowly stood. Gingerly he went to his large heavy oak desk. He sat down in the comfortable leather chair with equal care, laid the papers out in front of him, and began to read. Then to reread, and then to reread again. The words could have been Chinese for all he comprehended of them.

He couldn't comprehend anything but the fact that Charity didn't believe he was capable of loving—and he couldn't disprove it. The self-hatred inside him was eating him alive. All he knew was that he would never feel anything but sadness again.

* * *

It seemed a very short time after Theodore had returned with the coffee that he once again appeared in the doorway. Jason looked up from the brief with raised brows.

The assistant spoke hesitantly, "There is someone here to see you, Mr. Trenton."

Jason closed his eyes. He wasn't expecting anyone, nor did he want to see anyone. "Tell them I'm not available."

"It's Mr. Morton."

Michael. What would he be doing here this morning? Jason had told him that he would be happy to answer his questions about Grisak, but he could hardly face doing so today. Yet he couldn't send Daphne's brother away.

He nodded. "Show him in."

Michael hesitated at the door when he saw Jason. "What happened to you, my friend?"

Jason scowled. "What do you mean?"

Michael was not deterred. "You look as if you've been run over by a speeding train."

Jason thought of the whiskey bottle which he had stuffed under the corner of the settee. He didn't want to talk about that, not even with this old friend. He said instead, "I suppose you've come to talk about Daphne?"

Michael shook his head, then shrugged. "Well, I suppose I have, but—" He looked at Jason closely. "—Charity is a lovely woman, Jason."

His scowl deepened. "Yes. . . . Yes, she is." Where was Michael headed?

The other man continued to watch him as he went

on. "I realized last night when I met her that—" He raised his head. "—There is something that I should have told you a very long time ago. I just didn't see that it would do anyone any good before I saw you with Charity. And I had given Daphne my promise." He ran a hand over his face. "Grisak is dead now, Jason, and you have a chance to make a new life with Charity. I have to speak because it seems as if you still feel you are to blame for what happened to Daphne."

Jason took a deep breath. "Well, am I not?"

Michael shook his head. "No, Jason. Not for any of it."

Jason knew that no matter how hard it was to admit the truth to Daphne's brother, he had to do it. "If I had ever loved her, Michael, shown her any real affection and care, she would be alive now."

Michael stood and went to the window, gazing out unseeing as he said, "No, there was nothing you could have done to make Daphne want to be with you." He swung around. "You see, Jason, Daphne was never in love with you either."

Jason faced him. "I know that. We did not lie to each other when our parents suggested the match. But I do believe she would have grown to love me if I had made more effort to fit her into my life. She could have been happy."

Michael came to stand in front of him. "Jason, it wasn't going to happen. Daphne was in love with another man."

Jason stood. "What are you saying? She never betrayed me. I won't believe that of her—"

Michael broke in. "Of course she didn't. She wouldn't have done such a thing. But that didn't change the fact that she loved a man named Donovan Reilly. He worked in my father's mill, and was completely unsuitable for her. He died on the night they meant to run away together, but that didn't kill her love for him."

Shocked beyond ready comprehension, Jason shook his head. "I don't believe this. Why would she agree to marry me if that were true?"

Michael shrugged. "Largely to please Mother and Father. I have been such a disappointment to them." His lips twisted in a self-deprecating smile. "They were horrified when they learned about Donovan Reilly, even though he'd been killed before she could run away with him. They pushed for a marriage, and when they spoke of you, Daphne recalled that you had been kind to her when she was small. And we were friends. She said yes. I do believe that she thought she could make you a good wife." His voice grew husky with sadness. "She just hadn't realized how hard it would be for her to live with one man while wishing desperately that he was another."

Jason's head was spinning with shock and confusion as he realized that everything he'd believed about his marriage had been an illusion. "It's too incredible."

The other man took a deep breath. "It is all, sadly, quite true. As I said, last night I saw that you have a chance with Charity. She loves you, but you are holding back. Don't hold back this time, Jason. There was nothing you could have given my sister. Let her go. We have all mourned her. But you need to stop feeling responsible for her death."

Jason raked a hand through his hair. Michael could only be telling the truth about Daphne. She's been his sister, and he'd loved her dearly. All this time Jason had thought it was his fault that she was so miserable in their marriage. In some part of him he knew that he would always feel he could have done more. Perhaps if he had tried just the slightest bit harder, she would have told him the truth. But he had not given her the chance.

Yet at the same time as these thoughts ran through his mind, he realized that Daphne had made her own choices, had married him knowing she loved someone else. He spoke slowly. "I don't even know what to say. I am grateful, but it's too late for Charity and me. I have hurt her so badly with my inability to open my heart, that she will never forgive me."

"I don't know what you have done or said to your wife, Jason. I will tell you this though, she loves you deeply."

He knew a wave of sadness. "Charity doesn't love me. Oh, she did in the beginning, but I've let my hatred and guilt stand in the way so long there is nothing left."

Michael's eyes grew round. "I've seen the way your wife looks at you. She loves you, Jason. It's only your own blindness that keeps you from seeing it."

"But she's said . . ."

Michael stopped him with a raised hand. "Has she said, 'Jason, I don't love you'?"

He shook his head roughly, the pain of remembering bringing a tightness to his chest. "No, but she's made her feelings very clear."

"Have you told her that you love her?"

Jason felt a jolt of shock ripple through him. No, he'd never said he loved her, had not allowed himself to think it. Charity had accused him of being incapable of loving, but Michael's words made him see the truth for what it was. If what he was feeling, the degree of emptiness he felt at her not loving him, was any indication, he did indeed love her. He looked at Michael with haunted eyes. "Do you think she might . . ."

A loud knock interrupted him.

With a muttered oath, Jason went to the door and jerked it open. "What?"

Ted looked as frazzled as Jason was feeling. "I'm sorry, Mr. Trenton, but your butler is here, and he is insisting . . ."

Soames's uncharacteristically perturbed voice interrupted him. "I am sorry to disturb you, sir, but . . ."

At that moment, Jason's father appeared in the doorway of his own office. "What the devil is . . ." He stopped, his gaze taking in the fact that his butler, looking quite unlike his usual imperturbable self, was standing in the hallway.

He frowned as he came down the hall. "Soames, what are you doing here?"

The butler made no effort to answer him as he turned back to Jason. "It is Miss Charity, sir. She has gone to the train station."

Jason could hardly take this in. "What are you talking about?"

"Miss Charity asked me to send the carriage around for her this morning." He paused. "I did what she said, but I thought I should come here and tell you that I had. I also told Wilson to stay there with her until the train came, which won't be until noon."

From behind him, Michael cried, "You *aren't* going to let her go!"

Robert Trenton took a deep breath and spoke with

forced calm. "I want to know what is going on, and I want to know right now." Other assistants and junior barristers were beginning to poke their heads out into the hallway.

Trying to think, to make some sense of it all, but not wanting to do so in front of all these people, Jason said, "Can we all go into my office?"

As soon as the door was closed, his father said, "I insist on knowing what is happening. Is your wife leaving you, Jason?"

Before he could answer, Michael said, "It would seem so. It would be worse than a shame if he lets her go. Charity could be his one chance at happiness."

"What makes you the authority on my son's happiness?" Jason's father returned.

"I came to tell him the truth about my sister, about the fact that she loved another man and that all of us sat by and watched that marriage grow more painful with each passing day, and did nothing."

Wiping a hand across his stunned face, Jason's father sat down on the settee. "Dear heavens."

Michael turned back to Jason. "Well, you're going after her, aren't you?"

Jason shook his head, that numbness holding him in its grip. "I don't have the right to make her stay."

Michael groaned. "You won't have to *make* her stay. Just tell her you love her. She'll follow you to the ends of the earth."

"You don't know. You don't understand how it is. She doesn't want me. She believes I can't really ever care for her, and I can't argue that. I've not been able to give myself to anyone. I don't know how. I've hurt her so badly, brought her here and expected her to fit in to my life, when the one she gave up is the one worth having. I've never felt the kind of peace I knew living on that farm in Wisconsin, being with her family."

Suddenly realizing what he had just admitted in front of his father, Jason blanched.

His father's face suddenly registered sadness, but also determination. "Don't feel guilty about telling me the truth, son. It's high time you did so. Michael is right. We've all of us made some dreadful mistakes. We should have realized that Daphne . . . You've got to go after your wife, son. And don't bring her back. Go with her. I see that you aren't happy here, that perhaps you never were. The law was my dream. Follow your own, and do so with my blessing. Perhaps if you do, you'll begin to see just how much you do have to give her."

"What about Mother? I don't mean to humor her anymore, and I won't bow to any threats to disown me, but neither can I find it in me to cut her off completely. She is my mother, and I love her."

He seemed taken aback for a moment. "I had no idea she . . ." He took a deep breath and let it out slowly. Your inheritance will never be in question, no matter what you do. Your mother will be all right when she realizes that this is what's best for you. She has always loved you. She just wanted you to be happy, in spite of appearances to the contrary. She would never disown you, son. And I would not allow it if she tried. You know, she's never felt she was good enough herself either. And strangely enough, it's all I ever wanted from her. Perhaps if I try a little harder there myself, she will . . ." He drew himself up straight. "But that is not your worry. You have your own life to live."

Jason stood paralyzed. He couldn't think, couldn't make any sense out of all he had heard, or his own scattered feelings. He had not caused all the problems between himself and his first wife. He had carried that around for so long, for no reason.

Suddenly, in the midst of it all, he had one clear and irrevocable revelation. None of this had ever really mattered as far as his relationship with Charity was concerned, including what he had just learned about Daphne. All that had ever mattered between them was his ability to love and be loved.

Why was he standing here wasting time?

He loved Charity, loved her with all his heart and soul. He had to go after her no matter what she might say. There was no other option. She'd said she didn't want to be with him because he couldn't love. Well, he loved, and with a desperation that he hoped might reach her. He looked at his father. "Thank you."

"Soames, how did you get here?"

"By horse. But you can take it, sir."

"You're a good man. Thank you." Without another word, Jason flew out of the offices.

He could only pray that his wife would not turn him away.

Charity stood with her carpetbag in her hand. She looked at Wilson in apology. "I cannot keep thee here for the whole morning. Thee are free to go."

The man shook his gray head, his blue eyes determined. "Soames told me to stay, madam, and I do as he tells me to."

She bit her lip, sorry that he was being so stubborn, yet feeling an undeniable relief that she would not be left here alone. She simply could not go back to the Trenton house to wait. The man who had sold her a ticket for the train, which did not leave until noon, had seemed nice enough. But there were so many people coming in and out of the station, and all of them seemed to be in a hurry.

Wilson gestured toward the benches that could be seen through the windows. "Would you care to sit outside while we wait, madam?"

She nodded. Perhaps she would not feel quite so conspicuous sitting out in the fresh air as she did standing here with her bag in her hand.

Outside, the late October air was somewhat crisp, but her coat was quite warm. She took a seat on the bench and settled down to wait. She tried to keep from thinking about Jason, and the fact that she was leaving him behind forever.

Thus, when she heard the sounds of commotion from inside the station only moments later, she looked up eagerly, grateful for the distraction. It was with no small amount of surprise that she peered through the windows and saw none other than her own husband inside, waving his arms about like a madman.

As if sensing her attention, he turned and saw her.

Her heart rising in her throat, Charity stood as he started toward her. She did not know what she was going to say to Jason when he came through that door, but she would make him see that she could not remain here any longer.

The haunted expression in his eyes as he burst out onto the boardwalk gave her pause, made her pulse quicken. He hesitated there, as if uncertain of what to say now that they were face to face.

She waited, even as her eyes took in the golden highlights in his hair, the masculine beauty of his lean-jawed face. Even as her wayward heart skipped a beat, he took a deep breath and came forward, stopping just out of arm's reach of her. Without looking away from her, he said to Wilson, "Would you mind leaving us alone for a moment?"

She felt the driver slip away, though she could no more look away from Jason than cease breathing.

"Charity."

"Jason."

His voice came in a husky whisper. "You *are* leaving me."

She swallowed hard, nodding though the admission was dreadfully painful. "I can't live this way any longer."

He spoke softly. "Michael told me that Daphne was so unhappy because she was in love with another man."

Charity tried to be happy, for the fact had to give him some comfort from his guilt. But she could not be, for it had never been his relationship with Daphne that had stood between them, but Jason himself. "I am sad for her, and will hope that this will give thee some comfort, Jason."

He closed his eyes, and when he opened them again they were dark with regret. "I will always be sorry that I could not give you enough to keep you."

She felt her throat tighten with a sorrow she refused to feel. "I did not want anything thee were unwilling to give."

He faced her then, his gaze holding hers, his eyes desperate. "Not even my love?"

The words left her weak, their meaning washing over and through her with the force of a breaking dam. Yet she could not give them credence. Then, as he continued to look at her, making no effort to disguise the agony in his soul, softly, breathlessly, hopefully, she whispered: "Thy love is all I have ever wanted. It is all I will ever want."

He stood there staring at her, his face registering shock and disbelief. And she suddenly realized. He truly did love her, loved her so much that he could not believe she would accept that love.

Charity held out her arms, knowing that if he loved her, nothing else mattered, no problem was too difficult to overcome. Her joy was a radiant light inside her. "Come then, my love, thy precious gift is safe in my heart."

Jason came to her then, enfolding her, holding her so tightly that she could not draw breath. And Charity reveled in his ardor. She'd waited so very long for this moment, had lost hope that it would ever come.

When he drew back to kiss her, she returned that kiss with all the longing inside her.

Pulling away, he hugged her again, laughing shakily. "We had best go back inside and order a sleeper."

She pulled away from him, her gaze searching. "What?"

He was smiling at her, his eyes glowing with love. "I want us to start a new life. One that is *ours*."

She was afraid to believe the implications of his words. "Thee want to go back to Wisconsin?"

He sighed, a trace of uncertainty shading the happiness in his dark eyes she loved so dearly. "I would love

311

to try my hand at farming. But I could use some lessons. Perhaps, in time, your family will be able to forgive me and accept me as I am."

She smiled at him, her eyes telling him that she meant what she was saying from the bottom of her heart. "It would be so good to go home, to be near my family again, to have their support. But know this, my love, if they do not come to love and accept thee just as thee are, I do not need them by me."

She paused and put a hand to his dear face, "Where thee go, I shall call home."

She realized that she would never again doubt his love as he looked at her and replied, "Where thee are is my home."

SWEET FURY

CATHERINE HART

She is exasperating, infuriating, unbelievably tantalizing; a little hellcat with flashing eyes and red-gold tangles, and if anyone is to make a lady of the girl, it will have to be Marshal Travis Kincaid. She may fight him tooth and nail, but Travis swears he will coax her into his strong arms and unleash all her wild, sweet fury.

___4428-5 $5.99 US/$6.99 CAN

Dorchester Publishing Co., Inc.
P.O. Box 6640
Wayne, PA 19087-8640

Please add $1.75 for shipping and handling for the first book and $.50 for each book thereafter. NY, NYC, and PA residents, please add appropriate sales tax. No cash, stamps, or C.O.D.s. All orders shipped within 6 weeks via postal service book rate. Canadian orders require $2.00 extra postage and must be paid in U.S. dollars through a U.S. banking facility.

Name_____
Address_____
City_____ State_____ Zip_____
I have enclosed $_____ in payment for the checked book(s).
Payment <u>must</u> accompany all orders. ❏ Please send a free catalog.
       CHECK OUT OUR WEBSITE! www.dorchesterpub.com

Silken Savage

CATHERINE HART

Captured by a party of Cheyenne while traveling through Colorado Territory, beautiful Tanya Martin refuses to let her proud spirit be broken or her voluptuous body abused. But she has not anticipated the reaction of her heart to A Panther Stalks, the brave who has claimed her as his prize. Tanya soon becomes her captor's willing slave, overcome by a passion she cannot resist.

___4462-5 $5.99 US/$6.99 CAN

Dorchester Publishing Co., Inc.
P.O. Box 6640
Wayne, PA 19087-8640

Please add $1.75 for shipping and handling for the first book and $.50 for each book thereafter. NY, NYC, and PA residents, please add appropriate sales tax. No cash, stamps, or C.O.D.s. All orders shipped within 6 weeks via postal service book rate. Canadian orders require $2.00 extra postage and must be paid in U.S. dollars through a U.S. banking facility.

Name_____

Address_____

City_____State_____Zip_____

I have enclosed $_____ in payment for the checked book(s).

Payment <u>must</u> accompany all orders. ☐ Please send a free catalog.

DESPERADO

SANDRA HILL

Major Helen Prescott has always played by the rules. That's why Rafe Santiago nicknamed her ''Prissy'' at the military academy years before. Rafe's teasing made her life miserable back then, and with his irresistible good looks, he is the man responsible for her one momentary lapse in self control. When a routine skydive goes awry, the two parachute straight into the 1850 California Gold Rush. Mistaken for a notorious bandit and his infamously sensuous mistress, they find themselves on the wrong side of the law. In a time and place where rules have no meaning, Helen finds Rafe's hard, bronzed body strangely comforting, and his piercing blue eyes leave her all too willing to share his bedroll. Suddenly, his teasing remarks make her feel all woman, and she is ready to throw caution to the wind if she can spend every night in the arms of her very own desperado.

_52182-2 $5.99 US/$6.99 CAN

FRANKLY, MY DEAR...

SANDRA HILL

Selene has three great passions: men, food, and *Gone With The Wind*. But the glamorous model always finds herself starving—for both nourishment and affection. Weary of the petty world of high fashion, she heads to New Orleans. Then a voodoo spell sends her back to the days of opulent balls and vixenish belles like Scarlett O'Hara. Charmed by the Old South, Selene can't get her fill of gumbo, crayfish, beignets—or an alarmingly handsome planter. Dark and brooding, James Baptiste does not share Rhett Butler's cavalier spirit, and his bayou plantation is no Tara. But fiddle-dee-dee, Selene doesn't need her mammy to tell her the virile Creole is the only lover she gives a damn about. And with God as her witness, she vows never to go hungry or without the man she desires again.

___4617-2 $5.50 US/$6.50 CAN

TEXAS PROUD

CONSTANCE O'BANYON

Rachel Rutledge has her gun trained on Noble Vincente. With one shot, she will have her revenge on the man who killed her father. So what is stopping her from pulling the trigger? Perhaps it is the memory of Noble's teasing voice, his soft smile, or the way one glance from his dark Spanish eyes once stirred her foolish heart to longing. Yes, she loved him then . . . as much as she hates him now. One way or another, she will wound him to the heart—if not with bullets, then with her own feminine wiles. But as Rachel discovers, sometimes the line between love and hate is too thinly drawn.

___4492-7 $5.99 US/$6.99 CAN

San Antonio Rose
Constance O'Banyon

Sam Houston knows he needs all the help he can get to defeat Santa Anna's seasoned fighting men. But who is the mysterious San Antonio Rose, who emerges from the mist like a ghostly figure to offer her aid? Fluent in Spanish, Ian McCain is the one man who can ferret out the truth about the flamboyant dancer. Working under Santa Anna's very nose, he observes how the dark-haired beauty inflames her audience, how she captivates El Presidente himself. But as she disappears with a single yellow rose, he knows that despite the tangled web of loyalties that ensnare them, he will taste those tempting lips, know every secret of that alluring body. And before she proves just how effective she can be, he will pluck for himself the San Antonio Rose.

___4563-X $5.99 US/$6.99 CAN

BAD COMPANY

CAROL CARSON

Trixianna Lawless is furious when the ruggedly handsome sheriff arrests her for bank robbery. But when she finds herself in Chance's house instead of jail, she begins to wish that he would look at her with his piercing blue eyes . . . and take her into his well-muscled arms.

___4448-X $4.99 US/$5.99 CAN

Dorchester Publishing Co., Inc.
P.O. Box 6640
Wayne, PA 19087-8640

Please add $1.75 for shipping and handling for the first book and $.50 for each book thereafter. NY, NYC, and PA residents, please add appropriate sales tax. No cash, stamps, or C.O.D.s. All orders shipped within 6 weeks via postal service book rate. Canadian orders require $2.00 extra postage and must be paid in U.S. dollars through a U.S. banking facility.

Name_____
Address_____
City_____State_____Zip_____
I have enclosed $_____ in payment for the checked book(s).
Payment <u>must</u> accompany all orders. ❑ Please send a free catalog